BY DESIGN

Lauren stood in Nick's den holding a glass of brandy. She didn't need it—the way he'd touched her on the ride across the Brooklyn Bridge had been more than enough to keep her warm. She'd made the decision as the sounds of the orchestra tickled her ear and his hips moved against hers that she was going to explore the attraction between the two of them.

His eyes met hers and her tongue darted out over her lips. Nick's magnetic eyes pulled her in and warmed her up. She watched his eyes darken and gave him her best come-hither smile.

Lauren put her drink down and took a deliberate step closer to him. Like spring come to winter, she moved into him and he into her. Her hands framed his face and she touched her lips to his. Her tongue slipped through and began to explore the recesses of his mouth, announcing her intentions. She wanted him in the worst way. She wanted him to make love to her.

BOOK YOUR PLACE ON OUR WEBSITE AND MAKE THE ARABESQUE ROMANCE CONNECTION!

We've created a customized website just for our very special Arabesque readers, where you can get the inside scoop on everything that's going on with Arabesque romance novels.

When you come online, you'll have the exciting opportunity to:

- View covers of upcoming books

- Learn about our future publishing schedule (listed by publication month and author)

- Find out when your favorite authors will be visiting a city near you

- Search for and order backlist books

- Check out author bios and background information

- Send e-mail to your favorite authors

- Join us in weekly chats with authors, readers and other guests

- Get writing guidelines

- AND MUCH MORE!

Visit our website at
http://www.arabesquebooks.com

BY DESIGN

Angela Weaver

BET Publications, LLC
http://www.bet.com
http://www.arabesquebooks.com

ARABESQUE BOOKS are published by

BET Publications, LLC
c/o BET BOOKS
One BET Plaza
1900 W Place NE
Washington, DC 20018-1211

All Kensington Titles, Imprints, and Distributed Lines are available at special quantity discounts for bulk purchases for sales promotions, premiums, fund-raising, and educational or institutional use. Special book excerpts or customized printings can also be created to fit specific needs. For details, write or phone the office of the Kensington special sales manager: Kensington Publishing Corp., 850 Third Avenue, New York, NY 10022, attn: Special Sales Department, Phone: 1-800-221-2647.

First Printing: September 2003
10 9 8 7 6 5 4 3 2 1

Printed in the United States of America

One

There was too much magic in the early evening air to be blue, Lauren Hughes mused as she waved her French-manicured fingertips at an older married couple from her building. Dodging a dog walker being pulled by three poodles, she turned the corner toward home and stepped into a ray of sunshine. Strolling past galleries and flower shops, she paused, breathing in the quiet beginning of fall humming that filled the West Village. Lauren's lips curled into a smile as she let out a contented sigh. This was why she moved to New York from Chicago.

But it wasn't just the shops and people that had drawn her to the fast-paced city. It was the brownstones. She could go from south Brooklyn to the northern tip of Manhattan and see historic homes lining the intimate sidewalks. As an interior designer at one of the top firms in the country, she had her choice of office towers, pre-war apartment buildings, and lofts, but she preferred the elegance and charm of the city's brownstones.

Adjusting her grip on her portfolio, she used her key to open the brownstone's entry door, climbed the hardwood staircase, and let herself into the second-floor apartment. Dropping her keys on the side table, she kicked off her shoes. After her having spent half the day with suppliers, the sight of her pillow-decorated sofa was almost more than she could take. Bypassing the temptation of relaxing on the coach, she headed straight to the bedroom.

Lauren glanced at the Snoopy wall clock above her bed; she had one hour to get ready for the engagement party. The African-American power couple's celebration would be filled with the city's most notable residents.

Stripping off her work clothes, she put on her robe and headed toward the bathroom to take a quick shower. She didn't want to go to the party, but Alan had begged. Her best friend since preschool was afraid of going alone.

While she showered, Lauren found herself laughing. Alan Knight, New York City's newest pro baseball bachelor with a reputation of being a ladies' man, was nervous about being in a roomful of single women. She shook her head. He was too polite for his own good.

Lauren turned off the water and stepped out of the shower, dried herself off, and proceeded to rub shea butter over her skin and dab perfume on her pulse points. Putting her robe on, she went back into the bedroom and pulled her favorite dress out of the closet.

Not bad for someone looking at the back side of twenty, she thought, smiling into the full-length mirror. Lauren fingered the short indigo sheath dress she'd bought on a whim at a trendy boutique in SoHo. Her long legs were wrapped in sheer black stockings.

She pulled back her shoulder-length hair and styled it into her own version of a French chignon. Only a few strands framed her face, accentuating her deep almond-shaped eyes. She'd dabbed a light blush to her cheeks. All the women in the Hughes family had faces that were loved by the camera. Timeless classics with long, slender necks, generous lips, and delicate jawlines.

Lauren Hughes, you might look like your mama but you sure do have your father's eyes.

She shook her head at the memory. She'd lost count

of all the times she'd heard that statement as relatives from both sides of the family pinched her cheeks. But Lauren had been a stubborn little thing. Although she knew he wasn't coming back from the grave, every time somebody said she had her father's eyes she'd just tell them she'd rather have her daddy. Even after her mother married Ralph, she'd wish she had him back.

Lauren and Alan were fashionably late to the trendy club, but it didn't matter. As soon as they had entered the party, they were sucked into the crowd. Alan, the sports celebrity, was pulled into a group of fans and players while Lauren moved in front of the tall-framed windows. She took in the large room in a glance.

The first floor was about ten times the size of her one-bedroom apartment. The main room had exposed pipes and steel beams running across the open ceiling, which blended into pewter-colored metal-framed windows dressed by heavy velvet drapes, while a long crescent-shaped bar lined with a well-heeled crowd dominated the left side of the room.

Lauren smiled and waved at familiar faces as her stomach led her over to the food-laden buffet table. She made her way through the buffet line and filled her plate with small canapés, seafood scampi, and various other gourmet treats.

After securing her grip on her plate, Lauren moved toward the back of the room and took a seat at one of the midsized rosewood tables. She'd just sat down at one of the small tables when her sister-friend and fellow designer Cassandra joined her.

"Now you know she's a gold digger, right?" Cassandra said.

"What . . ." Lauren put down her cutlery before turning toward Cassandra. The petite Bermuda native with a flawless almond complexion and jet-black hair was busy giving the evil eye to the young magazine editor hovering around Alan. "Who?" Lauren said.

The woman's lips curved into a frown. "Little Miss Butter-Couldn't-Melt-In-My-Mouth over there next to Alan."

"You mean Brenda Sanders?" Lauren glanced toward the bar in time to see the statuesque woman leaning in close to her best friend.

Cassandra waved a dismissive hand. "Last week she was seeing an 'up-and-coming' singing sensation, last month she was about to be engaged to the Brooks Brothers fashion model. That girl picks up men the way a dog picks up fleas."

"Girl, stop that." Lauren looked around to make sure no one had overheard the comment.

"Don't get so uptight." Cassandra patted her mouth with a napkin. "It's not like you need to worry about anything."

Lauren picked up her fork. "Except for you getting kicked out by picking on the bridesmaids."

"It's not my fault Alan has to beat women off with a stick." Cassandra's eyebrow rose. "By the way, you're *supposed* to be his girl. Why aren't you looking after him?"

"Because he's a big boy and can take care of himself." Lauren watched the pro baseball player sign another autograph. With his signature angular nose, twin dimples, and strong jaw, Alan wore the well-cut black Armani suit better than any fashion model. She found it hard to believe he was the same skinny-legged boy she used to beat at dominoes.

Cassandra frowned and gave her a long look. "I don't know how you do it."

"Do what?" she questioned, turning from admiring the small band playing on the small elevated stage. Lauren was fond of all types of music, but jazz and blues were two of her favorite things. The sound of the trumpet set her toes to tapping.

Cass waved her hand through the air. "Be so blasé with all those women drooling over him."

Lauren shrugged and sat back trying to enjoy the music. "It's really not a big deal."

She and Alan had been joined at the hip from the time their mothers started dropping them off at the church day-care center. She knew him when he was just another ashy, scrawny neighborhood boy trying to get picked for spur-of-the-moment stickball games. He was the only man she knew who could make her feel like a pigtailed girl when she looked like a sophisticated woman.

"Well, if the maid of honor gets any closer to Alan, it'll take the Jaws of Life to get her away from the man."

Picturing the leggy woman being pulled away by the large metal clamps, Lauren laughed out loud. Afterward, she had to take a sip of water to get rid of the tickle in her throat.

Her best friend hadn't been at the engagement party thirty minutes before starting something. Lord, she wished she'd grown up with Cass as her little sister instead of Sabrina. She couldn't keep the frown off her face at the thought of her stepsister. She looked up in time to catch Alan's eye and, seeing the look of desperation on his face, she waved him over.

"Lauren, are you all right?" Alan eased down into the seat next to hers.

"I'm fine." She took a sip of her wine.

"What happened?" He patted her on the back.

She hurriedly shot Cassandra a warning glance. "Last bite went down the wrong way."

"Having fun yet?" Alan had leaned closer so she could hear him over the sound of the saxophone.

"Of course. What about you?"

"Getting a little tired."

"Your knee okay?" Lauren reached over and touched his shoulder. Alan had only been discharged from the hospital two weeks ago.

He nodded. "Just a little tender. To tell you the truth it's not the knee that's bothering me. I'd never have gotten away from the woman if you hadn't waved me over." He scooted his chair closer to the table and leaned in.

"You could have just walked away," Lauren suggested but knew Alan was too much a gentleman to be so rude.

"So where's the new man you've been telling me about?" he asked, changing the subject.

Cassandra jumped into the conversation before Lauren could answer. "She kicked his sorry rear end to the curb."

Lauren sighed and looked toward the ceiling. "We had a disagreement."

"They had a fight," Cass said, putting her drink on the table and tossing back her long wavy hair. "The man had the nerve to try and boss her around."

"That true, Lauren?" He stared at her.

She noticed Alan's brown eyes were serious. "No, I just discovered Phillip had some control issues he needed to work out." She toyed with her wineglass. Why was it, she asked herself, that relationships had to be so complicated . . . so emotional?

"Lauren." Cassandra let out an impatient sigh. "Phillip had more than control issues. The man was a walking, talking G.I. Joe. He says jump. You say, how high? He even called you every morning just to make sure you woke up on time."

"Cass," she hissed. Lauren was more than aware her friend was simply speaking the truth, but getting into a discussion about her horrendous dating life during a party was not something she wanted to have happen.

"Don't get mad at me," Cass said, waving her hand. "I'm just telling the truth."

Alan's right eyebrow shot up. "Are you still seeing this guy, Lauren?"

"No," she said, shaking her head. "I called it off last week."

"That's good." Alan leaned back in his chair and waved at a passing teammate.

"No, it's not." She tapped her finger against the table. "At this rate, I'm going to end up like Oprah Winfrey but without her bank account."

"Wrong again." Cass laughed. "Remember, Oprah's got Stedman."

"Thank you for making me feel better." Lauren crossed her arms and sat back.

Alan joined in the laughter and stood. "Don't worry, you could always marry me. Now, y'all stay out of trouble while I go catch up with some of the guys."

Lauren waved him away, then looked down at her food. The crab cakes and jumbo shrimp didn't look so appetizing anymore.

"I didn't mean to get you down, Lauren."

"I know." She looked toward the newly engaged couple. The bride's friends had put together the surprise dinner party in less than two weeks. The beautiful high-powered advertising exec was set to marry New York's newest district attorney. The future bride reminded Lauren of her stepsister except Sabrina had married for prestige and money, not love and family.

Lauren wanted to be happy but she couldn't be. The last engagement party she'd gone to still left a sour taste in her mouth while the wedding had left her stomach in knots. Her stepsister married Karl Jackson, a man twice her age, but the only one who could give Sabrina the money, power, and attention she craved.

She shook her head. Their marriage was a disaster waiting to happen. All the money and success in the world couldn't make Sabrina happy. Even having all of her stepfather's love hadn't been enough—she'd wanted exclusive rights to Lauren's mother as well.

"This is really getting to you, isn't it?"

Lauren turned her attention back to Cassandra. "You mean sitting here surrounded by happy couples watching the bride-to-be flash her ring, excuse me, the Rock of Gibraltar she has on her finger? The answer is yes."

She took a sip of wine. Just because she was never a bridesmaid didn't mean she didn't want to be a bride. She'd stepped into the engagement festivities when she agreed to do Alan a favor. Now, watching the happy couple made her feel as though she'd been sucker punched by envy. If she were to change colors, she'd be greener than the parsley on her plate.

"Look, it's not like Phillip is the last man on earth," Cass added.

"True, but the pickings are getting pretty slim." Lauren scanned the crowded room. Tall, handsome, and distinguished-looking men littered the room like confetti on New Year's. However, the women with the rings on their fingers, and the girlfriends by their sides, let her know that most of the men at the party were off the dating market.

"Come on, snap out of it." Cassandra shook her shoulder.

Lauren tapped her fingers against the table. Some memory was niggling at the back of her mind.

"Nine," she said out loud.

"What?" Cass asked.

"Phillip was number nine," she repeated with a gleam in her eyes. *I, Lauren Hughes, being of sound mind and post-freshman-fifteen body.* The after-graduation party with all the girls of Sista Row came back to her.

Cassandra looked at her as if she were crazy. "What did they put in your wine? Because you are not making sense right now."

Lauren planted a fake smile on her face and scooted the chair back. "What I was saying is that there are nine nice-looking gentlemen standing over near the bar," she improvised.

"Uh-huh." Cassandra eyed her suspiciously.

"So we should go and meet them," she suggested.

"And how are you going to accomplish that when they're drooling over that half-naked video model *Vibe* magazine had the nerve to hire as a writer?"

"You don't like Jeanine either?" Lauren stared at the fierce frown Cass had on her face. She could have sworn her tenderhearted friend had changed into Joan Rivers at the Academy Awards.

"Anyway." Cassandra let out a sigh.

"Well, since Alan will be taking us home, we don't have to worry about how much we have to drink, right?"

Her friend nodded. "Okay, love. What's the point?"

"So why don't we just stroll over to the bar and order something?"

Cassandra's eyes lit up when Lauren lifted her glass in a toast. A little oblivion could do her a lot of good at the moment.

Nick Randolph waved at a fellow attorney, remembering all the times he'd greeted Saturday and Sunday mornings with a hangover at a friend's place instead of at church. He heard the music and let his eyes rove over the dozens of beautiful women, but the thrill was gone. There wasn't a rush of adrenaline when he met a lady's glance and saw her eyes darken with interest.

Maybe he was getting old, he mused. Nick hurriedly glanced into one of the mirrors on the wall of the club. Nope, just tired and ready to kick back after four years of eighty-hour weeks and cross-country flights. He'd pushed hard to become a partner at the law firm. After selling his one-bedroom on the Upper East Side to move into a brownstone in Brooklyn, he was ready for a much-needed break.

Now that he had the house, the career, and financial security, Nick only needed one more piece to be complete: her. The one he'd bring home to Mama, the girl he and his family could love. *Best start by talking to Ami,* he made a mental note to himself, *she'll know some nice women.* His little sister could set up a dinner with one of her friends.

"Hey, Alan, how's it going?" Nick shouted as he made his way through the crowd. He'd barely managed to get out of the office before the cleaning women arrived. Having missed out on the bachelor party, he'd wanted to be on time for the engagement celebration.

"Everything's cool. Just showing support for a brotha about to jump the broom. What about you?"

Nick grinned. "Same ole same ole. Salary negotiations, licensing rights, and contracts."

He looked around for Alan's latest girlfriend—the five-eleven runway model with a chocolate complexion that could give a man nice dreams. The woman was perfection itself until she opened her mouth. Kendra's long speeches on why Versace was out of style and why sixties fashion was en vogue made him want to run out of the restaurant. "Where's Kendra?"

His friend shrugged. "Probably on a plane to Miami to check out the latest nightclubs and spa treatments."

"Sounds good to me." Nick raised his drink. "I wish she'd taken Theresa with her."

"What happened? Did the two of you get into a fight?" Alan asked.

Nick shook his head. "No, we haven't been an item for months but she still feels like she has to know my every move."

"That stuff must be in the air. Cassandra told me Lauren just broke up with some guy who wouldn't leave her alone."

His attention sharpened at Alan's mention of Lauren's name. "How's she doing?" he asked, trying to act cool.

Nick forced himself not to wince as he recalled the manner in which he'd treated her that night at the hospital. He'd hopped into a cab immediately after receiving the phone call that his pro baseball client had been in a car accident. A friend first and an attorney second, he had overreacted to the presence of the strange woman by Alan's bedside. When he walked in on what he thought was an invasion of Alan's privacy, he'd acted in Alan's best interests by having the woman forcibly removed from the hospital room.

Alan's tap on the shoulder brought him out of his reverie. "You can see for yourself. Lauren and Cass are sitting at one of the back tables."

Nick almost succeeded in spilling his drink at Alan's unexpected answer. Nick couldn't keep from scanning the room until his eyes zeroed in on Lauren fifteen feet away. In a sea of elegant black, she sat looking cool, calm, and collected in an indigo dress. The silky material clung to the woman in all the right places and showed off her vibrant mocha-colored skin.

No matter how far away she was, he could pick her out of a crowd. It was the way she held her head high and the easygoing flow of energy that radiated from her relaxed body language. His eyes trailed down from her slender neck to her long legs.

He followed the way she shook her head at something Cassandra said. He couldn't hear her laughter over the noise but he could imagine the husky sound. He'd seen her in old Polaroid pictures with Alan plenty of times. Even as a little girl, she'd had a beautiful smile.

"Hey, you want to talk with the girls for a minute?"

He turned in time to see a flash of pain on Alan's face. The knee. He'd forgotten about his friend's injury.

"Sure, just don't let Lauren get near me with a knife," he joked.

"You two still not speaking?"

"No," he said, shrugging. "I'm doing all the apologizing; she's just not in the forgiving mood."

"My girl seems to be going for a record, but don't worry, she'll come round."

The topic of their conversation took that moment to look up. Nick stared. Her warm gaze settled on Alan, and her face lit up.

Maybe it was the way her full bronze-colored lips curled upward or the way her husky voice sounded as she laughed, but Nick felt as if he'd run from the thirty-yard line to score a touchdown.

Yet, when those dark sparkling eyes focused on him, the evil glance Lauren threw Nick could have melted the North Pole. For a man used to getting nothing but admiring stares from young women and proud looks from the older ones, his broad smile disappeared as Lauren turned toward him. He'd tried everything from flowers to gourmet chocolate to persuade her to forgive him; nothing worked. The only results were to see his wallet a little emptier and to have his ears ringing from the sound of Lauren slamming the door in his face.

"What are the two of you up to now?"

Hearing Alan's voice, Lauren turned away from Cassandra. The smile on her face dimmed the moment she locked eyes with Nick Randolph. She lifted the wine to her lips and finished the glass. The man had the nerve to grin at her as though they were old friends.

He might have looked good in the dark blazer with the designer shirt, but she couldn't forget what had happened the first time they'd met. For that incident alone she disliked him more than cold grits on a Sunday morning.

"My, what a suspicious mind you have, Alan." Lauren batted her eyelashes.

"That's because I know you too well." A smile played on Alan's lips as he walked over and put an arm around her waist.

"Just like I know you're only holding me because half the women in here are staring at you like you're a piece of Junior's cheesecake sitting in the middle of a Weight Watchers meeting," Lauren murmured for his ears alone.

"That bad?" He glanced nervously around the room.

"Worse." She patted his shoulder. "If looks could kill, I'd be shot full of holes."

"Maybe we should check out early?"

"And miss out on the fun of being the object of jealousy and envy?" She shook her head. "Oh, no, you blackmailed me into coming, so you just smile and grab some drinks."

"Blackmail, Lauren?"

"You bet." She graced him with a devilish smile. "Don't tell me you forgot our little conversation? The one where you lied and told me that you were afraid that Pam, the man-eating praying mantis, would jump on you if I wasn't here to keep her away."

Paying not the slightest attention to Alan's discomfort, Lauren kept turning the screws. "Do the words, *if you don't come with me I might hurt my knee running away from Mariah* ring a bell?"

"Wow." Alan licked his lips. "I sure am thirsty," he said loudly.

She raised a well-arched eyebrow.

Alan started, "You know how I feel about causing scenes, Lauren."

She still wasn't moved.

"And I really shouldn't be standing too long." Alan gave her that puppy dog look that'd always gotten them both into trouble as kids.

"All right," Lauren said before turning toward Cassandra and Nick.

"I'm going to make a run to the bar for drinks. Any orders?"

"White wine for me," Cass replied, scooting over to sit next to Alan.

"I'll help," Nick volunteered.

Lauren barely stopped herself from swearing. The man was the last person in the world she wanted to talk to.

"Be my guest." She allowed him to escort her through the crowd.

Nick could barely stop himself from leaning in closer. Whatever she had on, pulled him like a magnet. The lush sensual scent made him want to lean over and lick the stuff off her beautiful neck. That thought brought him back to reality. Alan hadn't come out and said anything, but he wasn't going to start anything with the girl his best friend was interested in.

"Great party, don't you think?" he shouted over the music.

"Yes, it is." Her disinterested tone didn't seem to bother the man one bit.

"Do you know the bride or the groom?" he asked as they neared the bar.

"Both." She caught his look of surprise. "Alan introduced us months ago." She didn't add that she had put together the design for their loft renovation. "I take it you know the groom?"

"Bill and I sat for the bar exam together."

"How nice." She tucked a tendril of hair behind her ears before turning to greet the cute young bartender who could definitely get Lauren's confidence back. She couldn't keep from returning his appreciative smile even as she saw Nick's look of disapproval out of the corner of her eye.

She leaned over the bar. "I'd like white wine, an orange juice, and a French martini, please."

"Anything for the beautiful lady." Lauren beamed, hearing the bartender's lyrical Caribbean accent.

"I'll have a gin and tonic," Nick ordered.

Lauren wanted to move away but the crowd made it next to impossible.

"Is it okay for Alan to be having a drink so close to his knee surgery?"

Lauren blinked and cut him a look that read *You're still here?* but apparently the attorney needed glasses.

"I said—" Nick started.

"The French martini's mine." She enunciated slowly as if she were speaking to a child.

"Come on, Lauren. Can't we all just get along? I made an honest mistake."

Lauren looked at the smile on Nick's face, and her resolve came close to melting. However, the confident request for forgiveness wasn't enough for her to forget the first time they'd met. All it did was harden her heart at the memory of his callous treatment.

Angry at herself for even thinking about forgiving him, she added an even more impersonal tone to her voice. "Are you finished?" Lauren gave Nick a cool glance before smiling at the bartender.

"You haven't spoken one complete sentence since we met, Lauren. Are you going to be mad at me forever?"

She wiggled her finger back and forth. Long time . . . forever . . . extremely long time . . . Forever might be just enough time for her to forget the way he'd had her thrown out of the hospital, she mused.

She nodded. "For a lawyer it takes you a long time to catch on."

Nick rubbed his head. "Alan said you had a stubborn streak a mile long. I didn't believe him."

Lauren tipped the bartender and picked up two drinks.

"Apparently you must make it a practice of not believing your friends." She stood. "Now if you're finished pointing out the obvious, I'd like to give Alan his drink before the ice melts."

She turned away before he could see the grin on her face. In her mind she could see Yankee Stadium with its big scoreboard blinking: Lauren Hughes: 1, Nick Randolph: 0.

Nick stood there as Lauren brushed by him. The smell of her perfume had him thinking of some nice satin sheets and a bottle of red wine. He watched the enticing display of Lauren's nice round backside as she sashayed through the crowd turning heads along the way. He toyed with the championship ring on his finger. The woman was going to make him beg.

"Excuse me . . ."

He turned toward the bar. The young dreadlocked bartender was looking at him.

"Sorry I took so long with your drink, man."

"That's all right."

"That your girlfriend?" The man glanced in Lauren's direction.

"No," Nick said with a casualness he didn't feel. It bothered him, he realized. Lauren bothered him. But what bothered him more was that the young brother behind the bar got a piece of Lauren's smile and he was standing there hungry when there were dozens of beautiful women in the room.

The bartender continued. "She's straight-up fine, my brother. If I were you I'd definitely be trying to get up in her mix."

Nick took a drink, enjoying the slow burn of the gin and tonic as it swept down his throat. He had a better chance of being president of the United States than he had at getting Lauren out on a date.

He stood and pulled out his wallet. "Thanks for the advice."

"Good luck," the bartender replied before moving to the opposite side of the bar.

Nick left a big tip before grabbing the drinks. He shook his head remembering the way he had kicked Lauren out of Alan's hospital room. He'd been Alan's attorney and personal friend for almost two years but had yet to meet the infamous Lauren Hughes.

Walking in to see a woman leaning over Alan as he lay sedated, he'd written her off as another baseball groupie. He discovered who she was a day later and almost a friend short when Alan woke up. How was he to know the sexy lady holding his unconscious boy's hand was the same pigtailed tomboy Alan called his girl?

Two

It's not the end of the world, Lauren mused, looking out the window toward the pale sunrise. The early morning outside her apartment was colored yellow blue by dying leaves on skinny branches resting against a creamy sapphire sky. Heavy winds whistled through the trees, clearing off some of the autumn leaves.

If I had a dollar for every leaf . . . She closed her eyes at the memory of Paul lying in the pile of leaves into which his fellow firefighters had pushed him.

As the clock struck nine, Lauren swallowed two aspirins and felt her stomach perform circus flips from the combination of post-hangover upset and milky sweet Jamaican coffee. It'd taken her the better part of an hour to find the old paper among the other college items in her antique steamer trunk.

A serious and determined girl in college, she pulled in everything like a dry sponge. In high school both Lauren and her older brother, Nathan, had been voted most likely to succeed while Sabrina received the most popular vote. So when Amy, the psychology major of her friendship circle, challenged them all to name it and claim it, Lauren rose to the occasion. Full of champagne and good food, she hadn't raised a party maker after the graduation dinner. No, she'd picked up a pen and joined the group in writing down her ever-practical pledge.

The sound of Mrs. Peters leaving her apartment to

walk the dog snapped Lauren out of her reverie. Her
eyes drifted toward the desk calendar: October 15. Six
months. She had six months left to finish the list she had
started the day she got her undergraduate degree some
years ago.

I'm going to be thirty, she silently groaned, dropping her
pencil and looking up at the stuffed toy her brother had
won shooting hoops at Six Flags. She kept staring at the
Garfield cat sitting on top of the computer. The numbers three and zero seemed to grow larger in her mind,
and her eyes widened as the cat's lips twitched and whispered in her ear like a grandmother spilling secrets in
church. "Nothing beats a quitter but a try, young lady,"
she thought she heard him whisper.

As laughter pealed out, she held up the crinkled
college-ruled piece of notebook paper. She'd written her
pledge at 2:00 A.M. Chocolate stains from the cake her
mother baked littered the edges.

                                                    May 10

*I, Lauren Hughes, being of sound mind and post-
freshman-fifteen body, do seriously promise to accomplish
the following before I turn 30:*

1. *Receive my master's degree*
2. *Purchase my own home*
3. *Possess a nice portfolio (investment, not designs)*
4. *Own a decent old-school music collection*
5. *Travel around the world*
6. *Write a book*
7. *Be able to run a mile without falling out*
8. *Buy Mama that full-length mink coat and tell Sabrina I know she was the one who kidnapped my
   Raggedy Ann doll*
9. *Learn to cook like Grandmama*

10. *Jump the broom with Mr. Right (after dumping at least 10 Mr. Wrongs)*

Lauren blinked and picked up a pencil and circled numbers five and ten. Taking out two thumbtacks, she fixed the sheet to the fabric-covered bulletin board on the wall in front of her desk. She always kept her promises; only these two were to herself.

"About time I took a vacation," Lauren murmured, walking over to the couch. Sitting back on the cushy sofa, she took a sip of coffee, enjoying the silence of morning. There'd been a time when the sound of her father's booming laughter would send her running to the kitchen.

She stood, pulling the belt of her velvet burgundy robe tighter. Now Saturday mornings reminded her of the loud screaming matches she'd get into when Sabrina cranked up her little radio and start screeching to the music. To this day, close to a decade later, Lauren couldn't stand the sound of music in the morning.

"Lauren, you, Nathan, and ya mama is all I love in this world. I ain't ever gonna be leaving my girls." Her father's southern Mississippi voice washed over her. He'd promised to come back home in a few days. Only sorrow in the form of two police officers showed up on the front steps.

Sighing, Lauren opened the refrigerator freezer and pulled out a frozen waffle and popped it into the toaster. *It's that list,* she thought. For a minute she'd actually thought about settling down and raising a family. She'd even thought she'd found her soul mate. She poured out her lukewarm coffee.

Falling in love. She shook her head. More like falling in a pit of lies. She grabbed the waffle out of the toaster and dropped it on her plate. Love and forever were like New Edition and a reunion. Everybody knew they wouldn't stay together long.

"I don't need a passionate love," she said out loud. "I just need a husband and partner." She sat down at the table and poured blueberry syrup on her waffle. Love merely existed from the second the singer opened his mouth until the end of the song. It lasted a quick minute—the pain left behind lasted forever. She knew from experience grief wasn't a couple of pearl-drop tears like the ones Lauren saw on television. No, pain for her had a river flowing down to the pillow night after night.

She'd called it quits with the whole falling-in-love thing, but there was lust and longing. The kind that'd looked at her last night. She chuckled, picturing the look of frustration on Nick Randolph's face as she left him standing at the bar. Evil man, pretending everything was fine between them when she still hated his ugly guts.

Forgive him, please. Lauren made herself a fresh cup of coffee. The man expected her to forget the way everybody stared as security ushered her out of the hospital and left her to fight through the story-hungry press. Flowers and expensive chocolate couldn't wipe that memory away.

She couldn't see how Alan was friends with Nick. She would have detested Nick even if he hadn't gotten her thrown out. She cut into the waffle.

Tall, dark, and built with those street-smart eyes. The arrogant swagger and that "I got this" style. Just like Paul. She shivered despite the warmth of the room. The very things she couldn't stand about Nick broke loose butterflies in her stomach. But she'd learned fire burned. She was much stronger and wiser.

She swallowed a bite of the waffle; it tasted like sawdust in her mouth. Memories tried to flow through the dam she'd built around her heart and touch the shallow grave in her soul. The proud mahogany men she'd loved had raked hot coals over every nerve in her body. Her father's death had wrecked her childhood, but Paul's leaving her . . . She put the fork and knife down.

Love had tried to kill her twice. Lauren wasn't a fool—not everybody got married because of love. She got up and put her dishes in the sink. Six months. Six months to travel around the world and get married. It couldn't be that hard, she mused, remembering her Indian friend's tale of how she and her husband met through an arranged marriage. No. She shook her head. She wouldn't wait for a nonexistent Prince Charming to come along and break what was left of her heart. No, she'd go out there and get Mr. Dependable.

Lauren walked into the small alcove she called her work space and picked up her sketch pad and notebook from the table. All she had holding her back from packing her bags and leaving was work. She needed to finish Alan's place and submit the drawings for the new government office center. Six months. Flipping open her sketchbook, she sat down at the desk and began to draw.

Charlie kept it old-school, Nick thought, walking through the glass door. The empty shop smelled of lilac, aftershave, and alcohol. The owner was sitting in the barber's chair reading a newspaper. The one-room barbershop had been on the same Harlem block for the past two decades. But instead of wearing one of those white, doctor-looking tops that he remembered as a kid, Charlie had changed with the times. The heavyset black man was sporting a Nike sweat suit.

"Morning, Charlie." Nick walked back and took a seat in an empty chair.

"Right on time. How ya doing, Nick?"

"I'm hanging. Just moved into my aunt's place in Brooklyn."

Charlie nodded as he put the paper on the counter. "Say, Nick. You know a thing or two about taxes?"

He sat back in the leather chair and rubbed his chin. "I know enough to be dangerous. What's up?"

"Well, I'm having a little disagreement with the IRS, and I could use some help."

"Got the paperwork?"

"As a matter of fact, I've got it right here."

Before he could look up, Charlie had dropped the file on his lap. Settling back, Nick pulled a couple of pages and started to skim the documents as he heard the sound of the door opening and closing.

"Take it all off, Charlie. Give my boy a close shave."

Nick looked up from the legal documents to see Alan's reflection in the barbershop mirror.

"You're late, my man," he said, leaning back in the chair.

"You know what the traffic's like." Alan pulled off his sports jacket.

"Traffic?" Nick looked at Alan sideways. "It's six in the morning."

"In case you've forgotten, this is Manhattan, not New Jersey."

"True, but I drove in from Brooklyn and beat you here."

"Some of us have to sleep," Alan responded.

Nick waited for Charlie to get the clippers ready as the barber came to stand at the back of the chair. "So when are you getting back in the game, Alan?"

Nick watched his friend take a seat in the next chair.

"Don't know. I've got one more surgery and some physical therapy."

Nick sat back as Charlie turned on the clippers. He watched in the mirror as the older man shook his head. "Man, if I had a dollar for every time somebody asked when you was gonna be back on the pitcher's mound . . ."

Nick finished the sentence, "You'd still owe back taxes."

Charlie sighed. "So what's the verdict?"

"Nothing you can't handle. All you have to do is send in the extension request and get a new accountant. This one evidently is trying to put you in jail."

"Can I sue?" Charlie asked hopefully.

Nick raised his voice to be heard over the buzz. "Yes, but the attorney fees will set you back some serious money. My advice: get another CPA and make sure this one's reputable."

"You're a good man, Nick. Thanks for the advice," he said before removing the black cape.

Nick stood and stretched. Switching places with Alan, he stood behind the barber chair staring at the black-and-white photographs tucked in the corners of the mirror.

He couldn't help grinning at the old photo of himself at ten years old. He and some other neighborhood boys sat waiting to get their hair cut. Nick's head belonged on the front cover of *Ebony*. With his Afro, he could have doubled for a miniature Don King.

He remembered the days he'd spent sunup to sundown in the park playing dominoes with the older boys or dirty dozens with his crew. They'd mess around until the streetlights came on and their mothers came out the front door calling their names. Friends for life, he mused. Too bad it couldn't have stayed that way. His parents never looked back after they packed up for the move to New Jersey.

Nick had sacrificed having close friends for a degree and a football. Nothing else mattered but the books and game plays.

"You always have to love what you do and who you are, son," his father would say as his hand rested on Nick's head when his father put him on the yellow school bus every morning.

His dad was proud as a peacock, and it made Nick's chest swell to see how well his brothers and little sister were doing. Yet, something had gone missing since he left Harlem. Now, instead of having old friends from the neighborhood and connections to his childhood, all he had was his family, his career, and a weak knee.

I guess that should be enough, he mused, *but I want more.* He leaned against the same white barbershop wall. It hadn't been long after he'd sold his co-op before the voice in the back of his head had started telling him something was still missing from his life. His mother's hints of grandchildren and retirement only added to the feeling that he needed to make a change. Sighing as he watched Charlie shave what little hair was on Alan's head, Nick wished he had all the answers.

"So how's your family?" Alan asked thirty minutes later as Nick finished the last bite of the southwestern omelette in a local diner.

"They're good. Mama left me a message last night that Uncle Raymond was going to be coming by the house next week and wants to talk to me."

"What's he into this time?"

"Investments and wealth management. He's doing pretty good, I've heard. Think he's trying to build up his client base."

Alan nodded as he cut a piece of steak. "You couldn't get any better than yours."

"Yeah, well, it took a while. I've got you to thank for a lot of it."

"No, you know you're one of the best. If I ever got into trouble I'd call you." Alan sat back and rubbed his newly shaved head.

"Then I'd have to call in a favor from another lawyer. I'm a paper attorney, Alan. I'd get my tail kicked from here to Trenton if I had to step back into the courtroom."

Nick surveyed the quiet restaurant. At 7:30 on a Saturday morning, the popular neighborhood diner was practically empty.

"We should play some ball."

Nick looked at Alan funny and started to say something about the brace on his leg.

"Not *real* basketball," Alan explained. "Lauren finally let me back into my den on Thursday. The electronics guys finished installing the entertainment system. Video games look awesome on the big-screen TV. Man, it makes you feel like you're really in the game."

"Serious?" Nick leaned forward, placing his arms on the table.

"I kid you not." Alan raised his fork. "I don't know where Lauren found the man, but he worked a miracle. The house is great but my girl made sure the den design was just right. Even spent a couple of days testing out the gear. I've got surround sound and everything else that comes with a state-of-the-art entertainment system."

"Lauren put it together?" Nick asked, curious about the woman. He couldn't see the sophisticated lady playing video games.

"She's almost finished renovating the whole house. It'll look like something out of a decorating magazine when she's finished."

"Really?" Nick chuckled. "I would have put you in more of a Hugh Hefner playboy mansion kind of thing."

Alan shook his head. "You know that's not my style. Mama and the boys gotta feel comfortable. I had Lauren design a room just for Mama and Pop."

Nick rubbed his chin thinking about the empty brownstone he'd recently inherited. Aunt Roxie had given all her furniture and clothing to charity. The place needed some color, but he didn't have the time to plan anything.

"She's doing that good a job?"

"The house is great. Only problem is having all that

space to myself." Alan put his hands on the table. "It's got me thinking about family and kids."

Nick didn't even blink at Alan's comment about settling down. His friend came from a close-knit family. After the car accident, it was natural for him to be thinking about putting down some roots. "So you think Lauren would do a good job on my place?"

Alan grinned. "Only if you could get her to take it. I'm her best friend, but it took her a month to free up the time. Lauren is hot right now."

"All right then. Why don't you give one of those giggling waitresses a look so we can get out of here?"

"They're looking at you, not me," Alan said, grinning.

Nick shook his head and laughed. Only Alan could be so blind.

He looked at his watch. "Man, I have to run. The exterminators are coming by to spray the new place."

"See ya later."

"I'll be dropping off some things at your place on Monday."

"What's up?"

"We need to talk about your new licensing agreement."

"All right."

Nick hit the door with the image of Lauren playing video games floating in his mind.

Please, Lord, just hold off a little longer, Lauren prayed. She'd left the hair salon that afternoon humming bon voyage and thinking of long romantic walks along Paris's Champs-Elysées and hours wandering through the bazaars of Marrakech. Knowing that in a few weeks she'd be headed for new places and seeing new faces made even a cloudy New York City day look brighter.

Feeling a cool wet breeze, Lauren eyed the dark clouds. Normally she enjoyed the walk to Alan's house.

The quiet Harlem brownstone-lined neighborhood never failed to make her proud. She stepped over a pile of some small doggy's gift to the city. When the first cold, wet drop landed on top of her newly touched-up perm, she broke out the umbrella.

"Damn," she muttered, pressing the automatic release like an old elevator button. The wind took that moment to start blowing harder and the umbrella spoke refused to move. The sound of fabric ripping was as loud as the honking of a yellow cab. Letting out a groan, Lauren dumped the thing in the next wastebasket. She kept darting looks at the sky.

She prayed harder and walked faster. She turned the corner. God ignored her. Right as she was crossing the street, the bottom fell out and the rain poured down. By the time she got to the familiar half-spiral stairs of Alan's place, she was ready to call for the coast guard. She raised a shivering hand and put her key in the lock.

The warm smell of vanilla greeted her as she walked into the entrance parlor. She dropped her bag and glanced into the antique gold-rope-trimmed mirror she'd picked at an outdoor flea market. Lauren looked like a drowned rat. It didn't matter that she'd spent two hours at the beauty salon getting her hair done. The Lord had declared it was not going to be her day.

"Alan!" her voice echoed through the house.

"In the kitchen," came a response.

She paused from the act of taking off her overcoat and looked down. Her eyes followed the passage of a water droplet as it fell from her nose. Big puddles had formed on the newly restored hardwood floor. Lauren sniffed and felt tears pool behind her eyes. This house was one of her best works. She'd spent weeks planning everything from the Victorian chandeliers to the sienna-colored kitchen walls.

"What happened to you?"

She looked up to see Alan walking toward her.

"My umbrella broke." Her voice wobbled like a square table with an uneven leg.

"Well, don't just stand there," he said, shooing her. "You've got to get out of those wet clothes."

"I've made a mess of the new floor and I'm probably going to catch pneumonia. The worst part is that I was having such a wonderful day," she griped.

"What happened?" He took her wet coat.

"I'm taking a vacation." She leaned over and pulled off her water-filled shoes and soggy trouser socks.

"What? Are you sick?"

"No."

"Lauren, you haven't taken a vacation in years. When I was still in Chicago, you only dropped in for Christmas and Thanksgiving."

"True." She pushed her hair back and followed him upstairs. "This time, however, I'm really going to take some serious time off from work."

"Any plans?" Alan asked as they reached the second floor.

"Oh, yes." She nodded. "And I'll let you know all about them as soon as I get out of the shower."

Alan grinned. "I'll get you something to put on. You know where everything is."

She nodded and turned around as he closed the bathroom door.

This was one of her favorite rooms in the house. She'd spent hours working liming wax into the floorboards to give the floor that perfect silvery white bloom. The large bathroom was filled with a warm, ambient light from the Afrocentric wall sconces on every wall.

Letting out a sigh of content, she eyed the cast-iron claw-footed tub she'd found by accident while scouting out an estate sale in Westchester County. The plant-lined windowsill and handmade toiletries were a woman's dream. More like Alan's mama's dream come true, she mused. Lauren wished she could be there when Mrs. Knight came to visit the following month.

She breathed in the scent of rosemary and shivered a little. *No bath for me,* she thought. Positioning the shower-head toward the wall, she turned on the water. Stepping out of the large shower stall, Lauren took off her wet clothes and hung them on the empty towel rack. She headed back to the glass shower stall and stepped underneath the hot water. Rained on again. Only this time, she was reaching for a towel and not a broken umbrella.

"So where are you going?" Alan asked as soon as she had made herself comfortable on the couch. She'd created a relaxing mood in the living room by using light furniture as her canvas and then dressing the space with a mix of textures and African objects.

Lauren curled her bare legs under her, rolled back the sleeves on his oversize baseball jersey, and reached out to take the cup of Irish cream–laced coffee from his hands. "Around the world."

"Cass going with you?" He sat down on the sofa.

"Not this time."

"So you're going by yourself?" He took a sip of coffee.

"The hope is that I'll be bringing someone back," she replied warily.

"Huh?" His brows bunched together.

"I'm going to travel around the world and . . ." Lauren took a deep breath. "I'm getting married."

"What?"

"Don't you spill coffee on this couch! It took me two weeks to find the right style and color," she scolded, giving him a dirty look.

Alan's voice rose. "Forget about the damn couch. Did you just say you're getting married? Have I even met this dude?"

"No." Lauren crossed her arms. She smiled a little,

hoping to lighten the situation. The combination of a relaxing shower and warm liqueur had taken the edge off her nerves.

"Wait. I thought you had broken that thing off with the control freak."

She nodded. "I did."

Alan sat up straight. "Well, then, who is he?"

"I don't know yet."

Alan's eyes narrowed and his lips opened and closed. "You don't know yet?" he echoed. "You plan on getting married and leaving the man for a trip around the world?"

"I'm going to find him while I'm on vacation. You know, like in those old movies your parents used to let us watch, except this'll be a little more premeditated."

"Lauren, I know that I didn't hear you just say you're planning to go around the world and get a man."

"Husband," she clarified.

He frowned. "Have you lost your mind?"

"No, I've lost my patience. I'm going to be thirty years old in six months, Alan." She looked at him expectantly. If anyone could understand, it was her friend.

"Oh . . . Now I get it." He sat back and gave her a satisfied smile. "Your clock is ticking or whatever you women are calling that time-to-settle-down stuff. They have drugs for that, you know. There's no need to rush."

She glared at him, knowing that Alan was no longer taking her seriously. "I don't need drugs."

"How about some Prozac?" He laughed.

"I don't need antidepressants, Alan. I need vaccinations. I don't have time to get sick." She took a sip of coffee and continued, "I've got two things left on my list to do before I turn thirty." She counted on her left hand. "Get married and travel around the world. The way I see it I'll be killing two birds with one stone."

"No. I'm not letting you go on with this crazy scheme

of yours. All you're going to do is get into trouble, and I can't be flying to some strange country to bail you out."

"'Let me,' Alan?" She raised her eyebrow and her voice in response to his authoritative tone. "You don't have to 'let me' do anything. I'm going on this trip. I've already asked for the vacation, I've made an appointment to get a checkup, and I've also scheduled a meeting with a travel agent next week."

"Have you talked to your family yet?"

"No. I haven't told a soul and you aren't either."

He seemingly ignored her warning. "Not even your best friend, Cassandra?"

"Not yet. I'll wait until I have an itinerary and the tickets." She watched the smile disappear off his face. Alan was finally beginning to take her seriously.

"Lauren—"

"Don't Lauren me." She cut him off with a wave of her hand. "I'm going through with this."

"What about love? You can't fall in love and marry some foreign stranger while you're on vacation."

Lauren took a sip of coffee and looked Alan dead in the eye and replied in a cool voice, "What about love? I never said anything about love."

He gave her a sharp glance. "You're not fooling me, Lauren. This is happening because you're not willing to give another brother a chance."

"Wrong. I've given plenty of men chances."

Alan held up his mug. "Please, when the man shows any kind of serious interest, you send him packing."

Lauren gritted her teeth. "This is different. I'm going to get married."

Alan pointed his index finger. "You can't get hitched to somebody you don't love."

She put her cup on the table. "And why not? I gave up on love a long time ago. All I want is someone I can trust.

I'm looking for a responsible, stable, intelligent, trust-worthy man I can raise some kids with."

Alan put his coffee cup on the table beside hers, then moved over to put his hand on her shoulder. "Look, why don't you tell me what's really going on here? Is this because of—"

"Don't say his name, Alan," she warned.

He went ahead and said it anyway. "Paul. Hell, I miss him too, Lauren. He was one of my best friends. But he's not coming back, and you can't give up."

"I'm not giving up," she said softly. "I'm recognizing the truth. I can't live with love anymore. I'm not willing to take another chance like that again. It almost killed me."

"Look, Lauren," he started.

Lauren barely stopped herself from breathing a sigh of relief at the sound of the door chime. She moved to stand, but Alan beat her to the punch.

"Don't move. I'll get it."

She leaned over and put down her cup. "Who would be crazy enough to be out in this kind of weather?"

"That would be the pizza man."

Lauren's face broke into a smile. "You ordered pizza?"

"While you were in the shower."

"With mushrooms, olives, and extra cheese?" she asked, grinning.

"Of course." Alan grinned back.

Leaning forward on the sofa, Lauren reached up and began to rub her wet hair.

Five minutes seemed to pass before she heard the sound of shoes on the floor. "Did you remember to get Buffalo wings?" she asked without looking up.

"You'll have to ask Alan as soon as he finishes paying the deliveryman."

Lauren lost her balance at the sound of the deep voice; she moved the towel in time to see Nick standing in the entranceway. He stood there all nicely dressed in a dark navy pinstripe suit and silver tie.

As a designer, she couldn't help appreciating the way the jacket hugged his broad shoulders. Hot golden cinnamon buns straight out of the oven was the only way she could describe how he looked standing under the high-beam halogen lights.

That's what she'd thought the night he walked through the hospital door. She'd soon discovered that he wasn't sweet. The way he'd grabbed her arm as if she were some criminal still rankled her. Nick wouldn't listen as she tried to explain her relationship with Alan. He called her a liar when she had told him she was Alan's best friend.

"Oh, it's you."

She cut him a glance. The man didn't even have the decency to look wet. Lauren stared into his dark eyes and was extremely conscious of her lack of clothing. Nick was the last person she wanted to see, but he was still handsome as sin. Even after looking away, she couldn't resist peeking up at him from underneath her eyelashes. She proceeded to ignore him and went back to rewrapping the towel around her hair.

"Yes, Lauren, it's me. How are you?"

"I was doing quite fine until you dropped by," she mumbled.

"Aaaa' right, people." Alan's voice filled the silence. "Look who else I found at the door."

Lauren looked past Nick to see Cassandra standing next to Alan.

"Hey, Cass." She smiled and moved to stand.

"Lauren, you forgot the fabric samples."

She looked at her friend closely. The edge of coolness in her tone was enough to give her frostbite.

Alan moved farther into the room and started to lay the pizza on the coffee table. "Well, we don't want to let the food get cold. I got some beer in the fridge. What you say we go downstairs to the den and watch the baseball game?"

"Oh, no!" Cass and Lauren said together.

Cass continued, "The furniture in the den is too new for you to be ruining it with your beer spills and pizza stains, Alan Douglas Knight. There's a television in the kitchen, we can start watching it in there."

"Man, Nick. See what happens when you let women in your house?" Alan scooted backward into the hallway.

"And what's that?" Cassandra challenged.

The tall baseball player grinned. "They start taking over."

Nick took the amber-filled glass Alan handed him. As soon as the front door closed behind Lauren and Cassandra, his friend had gone all serious.

"What's up?" He leaned back in the soft leather chair. The new paint and furniture smell still covered the den. He knew Alan didn't drink unless something was bothering him.

"I need a favor, Nick."

His eyes narrowed as Alan took a seat in the chair across from his.

"Okay, what can I do for you?"

"It's about Lauren." His friend leaned forward.

Nick's fingers tightened around the glass as he brought it toward his lips. He couldn't shake the image of her beautifully shaped legs from underneath Alan's baseball jersey.

"What about Lauren? Is she all right?"

"I don't know. She told me about some crazy plan she has about going around the world."

Nick frowned. "Nothing wrong with that."

"She wants to go alone and . . ."

Nick narrowed his eyes at Alan's hesitation.

"And she plans on finding a husband."

"What?" Nick choked on the Scotch and put the glass down hard.

"She's got this idea stuck in her head that she has to get married before she turns thirty."

"Are you serious?" Nick scowled.

"As a heart attack." Alan rubbed his brow. "The thing is, I know she'll do it. Once Lauren sets her mind to something, she won't let loose."

Nick frowned. "Is she trying to get you to propose?" As the words came out of his mouth, a knife seemed to go through his stomach.

Alan waved his hand. "No, Lauren won't marry me, not after what happened to Paul. That's why I've got a mess on my hands."

"Paul?" Nick grabbed hold of the information like a dog with a bone. "Who is Paul?"

"Her ex-fiancé."

"Lauren was engaged?" It shouldn't have surprised him, but it did.

Alan nodded. "Paul was a firefighter. He died trying to save a little girl from a house fire. It was three months before their wedding date."

"Damn. That's rough." Nick ran his hand over his chin.

"It hurt her something deep. Lauren didn't speak for weeks afterward; then one day she just packed up and moved to New York."

Nick tossed back the rest of his drink. Affairs of court, negotiations, and contracts were his fields of expertise. The affairs of the heart were uncharted territory for him.

"I don't know what I can do for you." He was the last person to give advice on women.

"I need you to help me keep her here."

The other man's request hit him like a ton of bricks.

Any hope he might have held that his friend wasn't involved with Lauren disappeared. No man on earth went through all these machinations unless he was committed.

Nick put down the half-filled glass and sat forward. "Now how am I going to do that? I'm the last person Lauren would listen to."

Alan nodded. "You really messed up."

"No need to remind me."

"Look, I only need to keep her here until Mama comes for a visit. If anybody can talk some sense into the girl it's my mother."

"How long is that?"

"Five weeks."

"When is she planning on leaving?"

"As soon as she finishes my place. Probably within the next ten days."

"So what do you need me to do?" Nick prompted.

As soon as the words left his mouth, Nick shifted in his chair. He was walking a razor-thin line. As a friend he'd do anything for Alan; as a lawyer he'd pledged his life to upholding certain principles. He'd sat at the negotiating table enough times to know when something was about to go wrong.

Alan rubbed his chin. "I need you to decorate."

Nick narrowed his eyes at the grin on his friend's face. He could name it because he'd seen that look before. In fact, he saw it often when he looked in the mirror: victory.

Three

Lauren put down her pencil and rubbed the back of her neck. She'd been working since six o'clock that morning. If she kept this up she could wrap up her projects and be on a plane in less than two weeks.

She looked down at one of the design plans on her desk and smiled. The sketch would be perfect for kids. Alan had wanted a room for when little cousins came for the holidays or summer vacation. She could have the walls painted by Friday and the furniture delivered within the week.

She added a note to the sketch to paint the room with darker shades. She'd met some of the Knights' younger members. The sticky fingers and messy faces still made her giggle. Her eyes strayed to a magenta fabric swatch she'd picked up the day before.

She used to love the color red, seeing Paul leaning against her car in his loose-fitting firefighter's suit. Maybe if he hadn't wanted to be a hero. The old grief surfaced again as she reached over and put the sample away. Lauren stood and turned to look out the window. Her moist eyes focused upward on the moving clouds; they were sending a message. She didn't have the luxury of maybes; whatever happened in the future, she was going to be in control.

Before Lauren could pick up the phone to call the contractor, the intercom buzzed.

"Yes," she answered.

"Lauren, Brad needs you in his office."

"Can it wait a minute? I was about to make a phone call."

"Umm . . ."

Lauren rolled her eyes. The secretary's hesitation was all she needed to know that Brad was in one of his moods again. The senior partner of the design firm had the creative instincts of da Vinci but the temperament of a prima donna.

"Tell him I'm on my way," she said, sighing.

"Thanks," the young woman replied.

Twenty minutes later, Lauren jumped up from the chair and started pacing. "You can't do this to me." She stopped in front of the oval desk.

She watched the older man. Brad was dressed in his usual monochrome black style. Black pants, black cashmere turtleneck, and black wire-rimmed glasses. His salt-and-pepper hair was perfect, just like everything else about him. Brad liked to be trendy but classic and his clients, along with the New York society women, loved him. Lauren knew that he'd shed blood, sweat, and tears to start the firm. She also knew that he was grooming her to help run the business when he decided to slow down.

"Honey." He stood and waved his hands. "I'm sorry, but we can't afford to turn down this business."

"Why? We're not hurting for new clients." She looked around his large modern office with honey-colored carpet and perfectly designed curves and cocoordinated furnishing.

Brad sighed and shook his head. "The man knows a lot of people. The same people we want to know. He's also in good with the president of the NBA and you know they've got that bid out for their office redesign."

She waved her hand. "I already put in for my vacation."

Brad moved around the desk. "I know, but think about

it, Lauren. Brooklyn brownstone, fifteen-foot ceilings with original details. He's willing to give you a free hand and a blank check."

She stopped pacing and tapped her fingernails against the desk. "Where is it?"

"Park Slope in Brooklyn," he said nonchalantly.

"How old is the house?" She barely managed to keep her voice even.

"It was built in 1910. Underwent major renovation twenty-five years ago."

"What kind of shape is the place in?" She felt a flash of excitement at the possibilities.

"Excellent. I went over to see it last night. He hasn't touched a thing. Most of the rooms are empty."

"How much space are we talking?"

"About 3,500 square feet, four floors, a beautiful deck, and a half lot in the back."

"Are they going to break it into rental units?" That was the linchpin; she couldn't take the thought of destroying the original structure.

"As far as I know he has no plans to do that."

She looked up as Brad leaned on the desk in front of her.

"Please, Lauren, say yes. You're the only one who can do this. You know you want to do it. Think of the crown moldings, the stairs, the fireplaces."

"I don't know." She dropped into the chair. "I have to go on this vacation."

It was becoming an obsession. Every morning she woke up thinking another day had gone by and she was wasting time. Time that she could be spending exploring some new country or dining with a new man.

Lauren chewed the inside of her lip. Brad had believed in her from the snowy afternoon when she'd shown up at his office with nothing but a handful of sketches and a mind full of ideas. He'd taken a risk bringing an unknown black woman into the firm.

She'd come to work at six o'clock in the morning and left at ten o'clock at night. Pushing herself to the limit, she'd spent weeks learning the newest modeling technology, hours visiting stores, as well as taking the time to begin building a furniture supplier and client base. Through it all, her boss had been her mentor and at times a bellwether when the stress of pressing deadlines and finicky clients got to be too much. She owed him and now she'd have to pay up.

"Have you booked the tickets yet?" He toyed with his watch. She'd stood next to him when his superstar client had given him the Rolex as a token of her affection.

"Not yet." She crossed her legs.

"I'll pay for the tickets, Lauren."

She did a double take and looked at him suspiciously. No. She shook her head, seeing the number thirty light up like a neon sign. "I have a timetable . . ."

"Okay." He waved his hands. "Just do the preliminary designs and start the work plan. I'll have someone else take over."

"How long?" She narrowed her eyes at the Cheshire grin on his face.

"Three months."

"One." She raised her chin and gave him a small, confident smile.

"One and a half."

She leaned back in the cushy chair and placed her hands on her lap. "First-class tickets, Brad."

He nodded. "Let me know the price."

Before he could change his mind, Lauren nodded. "Deal."

Nick put down the legal brief and closed his eyes. He'd been trying to read through the case document for the past hour. No matter which way his thoughts went, they came back to Lauren.

The woman was hell on a man. Jazz and whiskey. All the stuff that could bring a man like him to his knees. Any minute she'd be ringing the doorbell, and he'd have to talk her out of leaving. He wasn't even sure about whether or not he wanted to succeed in helping Alan with his crazy scheme. Getting the design firm to take the project had taken only a few names and bank account numbers. Lauren, however . . .

The sound of the phone brought him out of his thoughts. He picked the receiver up after two rings. "Nick Randolph."

"Mr. Randolph." His paralegal's crisp voice came over the phone line.

"Yes."

"Vincent Baker's offer letter just arrived."

"Good, would you have a messenger bring it over to my house? Then have Mary set up a conference call with Mr. and Mrs. Baker for seven o'clock tonight."

"Yes, sir. Anything else?"

"No. That's it."

After hanging up the phone, he took a sip of coffee and nearly spat. Stone cold. Getting up from the hand-me-down desk he'd had since college, he made his way to the kitchen for a refill. He stopped before going back into the room he'd picked to be his study.

Every time Nick walked into the makeshift office, he grinned. His days of coming home late at night to hear the buzzing sound of a neighbor's television and the honking of car horns were over. He liked Park Slope. The area with its mix of middle-class professionals, college students, and ethnic families was appealing to his nature. He enjoyed being able to jog in the park without having to put up with suspicious stares from other Manhattan Upper East Side residents.

The morning commute might have gotten longer but the satisfaction of having his piece of the American dream made it worthwhile. Then there was the history. Of all his aunts and uncles, Aunt Roxie had been his favorite. His widowed aunt had been the only one who understood his need to be away from his large family.

He'd grown up the son of a politician and a doctor. The Randolph family meant success in Princeton, New Jersey. All of his siblings and cousins had graduated from prestigious universities and settled into successful careers. His father had finally semiretired from practicing medicine while his mother still kept her hand in the political mix.

Nick still received calls every election year from his mother's political party. After his graduating magna cum laude and passing the bar on his first time out, people still wanted Nick Randolph, the first-year National Football League MVP, to come home. Even family members urged him to take up the family business and coach the high school football team.

Nick Randolph never stopped running and never fumbled the ball. Football honors aside, he was an entertainment and sports lawyer, and that meant using charm and smarts to get the deals done. He'd need all of it plus his mother's gift of working miracles to win this next assignment.

He walked around the pile of law books on the floor and went to stand by the windows. Looking out toward the tree-lined street, he took a sip of coffee. Most of the six-bedroom brownstone stood empty waiting to be filled. Except for the new furnace and hot-water heater he'd had installed last week, nothing had been done to the place. What he needed was to turn the brownstone into a home. Now, he had to convince Lauren of that.

* * *

Father's daughter back in the neighborhood, Lauren mused. Three miles east of Wall Street and a thousand miles from Chicago, her pop had strolled down these Brooklyn streets.

She looked toward the Brooklyn Bridge in time to see a train go across. Her father had loved riding the rails. For all the agony she went through when the policemen came and told the family he'd died when his train derailed, the only measure of peace she carried was that he passed while doing the very thing he loved.

Shaking her head, Lauren lengthened her stride, quickly passing Victorian row houses to reach her destination. She paused on the steps to look at the outside of the brownstone. The exterior was in excellent condition. Lauren loved the way the sandstone brick home looked in the afternoon light. She nodded in approval of the solid dark rosewood double doors and antique brass door knocker.

She studied the long white-trimmed French-style windows, openly admiring the multipaned glass. The windows could open like doors in the summer, letting in the cool morning air. Without a doubt the previous owner had spent time and money on the stately brownstone.

Lauren was about to press the doorbell when the heavy wood door swung open.

"Hello, Lauren."

Nick Randolph stood dressed in dark navy pants and a wool sweater. His eyes matched the wide grin on his face. She frowned in surprise. "I'm sorry, I've got the wrong house."

"No, Lauren, you're at the right place."

She looked at Nick, then to the house number, back to the address on the contract, and then settled on the man standing in the doorway.

"You're not Roxanne Howard." Lauren felt a little dumb at stating the obvious.

"No, that would be my aunt. She passed away two months ago."

"What kind of game are you playing, Nick Randolph?"

"No game. My aunt left the brownstone to me in her will."

She tightened her grip on her briefcase. "You lied, counselor."

Nick shuffled his feet. Her accusation hit close to home. "No, the estate over which I am executor doesn't settle until next week," he stated in his lawyer voice. "Technically, my aunt's estate is the owner."

Lauren looked at Nick, remembering the cold, hostile voice he'd used when ordering her out of Alan's hospital room. The price for taking this job was too high.

"I can't work with you."

His eyebrows rose. "Can't or won't?"

"Won't," she snapped back, raising her chin. She looked him in his brown eyes and felt a spark that had more to do with attraction than anger. Lauren was well aware of the handsome man with his broad shoulders and warm hands.

Nick saw the flash of defiance in her eyes. He'd known this would be a battle and had prepared. "You don't have much of a choice. Your firm committed you to this project. If you pull out, I'll be forced to take you to court for breach of contract."

"Why?" It was the only thing she could think of. His threat to sue the firm poured ice water over her anger.

His tone softened. "Because you're the best, Lauren. I want this house to be a home again. Now how about we discuss this inside where it's warm?"

He stepped back and gestured for her to enter.

She shivered. Lauren, the woman, wanted to turn around and leave. Lauren, the professional, wanted to see the rooms beyond the doorway.

Pushed by adrenaline, she breezed by him with her

head held high. No one got the best of Lauren Hughes. Nick Randolph was going to find that out the hard way.

Nick had earned the nickname Mr. Frosty at law school. Exams, mock trials, and surprise visits from his parents never caused him to lose his cool. But Lauren wearing a long leather coat in his empty living room had his palms sweating.

"Can I get you something to drink?"

"Coffee would be nice."

"Cream and two sugars," he added.

Nick saw the question in her eyes and shrugged. "I've got a good memory."

"I've never had coffee with you." Her voice was clipped.

"True. That would imply speaking to me. We were seated at the same table during the Urban League Awards."

He moved toward her. "Let me take your coat." He had his hands on her shoulders before she could protest. Shrugging, Lauren allowed him to pull it away.

She watched Nick as he left the room. Running her fingers through her hair, she let her gaze roam round. Fifteen-foot ceilings filled with possibilities. Her lips curled as she took a step over to the fireplace. She could almost see the flickering of a roaring fire. The wide mantel was the focus of the sparsely furnished room. Already her mind was imagining the lighting, colors, and window themes.

She studied the floor and nodded in approval. Square parquet flooring with mahogany inlays around the border. She imagined that the house would be filled with beautiful wooden floors. It would make her job easier. She walked over to the window and placed her palm against the pane. The original antique period glass felt cold and smooth to the touch.

Nick stepped through the doorway into the living room and paused. She was wearing burgundy and black. Only Lauren could pull off wearing the short skirt and blouse. A silver pendant lay still against her graceful neck.

Remember, she's Alan's girl, he thought as his fingers tightened on the coffee mugs. "It's not gourmet, but it'll warm you up."

"Thank you." She smiled automatically, turning at the sound of his voice.

An answering smile hung on his lips. He watched as she reached up to tuck a stray lock of hair behind her ear. For a moment her eyes had warmed before the warmth was replaced with icy indifference.

"Have a seat." He gestured to the only piece of furniture in the room.

"I prefer to stand." She held the mug with both hands.

"Suit yourself. We're going to be a while." His pop had taught him early on that the best defense was a good offense. He was going to use the truth to get past Lauren's defenses.

He took a seat on the lumpy pullout sofa. Crossing his legs, he sat back. "Before we get down to business, let's get some things straight. I made a mistake. One that I regret. My forcing you to leave the hospital was a knee-jerk reaction. I was rude."

Her eyebrows lifted. "You were cruel."

He nodded. "I should have listened and not jumped to conclusions."

She leaned her head to the side. "As a lawyer, aren't you supposed to get the facts first?"

She was making this hard. Nick eased back, feeling hopeful. It was the first time the sarcastic edge in her tone hadn't drawn blood.

"I was reacting as a friend that night," he explained.

"So was I," she pointed out.

His next words came out easier than he thought they would. "I'm sorry, Lauren. And I've done everything I know of to ask for your forgiveness." Nick looked up into her eyes. "If I could do it all over again, I would have listened."

Lauren blinked twice as his words erased the biting retort waiting on her lips. The sincerity of his voice did it. Unconsciously her grip on the coffee cup loosened.

She'd been angry for the past two months, unwilling to accept his calls or the flowers. Now, she couldn't ignore the sound of regret in his voice. Her anger drained away, leaving her empty. He really did care about Alan, she realized. *Maybe it's time to accept Nick's white flag,* she mused. *Maybe I've held on to my anger for too long.* "I think," she said, moving to take a seat on the sofa, "maybe we should start over."

He'd expected many things from Lauren, but that wasn't one of them. Nick let out a breath he hadn't realized he was holding. He was a proud man, but his father had taught him to be a smart one. He'd recognized that he'd wronged Lauren and all he wanted was her forgiveness.

"Sounds good to me."

She extended her hand, which his fingers enclosed in a firm handshake. Looking into her dark eyes and warm smile, he felt his throat going dry. He knew from the way he never wanted to let her hand go that the next month was going to be more difficult than he'd ever imagined.

"So when do I get the grand tour?" She blinked her long lashes, and the light in her eyes sent some serious heat to the lower region of his body.

"Now's as good as any time." He grinned and escorted her out of the room.

Nick led her downstairs to the bottom floor. The fully

finished belowground room received a great deal of light from two front windows.

"What is it you want done with this floor of the house?" Pen poised on the first line of her notebook, Lauren looked up at Nick.

"Well, I promised my younger brother a place to call his own when he was in New York for an assignment. It would be great if we could turn this floor into a private apartment."

"Would you need separate amenities such as a kitchen, bathroom, et cetera?"

"I don't know, what do you think?"

"If you should decide to sell the property in the future, having a fully functional private living space would only enhance the selling value."

"Good point. I'd like you to make it into a separate apartment."

"By the way, is there anyone else that should be involved with the project?" Lauren asked as her heart rate sped up.

"What do you mean?"

"Someone else's input I should receive. A fiancée or girlfriend perhaps?"

He shook his head. "Sorry, Lauren. It's just going to be you and me."

Looking down at her pad, Lauren let go of her sharply inhaled breath. Pinning a smile to her face, she followed him back up the stairs.

By the time they reached the fourth floor, Lauren knew she had her work cut out for her. The interior structure was perfect but the empty rooms, old carpeting, and unevenly painted walls would have to be completely redone.

She poked her nose in every corner and crevice, taking time to look in the closets and the attic. Whoever had previously renovated the place had done a phenomenal job. The feel of the brownstone was timeless, but the additions and changes made it into the most modern of homes.

The screened-in back porch was a wonderful addition to the house. All it needed was a fresh coat of paint and some comfortable chairs and a table. She'd have to come back with her tape measure and sketch pad. For the moment, all she wanted to do was explore.

"And this is my temporary home office. It used to be what my aunt called the sitting room."

Lauren barely managed to keep from tripping over a pile of books sitting haphazardly close to the large entranceway.

"Shelves," she muttered as his hand came out to take hold of her arm. Unexpectedly, something warm and inviting passed between them, and she cursed under her breath.

"I'm sorry. I didn't catch what you said." Nick pushed the books away with his foot.

Lauren was close enough to see the corners of his mouth twitch. "You need bookshelves. Lots of them, built into the walls."

He nodded. "You know what's best."

She couldn't keep from wincing at the sight of the room. The small desk was covered in papers; brown accordion folders sat everywhere, and a laptop computer lay precariously perched on the windowsill.

He didn't just need interior design, she mused, he needed a keeper.

"That bad?" he asked.

Lauren turned her attention back to the man standing beside her. Her breath caught at the amused look on his face. She shook her head. "Worse. This place is a fire hazard."

"I haven't had time to catch up on my filing."

She gave the room another look over. There were no

filing cabinets in the place. Instead of pointing out that fact, she humored him by nodding. "I'll make sure the design plan includes plenty of filing cabinets."

"Sounds good."

"Are there any particular themes, designs, colors that you like, Nick?"

Preoccupied by the sound of his name coming from her lips, he took a while to answer.

She prompted, "Any styles? Modern, natural, oriental?"

"Comfortable," he answered, leading her out of the room.

"What does that mean exactly?"

"I don't know. But I'm not a fancy man, Lauren. I don't expect to do a lot of entertaining. I want this place to be a home again, just like it was when I came to visit my aunt during the summer."

"Do you have any pictures of the house before your aunt died?"

He rubbed his chin. "I think my brother has some."

"It would help if I could see them," she added.

"I'll give him a call tonight."

"In the meantime, I'll need a key so that I can come by and draw up a floor plan."

"Whatever you need."

She pulled out her pad and began taking notes. "Is it acceptable to relocate some of your existing rooms?"

"For example . . ."

"You have a lot of space and light on the fourth floor."

It was an understatement. The empty room with mahogany wall paneling and the large window cried for color and furnishings.

"The attic?" he asked as they entered into the kitchen.

"Yes, we could turn that into a home office. You'll have plenty of privacy, and the openness of the room would be more conducive to work."

"I like the sound of that."

Lauren nodded. "Just a disclaimer. I'll only be on the project for the initial phase."

His gaze sharpened. "Explain."

"We start with the design phase. This is where you and I pick themes, colors, space, furniture style, et cetera. Then I order furniture, appliances, and fabric. Last, we install."

"How long do you think this will take?"

"About three to four weeks, give or take a few days. A lot of this depends on you." She turned back to the kitchen table and began putting papers into her brief-case.

Nick's eyes strayed to her nice backside. "Depends on me . . ."

"On your knowing what you like and dislike."

He gave her a discerning look. "Oh, I tend to know what I like the minute I see it."

Lauren picked up her briefcase. "That's good. This is a team effort. I'll need your full cooperation."

"You've got it. We could start tonight." He gave her the smile that had graced the cover of *Sports Illustrated,* but it withered moments later as she frowned back at him.

Nick moved swiftly to catch up with Lauren as she walked out of the room.

After seeming to stop in front of the coat closet, she faced him. "Interior design is an art, not a contract you read through, make changes, and sign. This is about cre-ating a place for you to live."

He reached into the closet and brought out her coat. "And that's why I've got you."

She turned around and let him help her into her coat, then waited for him to move away.

"All right." Lauren broke the silence, taking a step back. She handed him a business card. "Give me a call tomorrow, and we can set up some time to look through designs and sketches. I would also like to take you on a tour of some of the furniture stores and interior design workshops I've used in the past."

"That's all?"

"For the most part." She gave him a puzzled glance.

"Well, Alan said . . ."

"Yes . . ."

"Uhh, I guess I expected more."

She raised an eyebrow. "Such as . . ."

Nick gestured toward the hall stairs. "I was thinking we'd have to make big changes like knocking out walls or tearing up floors."

Something flickered in her eyes. "There's no need. I like to build, not tear down."

He wanted to know what lay behind her words. "I'd like to build our friendship as well, Lauren."

She was glad she had a good grip on her briefcase or she would have dropped it. The corners of her mouth moved upward. "Give 'em an inch and they'll take a mile, isn't that right, Nick?"

Mile? He'd settle for the three feet that stood between them.

"Any friend of Alan's is a friend I'd like to call mine as well."

The mention of Alan's name stopped her cold. "I'm sure we can work together to create the home you want. We'll have to wait and see about the other part." She enjoyed the look of surprise on his face. "Now if you'll excuse me. It's late, and I need to be getting home."

She was halfway to the door before he called out, "Lauren?"

Her heart skipped a beat. "Yes?" She swallowed before turning to see him dangling something from his fingers.

"You forgot your keys."

She stalked back toward Nick. Without batting an eye,

she went to snatch the keys from his hand. But the second her fingers touched his, Nick's hand closed.

She groaned inwardly after making the mistake of looking into his eyes. A shiver raced over her skin as her heart started to pound. She was near enough to inhale the crisp scent of him, close enough to feel his body heat. It felt like a blanket of hot silk brushed against her skin. Not one to lie to herself, she acknowledged the physical attraction evidenced by the way her fingers tingled and her lips parted in anticipation of Nick's kiss.

His mouth slowly came down. Nick never felt hungrier in his life. *Just one taste,* the devil whispered in the back of his mind, *a little kiss never hurt anyone.*

The sound of the door chime broke the spell. Lauren's eyes widened and she drew a quick breath. Not even bothering to say good-bye, she pulled back from his embrace and broke for the door.

"Excuse me," she said hurriedly, not giving the woman on the stairs a second glance. She didn't care. All she wanted was to get as far away as she could from Nick Randolph.

As she walked down the street dodging strollers and pedestrians, she didn't pay a bit of attention to the cold wind. Lauren was flushed with that toasty feeling after a deep blush. She'd felt Nick's smile all the way down to her feet.

No, not now, not ever, she repeated. She had promises to keep.

Four

Lauren rolled out of bed after the alarm went off for the third time. Covering her mouth to hide a giant-sized yawn, she gazed out the window to a semilight sky, then back to her nice rumpled bed. For a minute, she actually thought the lavender and gray pillows were calling her name. Instead, she heard the sound of the phone ringing.

"You're late," she said after picking up the portable.

"Lauren?" came a distinctly masculine reply.

"Nick." Her voice went up an octave. She'd expected to hear Cassandra's voice on the other end.

"Hope I didn't wake you up . . ."

"No, you didn't. I have to meet someone before I meet you." She switched the phone to her other ear. "Do you need to cancel?"

Nick swore he heard relief in her voice. "No, just wanted to let you know I might be a little late."

"Oh." She tapped her foot. "How little is little?"

Nick's grip on the phone eased. The smile in her voice came straight through the phone, making his lips curve upward.

"Little means about thirty minutes."

"I hope it's worth ticking off your interior designer," she scolded playfully to cover the disappointment that settled in her stomach. The baby of the family always wanted to be first.

"Well, I can't show you my aunt's pictures of the house if I'm not here when my brother drops them off."

"Hmm . . ." Lauren cradled the phone between her neck and shoulder as she pulled on her robe.

"So where are you off to?" he asked casually.

For some reason she resisted coming out and telling him that she was meeting Cass to get her eyebrows done. She'd been in a fabric store when a group of Indian women dressed in brightly colored saris entered the room. Their beautiful arches and smooth eyebrows had been a painful reminder that she was long overdue for some personal time.

"Greenwich Village."

"That sounds good."

Lauren smiled at the puzzled tone in his voice. "Not the answer you were looking for, huh?"

"Not quite," he said, laughing.

"Got to ask the right questions, counselor." She poured herself a cup of coffee.

"I'll remember that."

"And I'll see you in a bit." She smiled before hanging up the phone.

Nick looked at the phone before putting it back on the cradle. Placing his hands behind his head, he sat back in his chair and grinned. After the difficult night he'd had trying to convince Theresa to move on, his day had just gotten a lot more interesting. Lauren Hughes. He shook his head, remembering the sexual tension that had flared between them the night before.

Nick looked down at this watch. Nine o'clock and his younger brother was nowhere in sight. After two hours of intermittent pacing and reading, the doorbell rang.

"You're late," Nick pointed out with gruff affection.

Chris clapped him on the shoulder before strolling through the door. "Good morning, bro. Aren't you going to offer me a cup of coffee or something?"

"How about some aspirin for that hangover?" Nick tossed back, shutting the front door. Chris's bloodshot eyes were redder than the peppers his pop liked to put in his signature Texas-style chili.

"I wish I had a hangover. No, I just got off the red-eye from Los Angeles."

"You didn't tell me you were on the West Coast." Nick frowned.

Chris took off his coat. "When you get the call, you jump on the plane. I've been trying to book a photo shoot with this one model for months."

"I take it things went well?"

"Like magic." Chris formed a camera frame with his hands. "A couple of clicks and a few rolls of film and that's all she wrote."

Nick reached into the hallway closet and grabbed his coat.

"That's good. Now, where are the pictures of the brownstone?"

"What about that coffee?" Chris grinned.

Nick shook his head. "You know where the kitchen is."

"No doubt the cabinets are bare."

Nick smiled. His little brother wasn't too far off the mark. Although he'd picked up some groceries the week he moved into the house, Nick hadn't eaten anything outside of restaurants and takeout, so he hadn't needed to go food shopping.

"Coffee's in the freezer," he added, picking up his house keys and wallet. Nick had made a disastrous first impression with Lauren and if he didn't get going soon he was going to be late for his first buying expedition.

Nick watched as his brother gave him a puzzled look.

"Why are you rushing out?" Chris asked. "Isn't like you've got a date or something. It's Saturday morning."

"Almost afternoon. I've got to meet Lauren."

"Lauren?" Chris's brows shot up. "Not Theresa?"

Nick sighed. "How many times do I have to tell you and Will, Theresa and I are history?"

"When I stop hearing the sounds of wedding bells ringing every time she drops by our parents' house hoping you've come home for Sunday dinner."

"Damn it, Chris," he started.

Chris waved his hands. "All right, calm down, big brother. I was just kidding."

"Uh-huh."

"Seriously though, I'm a little put out that you haven't said a word about the new woman."

"That's because she isn't my woman," he replied, annoyance sharpening his voice. He and his sibling were extremely close, but for some reason he couldn't fathom, Nick didn't want to talk about Lauren.

Chris persisted. "Well, then, who is she?"

"Lauren Hughes is the interior designer I hired to fix up the place," he stated matter-of-factly.

Chris's brow creased. "The one who's going to renovate the downstairs so I can have a place to rest my weary head?"

Nick burst out into laughter. His younger brother's face looked like a kid's in a candy store. "That's right."

He blinked as Chris stuffed an envelope into his hands and started pushing him out the door. "What are you waiting for? You don't want to keep her waiting."

Laughing as he left the house, Nick jumped into his car and made his way into the city.

The small Indian salon hidden in Greenwich Village pulled in women like a sponge, Lauren mused. Cass didn't have to ask twice for her to go the first time. After breaking out in about four different rashes from getting her brows waxed at an upscale salon in Chelsea, Lauren wasn't about to go back to using wax.

It took less than five minutes to get her eyebrows done. Ranhi held one end of the thread between her teeth, and the other end was wound around a finger. Lauren closed her eyes and the hair was plucked by the swift motion of the thread.

She talked through the lightning-quick twinges. "So what are you up to after the flea market?" she asked Cass.

"Shopping for a to-die-for evening gown. There's going to be an entrepreneur awards ceremony next Saturday."

"You're going?"

"Alan asked me."

Lauren heard the hesitation in her friend's voice. "That's good. You'll have a lot of fun."

"You're not upset?"

"Why would I be upset?" She sat up and smiled at the woman as she handed her a well-earned tip.

The other girl was putting the finishing touches on Cassandra's slick brows. "You two are . . . well, you know."

"No, I don't know. Why don't you tell me?" She sat up.

"Come on, Lauren. We both know you're Alan's *girl*."

Her laughter echoed in the small plant-filled salon. "So that's what's been bothering you lately."

"Girl, this is no time to get cryptic." Cass let out an exasperated sigh.

"Cass." Lauren took two steps over and hugged her friend. "I might be Alan's girl, but I'm not his girlfriend. You're talking some serious incest here."

Cassandra still looked unconvinced. "But you two were joking about getting married and everything."

"We only did that so that Alan's mama would quit shoving all her church members' and friends' daughters his way."

"You're not just saying that?" Cass's eyes widened with hope.

"Have I ever lied to you?"

"No." She shook her head and adjusted her pocket-book. "But you didn't tell me about this vacation you're planning either."

Lauren's hand froze on the door handle. "Alan . . ."

"Brad mentioned that I might need to pull back on some of my smaller projects to take on a heavier work-load after you leave."

"Oh." Lauren relaxed.

"Why so hush-hush?"

"It's not set in stone yet. I didn't want to say anything until I got the tickets. You know . . . didn't want to jinx the thing."

"So wha'cha gonna do, wild child?" Cassandra grinned. "What beach are you going to be lying on and who are you going with?"

Lauren released the breath she didn't realize she was holding. "I am taking me, myself, and I on a trip around the world."

"For real?"

"Yes, Lord." She nodded excitely. "If everything works out I'll start out in North Africa, make my way south, and then keep heading west."

"Go on with your bad self."

Lauren gave Cass a high five before they went their separate ways. Her friend was headed to the Saturday outdoor flea markets. Lauren glanced down at her watch, wishing she could join her. She had about forty-five minutes before she met Nick. Adding a little pep to her step, she turned south.

She envied Cass because she loved going to the out-door flea markets even in the cold. The skillfully crafted African pieces always brought her back. A lot of the ven-dors knew her by name. She'd sat in their stalls, drunk their tea, and met their wives. Lauren always felt a little intimidated by the beautiful women from the Congo. Smooth round faces and sun-drenched laughter. But today she'd be hitting the designer shops and warehouses looking for the right kind of furniture that would transform Nick Randolph's empty brownstone into a well-designed home.

Nick spotted Lauren in the large furniture gallery and made his way toward the back. He checked the urge to look into any number of the wall mirrors. He'd barely had time to recheck his hair before running out the door. His younger brother was never on time. He shook his head. No wonder Chris chose photography. It was the only profession where being late was expected.

"Nice crowd." Nick stopped beside Lauren as she examined an oriental stool.

Her eyes slid to him. "It's early. Give it an hour and the place will be crawling with interior designers hoping to discover some odd one-of-a-kind decorator piece."

Nick scanned the room and wished he could grab Lauren and run for the door. Everything in the place screamed museum instead of home. For the life of him he couldn't figure out why she'd chosen to meet at the avante-garde furniture gallery.

"See something you like?" she asked.

He didn't look up from the rusted metal chair with a $14,500 price tag.

"You can't be serious." His face squelched up.

"What?"

Nick couldn't tear his eyes away from her mouth. The hazel-tinted corners were fighting a battle to stay straight. He wished he could kiss her lips and let her know that the brightness of her eyes gave her away.

"Please tell me someone isn't going to pay good money for this." He pointed to the chair.

She shrugged and put her hand on his shoulder, moving him along. "It'll be gone by evening."

He took her hand within his own. "There's nothing in this place I want in my house, Lauren."

"Sure?" She raised an eyebrow.

"Positive."

"So you wouldn't be interested in the handcrafted African chair and footstool I picked out?" she murmured close to his ear.

Nick forgot about the crowd, the ugly furniture, everything but the touch of Lauren's hand on his arm and her scent. It was the same perfume she had worn to the engagement party, he could recognize the sensual smell anywhere. One whiff sent enough electricity through his body to light all five of the New York City boroughs and half of New Jersey as well. He had to take a step away and gulp air as beads of sweat appeared on his brow.

Clearing his throat he looked around. "Now that's different. Where are they?"

"In the back. I'm having them polish the legs before delivery."

He raised an eyebrow. "Isn't that a bit presumptuous?"

"No." She favored him with a confident smile. "You gave me creative license, remember?"

No, he'd forgotten. *Must be slipping,* he mused. Nick wiped his brow, feeling the heat of the place for the first time. "You're right. It was in the contract, but don't you usually consult your clients before making large purchases?" He tried to turn it around.

"Large purchases, Nick." She weaved her way around a small group and headed toward the door. "I got the chair at a deep discount."

"How'd you do that?" He resisted the urge to touch her blowing hair by putting his hands in his pocket.

"Armond owed me a favor for placing a Greek urn that had been sitting on display for six months."

"So where are you planning on putting it?"

"The living room or the master bedroom."

"I like the sound of that."

She turned toward him as they stopped in the outer enclave of the store. Moving away from the milling groups of people, she tilted her chin toward Nick. "So did you get your pictures?" Lauren asked, reminding him of the reason for his late arrival.

He took an envelope out of his inner jacket pocket. "My brother Chris actually took these."

She studied the black-and-white prints. "They're beautiful," she said softly.

"Some of his recent exhibition photos were featured in an African-American style magazine."

"Wait." She looked up from the photos. "Christophe Randolph is your brother?"

"Unfortunately so."

"I've seen his work. He has a truly gifted eye," she said with awe filling her voice.

Nick shook his head. "Just don't tell him that. Chris already has a big enough ego."

"So this is what you'd like for the brownstone?"

"Well, not really."

Her eyes twinkled as they moved from the pictures to him. "You're not a fan of the combination Greco-Roman and Victorian style?"

He shrugged. "Don't get me wrong, it's nice, but it's not me. The furniture, the curtains and antiques. It's too formal."

"I kind of figured that," she said, stepping out the door he held open.

"So where to next, Lauren?"

"Since we're out and about, I wondered if you might want to check out some furniture I thought would be nice for the den."

"Now, that's more like it." He looked around noticing the neighborhood shops and restaurants. "Should I hail a taxi?"

She looked at him curiously. "Why?"

"Well, I had my eye on this nice stereo system at a spot two blocks from the office."

"Furniture, Nick. Let's choose a style before we start picking out entertainment centers."

His face fell like a ton of bricks and Lauren couldn't stop the laughter that pealed out of her throat. She reached over and patted him on the arm. "Soon, okay?"

"Promise?" He grinned.

"Promise." She nodded. Lauren looked at him closely. She liked Nick's smile. The way the corners of his eyes narrowed and the barest hint of a dimple appeared in his right cheek. And when he laughed, the husky sound was like Christmas filled with good things and good feeling. Only she wasn't feeling remotely childlike emotions toward the man walking beside her.

They entered the spacious furniture store about twenty minutes later. Lauren let her eyes drift around for a few moments before she signaled out something toward the back.

"Signora Lauren," came a smooth Italian voice.

"Paulo." She whirled around and smiled at the silver-haired gentleman strolling toward her. He was such a flirt, but she always got a kick out of the way her name rolled off his tongue. Lauren held out her hands and Paulo took them. "You look gorgeous as usual." The store owner smiled.

She tilted her face to receive his kiss on her cheek.

"What?" She was jerked backward and watched as Nick took Paulo's hand and shook it.

Lauren stifled a giggle as Paulo shot her a look and raised a heavy eyebrow. She mouthed back, "Client." His frown transformed into a smile before she could blink.

"Paulo Vencitti."

"Nicholas Randolph." He eyed the man's black clothes and ringless hand. He didn't like Pablo or Paulo one damned bit. The way the other man looked at Lauren coupled with the sight of him moving to kiss her cheek made him want to spit nails.

"To what do I owe the pleasure of this unexpected visit?" The Italian turned back toward Lauren.

"I'm looking for something nice for a masculine den."

Paulo glanced at Nick. "Leather."

She nodded, taking a step forward to stand by Nick's side. The attorney wasn't cigars and bourbon. At first, Lauren had thought Nick was down-home fried chicken and collard greens. But he had that edge. She saw him walking as comfortably in the world of jet-setters and caviar as he would with the beer and pizza crowd.

"You are in such good luck, signora. I have just the thing you are searching for."

Lauren nodded and pushed Nick to follow the store owner.

"What are we doing here, Lauren?" Nick scowled. The light mood of the day had started to disintegrate since they'd stepped into the upscale furniture store.

"Shopping." She gave him a serious look.

"And him?" He inclined his head toward Paulo.

"Helping us."

"No," he contradicted. "This man is helping himself to looking at you."

Lauren's smile widened, and she gave him a curious look. The edge in his tone and the protective look in his eyes were the last things she expected from the usually aloof attorney.

"Ahh, *bella*. This is it."

Lauren left the warmth of Nick's arm and slowly stepped around the sofa that Paulo pointed out. She gestured for Nick to approach. "Give me your hand," she ordered.

She took it within her own and placed his fingers upon the back of the sofa. "Now close your eyes."

Lauren spared a glance at Paulo and acknowledged his knowing smile. He'd seen her do this before, but this time she wanted a little privacy. Catching her glance, he left them alone.

The pale mushroom-brown nubuck leather sofa with matching pillows was perfect for Nick's den. Even under the harsh fluorescent lighting, it looked good.

"Feel how soft the leather is, almost velvety." Her voice was low and monotone. "Take a deep breath. Smell the faint whiff of comfort and warmth. Think of coming home and wanting to kick back and catch a basketball game."

Lauren wasn't unaffected by his nearness. She glanced up at Nick from underneath her lashes and a feeling of intense heat started at her scalp and worked its way down the rest of her body, making her hands tingle and her pulse jump. If she hadn't felt that sudden flush of desire before, she would have sworn she was having a hot flash.

Nick's heart rate sped up. She didn't have a clue as to what she was doing to him. He wasn't thinking about relaxing on the leather sofa with a beer. All he wanted to do was kiss her. He pictured Lauren lying naked on the leather sofa. He opened his eyes and stared straight ahead.

"I'll take it."

Still holding her hand, he turned to look at her abstract expression.

"I'll take the chair, the lamp, and the footstool. Maybe I'll buy the entire store," he embellished.

"Hmm." Lauren stepped back and looked up at him. "I don't think it'll all fit in the brownstone."

"Glad you're back, I thought I'd lost you there for a moment," he joked.

"Sorry." She shook her head. "I get lost sometimes."

"So where did you go?" he asked, guiding her to take a seat on the couch. His new couch. Nick enjoyed the soft leather as he sat down.

"I was somewhere between red and yellow."

"What?"

"The color of the den walls."

"Really?"

She nodded and focused on Nick. He looked right at home on the sofa. Then again the man looked at home everywhere he went. She'd never really seen Nick uncomfortable in any situation. "I think I've settled upon a color."

"Good, so why don't you tell me about the den?" He didn't care if she wanted to paint the room with pink elephants. All he wanted to do was look at the dreamy expression on her face. Even if he couldn't touch, he could watch.

"Orange," she murmured. "Terra-cotta, the deepest orange. It's a harmony of yellow and red."

"Uh-huh."

"It's a very welcoming color," she added.

"Definitely want to be welcoming."

She shot him a sharp glance. "Since the downstairs is configured to be a stand-alone apartment, this furniture can double as a contemporary living room."

"Signor, signora. Do you like?"

Lauren stood and went to stand next to Paulo. Being so close to Nick had her on pins and needles. He made her nervous and when she got nervous she started babbling like a starstruck teenager.

"It's a nice couch." She turned away from Nick.

"Yes. It arrived from a tannery in Florence last week. The initial buyer has been transferred to Hong Kong and cannot take it with him." Paulo shrugged. "He hated to give it up."

"His loss, my gain. How about we step to the back and have a chat, Pablo?" Nick asked.

"Paulo," the man corrected. Faint signs of annoyance had crept into his eyes.

"Lauren, I'll be right back."

"Nick . . ." She was about to remind him that this was her job, but she saw the look in his eyes. It was that male look that said, "Let me be the man."

Lauren held up her hands in defeat. "Just be careful."

Nick gave her a wide grin as she frowned up at him. "I'm a sports lawyer, remember? I cut my teeth on multimillion-dollar contracts."

Sensing that trying to talk sense into Nick was about as useful as banging her head against a brick wall, she started strolling in the opposite direction.

Thirty minutes later, she stood watching as Nick took one last look at his new den furniture.

"He got you for the sofa, recliner, and what?"

She'd known from the way Paulo beamed at her that Nick had fallen prey to the Italian's persuasive charm.

"I got twenty percent off," Nick boasted as he put on his coat.

"What else did you get?" Lauren gave him a stern look.

"The love seat."

"Nick."

"He threw in some of his mother's handmade pillows."

Not having the heart to tell him Paulo's mother owned a boutique housewares shop in Tribeca, she chuckled at the excited expression his face.

"Be careful. I may turn you into an interior designer," she teased.

"Did you do that same thing with Alan?" Nick asked. A part of him didn't want to know. The thought of her holding Alan's hand and running it over the plush leather didn't sit right with him. Even if the man was his good friend.

"No." She laughed, taking her eyes away from the steel side table. "He wasn't as hands-on as you. Plus, Alan was in Arizona most of the time. Cass and I picked out everything."

"Well." He shrugged. "I'm a hands-on kind of guy."

"I know. I like that about you." The honest reply caught them both off guard.

"That's good, I wouldn't want to mess up your flow." He stepped in front of her and opened the door.

Lauren stuck her hands in her pockets and smiled at him. "It's good that you want to be involved. This is, after all, going to be your home, the place that you'll share with your family."

"To be honest, I never really felt like my old apartment was really mine."

"And now?"

"The brownstone. It feels good." He shrugged, unable to put the rest into words.

Lauren reached out and placed her hand on his shoulder. "I know. It's one of the most rewarding aspects of my work. To transform a space into a home." She smiled.

Nick felt the heat of her hand through the coat and it set him at ease. She had no idea how much she affected him.

"On to the next store?" he asked.

She shook her head, amused at the eager expression on his face. "I think we've done enough damage today."

"That's it?" He didn't want the afternoon to end so soon.

"No." She tucked her arm under his. "We've got one more stop."

Twenty minutes later, they entered the office building that housed Lauren's design firm.

"Thanks for coming with me. I don't know what I was thinking when I forgot to bring the book home with me last night."

Lauren finished signing them both into the empty office building. She waved at the guard as the elevator doors closed.

"No problem."

She directed him to her office. "Would you like some water?"

"That'd be nice."

"I'll be back in a second. Make yourself comfortable."

Nick nodded and as soon as Lauren left the room, he started checking the place out. Relaxing. That was the only word he could use to describe her office. Books and knickknacks lined the shelves. The sand-colored carpet muffled noise and African copper-colored prints lined the walls.

Instead of taking a seat on the sofa, he leaned over her desk and studied the color photo in the silver picture frame. A distinguished-looking black couple with two children. The man held the little smiling girl in his arms while the boy waved an American flag.

"My family."

He glanced up at the sound of her voice. She stood leaning in the doorway.

"Here's your water."

He put down the picture frame and took the bottle she offered. "That was the Lincoln Memorial in D.C., wasn't it?"

She nodded. "It was taken on our first summer vacation. We took the train all the way from Chicago."

"Must have been a long trip."

"Didn't feel like it." She smiled. "I remember the way Nathan and I would take turns jumping off the top bunk."

"You must have driven your parents crazy."

Lauren's smile dimmed a little. "Pop got a little impatient with the both of us."

"I'm sure he's proud of you now."

Her eyes fluttered closed at the sting brought by the reminder of her father's death. Nathan had stepped into her father's shoes; she'd been too wrapped up in her own grief to see her mother's suffering. No one was surprised about her older brother's appointment to the judicial bench. Her aunts and uncles said he had an old soul. She disagreed; Nathan aged a decade in the course of a week. The quick-to-tell-a-joke mouth was replaced with deliberate quiet discernment.

She sighed. "I hope so. My father passed when I was twelve."

"I'm sorry." He watched her eyes darken.

"It's okay. Here's the book."

He took it from her quivering hands and placed it on the desk, then wrapped his arms around her in a hug. He felt her stiffen and then relax. After a moment her breathing evened out and he stepped away still holding her hands.

"Thank you," she said quietly, still feeling the hum that had washed over her body the moment she laid her head against his shoulder.

"Any time." He grinned. "I don't know about you, but all this shopping has worked up my appetite. How about I take you to lunch?"

"I don't think that'd be a good idea." She backed away from him. The reminder of her father's death had pushed aside the glow of the day.

Before he could add anything else, she pushed the book into his hands. "I've got some paperwork to finish up and then I promised to stop by a friend's place, later this afternoon." It was a white lie. She'd mentioned to Jessica that she might come by and see the nursery she and Ben had recently finished decorating.

End of the line. The warm, relaxed camaraderie they'd had earlier had ended. He could see her defenses rise up. Gone were the sparkles that filled her eyes, replaced with ice chips.

Nick lifted his shoulder and shrugged, puzzled at the sudden change. Instead of voicing the questions he had on his mind, he buttoned his coat. "All right then. Have a good weekend."

Lauren didn't look up from the papers she held in her hand. "You too."

She waited until he was out the door before she sat down and closed her eyes. A big hole had seemingly opened up in front of her and she stood on one side while Nick held out his hand on the opposite ledge.

Three steps and that'd be it. She could see herself falling hard. She pulled out the red fabric sample from her desk and focused on the image of her Paul. She closed her eyes, remembering the rawness of her throat as she had stumbled between Alan and Nathan. The surreal coldness of the snowflakes as they blanketed the cemetery, stinging her lips and cheeks. Her dreams of happily ever after lay sleeping in the grave. Taking deep breaths, Lauren rubbed the cotton swatch against her cheek.

Five

She was doodling. Instead of trying to pick out countries and cities, she was drawing. Lauren looked down at the rough sketch on the blank sheet of paper. Those arrogant eyes stared right back at her. No matter where she went these days, on the train, walking down the street, he was standing beside her. The man with his unfilled rooms and orange gold colors haunted her.

"Nick Randolph is going to drive me to drink," Lauren said, shoving the sketch pad back into her briefcase.

"Just put this in the back of your mind, girl," she muttered to herself, closing her eyes and counting to ten. "You've got things to do, trips to take, and men to meet."

"Ms. Hughes?"

Lauren opened her eyes and looked around the quiet cream-colored waiting room. Brad had recommended the exclusive travel agency. She couldn't help studying the pictures of exotic locations on the walls. She could see Brad's hand in the decorations. Soft black leather with a natural blending of wood and stone. She sat back on the sofa and took a deep breath of vanilla-scented air.

"Would you like something to drink? Mitzi will be with you in about five minutes."

She smiled at the young woman. "Water, please."

Lauren glanced at her watch. Three o'clock. Two hours before she had to meet Nick at the brownstone.

"Lauren, come on in."

She stood to greet the travel professional. Mitzi was a chic type of woman, midfifties with brown wavy hair streaked with silver, pulled back in a bun. She walked out of the corner office. "Sorry to keep you waiting."

Lauren shook her outstretched hand. "No problem, but I only have an hour."

"Plenty of time to get you started." Mitzi ushered her inside. The travel coordinator's office was filled with pictures from exotic places, and numerous ethnic objects lined her bookshelves.

"When Brad called me the other day I was tickled pink. He was quite irritated, you know. He's going to miss you like crazy."

Lauren had to smile as the woman continued.

"He went on and on about taking care of his girl. Like I wouldn't," she sniffed.

Lauren took a seat at the small round table next to the window. She could look down at the active streets below. The distinctive ring of her mobile phone caught her attention and she reached into her purse.

"Hello."

"Ms. Hughes?"

Lauren recognized the lyrical accent. "Yes, Abdul?"

"The new shipment of goods from South Africa you were expecting came in this morning."

"Great. When can I come by?"

"Give me a day or two to unpack the crates."

"I want first look," Lauren warned. She'd been his first client. After she had placed a few of his imports in a publishing executive's Northampton home, her small shop had been inundated with orders.

"Of course. I shall telephone you on the morrow."

"Thanks."

"Sorry about that." Lauren switched off the phone and dropped it in her purse.

Mitzi waved a braceleted hand. "That's all right, dear.

You're a busy woman. Now let's get down to the fun stuff. Tell me more about your plans."

While she'd been on the call, the young receptionist had generously brought her a bottled water. Lauren eagerly took a sip as her throat had gone dry. She was really going to do this. The idea of traveling around the world seemed almost too easy and clear. Now she was going to actually name places and set dates.

"I haven't had a lot of time to think about where exactly I want to go."

"Well, that's okay. I've got plenty of stuff for you to read. First, how long do you want to travel?"

She looked into the woman's warm brown eyes and smiled. "Forever."

"Can't do that. Brad told me to make sure I made this a round trip stopping back at JFK International Airport."

Lauren laughed. "I knew there had to be a catch."

"No such thing as a free ticket."

"All right. There are only two places I know I want to visit."

She watched as Mitzi picked up a pen. "Where is that?"

"Morocco and Africa."

"East, West, or South Africa?"

Lauren closed her eyes, seeing the brown and orange and coal earth-rich shades of kuba cloth.

"West."

Mitzi nodded. "Good. West African countries are easier for women traveling alone."

Lauren shifted in her chair, hearing the echoes of Alan's protests in her head. "So you don't think I'm crazy traveling by myself?"

"Of course not."

She watched as the other woman sat back in her seat and waved her pen. "When I decided to leave school and travel instead of settling down with a suitable young man from a good upstanding Long Island family, my own family was in an uproar for months."

"Really?" She could tell that Mitzi was used to the finer things in life from the way the woman carried herself. Mitzi wore an elegant pantsuit that had haute couture written all over it.

"Starting a travel agency? Please. My older brothers came close to laughing themselves to death. Now they come to me for both business and personal travel."

She unclenched her fingers and leaned back in the chair. "Are you interested in more of a historical tourist itinerary or something more in line with seeing the local flavor?"

"The latter. I want to take long walks, explore the countryside, and absorb some of the local culture." Her eyes brightened.

"And do some shopping of course?" Mitzi paused from taking notes.

The corners of her mouth inched upward. "Maybe find some new suppliers for the firm."

"That's more like it."

They continued talking and before she knew it the hour had flown by.

"Okay, Lauren. You've given me some good ideas. Now, I need you to look through these brochures and mark some of the destinations that you're interested in."

She nodded. "I've earmarked a set amount of money for this trip. I just want to make the most of my budget."

"Don't worry. For the amount of money you've told me you want to spend, we can send you around the world in style."

"Thank you for helping me with this."

"Any time. All you have to do is promise to come back and tell me all your stories."

"Of course."

"Lauren, do you have a passport?"

"Yes."

She'd spent a semester abroad in Paris during her undergraduate studies. Notre-Dame, La Tour Eiffel, and Le Louvre. Nothing had enchanted her more than the narrow brick streets lined with smoky cafés, filled with the scent of baking bread and brewing coffee. She'd dreamed of taking Paul there. Discovering Paris treasure troves of gardens, buildings, museums, and romantic boulevards hand in hand.

"Good. Depending on the countries you chose, you're going to need visas, which I'll take care of, and you might want to go ahead and talk to your doctor about getting vaccination shots."

"Shots?" Lauren's eyes widened. She'd forgotten about that.

"Come on. Surely a woman as adventurous as you can't be scared of getting shots."

She shook her head and reached up to nervously tuck her hair behind her ears. Adventurous? The word had a nice ring to it. She found herself warming to this idea but she couldn't forget about the mention of visiting the doctor. "It's not the shots I'm worried about. It's the needle."

The other woman reached out and touched her arm as they made their way to the door. "Just think about the food, Lauren. Imagine the bazaars, the markets, the people."

The images came quickly to Lauren's mind. As she stepped into the small elevator and nervously punched the button for the ground floor, small shivers of excitement ran down her spine. The thing was, she didn't know if they were in anticipation of her journey or seeing Nick.

Soon, this project had to be over. The man was getting to her in the worst way. She'd seen the looks he'd given her when he thought she wasn't looking. Long, intense stares that had nothing to do with the furniture catalogs she'd put in front of him. Her heart skipped a beat and that heat of physical attraction she'd banked after Paul's death sprang back to life.

Lauren stepped out of the elevator into the lobby. Her long legs carried her swiftly out of the marble-floored building. She didn't see heads turn at her passage; she pulled on her leather gloves before an icy wind blasted her as she pushed through the rotating door.

Heartbreaker. He had the eyes of a high school crush and the smile of a fallen angel. No playboy, this man, she mused. She couldn't afford to get involved with Nick. His price would emotionally bankrupt her. He wasn't the love 'em and leave 'em type.

She was, by choice and circumstance, emotionally unattached. But something moved in the air between them and no matter how much the wind blew, it clung to her.

"Morocco, Kenya, Malaysia, Vietnam, Japan." Lauren chanted the names of countries she'd always longed to visit as she stepped aboard the downtown express train to Brooklyn. Ever since the night they'd nearly kissed, she was certain that if she didn't get away soon, Nick Randolph would have her so tied up in emotional knots she'd never be able to cut loose.

Nick looked at the parents sitting in his office. One would think that his clients were some of the happiest people in the world. Their nineteen-year-old son, who was at the moment practicing for the Sugar Bowl, had been asked to leave his university and join the NFL.

Nick studied the older man. Mr. Baker was far from pleased and his wife was pointing her finger like a loaded gun.

"Wilma." Mr. Baker crossed his arms.

"Don't try to convince me, Henry. I'm not letting you talk me into letting him leave school."

"But—"

She cut him off. "Remember our dreams for our son? He was going to be the first to graduate from an Ivy League college."

"He can go back to school. Pumpkin, that's a whole lot of money you're asking the boy to turn down—"

"He can play after he gets his degree," she interrupted.

"The offer might not still be on the table," the husband countered.

"Is that true, Nickie?"

He winced at the use of his childhood name. Mrs. Baker had been his mother's roommate in college and one of her bridesmaids. It seemed that no matter how old he was, his mother's closest friends continued to call him by that childhood nickname.

"That's a good possibility. A lot of things can happen between now and when Thomas graduates. If he keeps playing like he is now, another year can only sweeten the pot. But if something were to happen, then all bets are off."

Nick hated seeing the uncertainty in their faces, but he had to be honest.

Mr. Baker rubbed his head. Nick sat forward and put his hand on the desk. "I can't tell you what to do."

"What would you do if you were in our shoes?"

He'd known that question would come. In this case it came sooner than later. His own parents had made that same decision. "I can only tell you what I already know. When my parents faced the same decision, Pop chose not to sign the papers. I graduated, went into the leagues, and blew my knee two seasons later."

"Now you're a big-city lawyer. I'm so proud of you."

Nick felt a glow from the older woman's smile.

"Yes, I am. That's only because I got that first degree. I'm a firm believer in having something to fall back on.

Thomas is smart, and if playing football fell through, it's a nice thing to have a solid education."

Nick escorted the couple out of his office and glanced at his watch. He had to be back at the house to meet Lauren. The thought of seeing her made his body tighten. His fingers curled into fists as he shook his head. She was his best friend's girl. He was only doing a favor for a friend, he lied to himself.

"Nick, I've got the broadcasting rights brief you requested."

He turned to see Mary standing by his desk. He hadn't heard her knock at the door. He took the folder and stuffed it into his briefcase. "Thanks."

"Early night, boss?" She looked at him curiously.

"Yes, it is." He smiled.

"Hmm, you didn't have me make dinner reservations after Theresa called."

He shook his head. His ex-girlfriend liked to go out and try out trendy new restaurants. Theresa St. John had the manners of a lady and the determination of a pit bull. They'd grown up together and spent summers at the same community center. Their fathers still met together every other Saturday to play golf. He and Theresa had dated for three months before Nick told her it wouldn't work out. His ears were still ringing from her angry accusations.

"No, I'm going to be eating at the house tonight."

He glanced out the window at the rapidly darkening sky. His mouth watered with the thought of a candlelight dinner complete with plates of pasta and garlic bread.

Nick put on his coat and hat, grabbed his briefcase, and headed out the door. Putting the cell phone to this ear, he hit the speed dial to the best Italian restaurant in Brooklyn. One train ride and two stops, one for wine and the other for food. Tonight he'd have dinner for two, only this time he'd actually enjoy it.

* * *

"What about this one?" she questioned.

Nick swore under his breath as his gaze centered on the top of Lauren's head as she paged through another design book. There were no candles on his kitchen table. They would have set the place ablaze. Plates full of pasta lay surrounded by photos, papers, and fabric samples.

His idea of a nice friendly dinner with Lauren had dissolved into business the minute she put down her fork. For the past two hours, they'd discussed plans for Nick's brownstone while enjoying angel-hair pasta with shrimp and clams, garlic bread, mixed field-green salad, and his favorite vintage of French red wine. He had met old hard-bitten defense attorneys with less dogged determination than the beautiful woman sitting across from him. It was about to drive him crazy, and for a moment he wanted to just give in.

He sat back and took a sip of wine. He knew as soon as she sensed a weakness she'd believe her part of the contract was fulfilled and be out the door and on a plane to find a husband.

It amazed him that a woman that beautiful thought she had to leave the country to find a husband. Any single man in his right mind would stand in line to have a chance to marry Lauren. He wasn't even sure that he wouldn't be waiting at the door. The thought of Lauren in some foreign Casanova's arms turned his stomach.

"Did you enjoy dinner?"

"Hmm . . . Yes, I did." She looked up at him. "Thank you."

"So how's Alan?"

"When I talked to him the other day he was fine." Lauren opened another decorating book. He liked the way the wire-framed reading glasses rested on the tip of her nose.

"How about this picture?" He enjoyed the sight of her long, slender fingers before moving on to the photo.

She continued. "Notice the colors and silk, this room has a definite Middle Eastern feel to it."

"For which room?"

"I was thinking about the master bedroom."

Nick couldn't shake his head fast enough. Curtains over the bed, red walls, gold, and velvet weren't his style.

"Look, Lauren. I'm sure this is the going thing for home design, but this really isn't me."

She snapped the book closed so fast, his finger almost got caught in the pages. "Then what is you, Nick? Help me out with this."

"I'm not sure." He leaned back. "Why don't you ask?"

"This isn't a court case, this is decorating."

"This was a meal and I spend most of my time at the negotiating table or in the office, not in a courtroom," he corrected. "Now, you just asked me about myself. What do you want to know?"

Lauren sighed but decided that it might be worthwhile to play his game. Anything to get the job done faster. "What's your favorite color?"

"Yours."

Lauren's brows drew together. "What?"

"Brown."

A blush rose on her cheeks even as she lowered her face. He definitely had the personality of a person who preferred brown. Very in control with a defined sense of right and wrong. She envied him for the way he seemed to be at such ease with life, that sense of belonging he projected. Nick fit the profile for the color but it surprised her all the same. The want for simplicity, his sense of duty and responsibility. The woman he would choose to spend his life with would never have to doubt his commitment. Her teeth clenched at the thought of Nick with someone else.

"What's yours?" he asked.

She slowly took off her glasses and placed them on the table. "This isn't about me."

He took a sip of wine. "Humor me."

"Blue," she reluctantly answered.

"Really?"

"Yes." She took a sip of wine. Once she'd treasured deep red mixed with brown. Now only the color of water moved her.

"I don't see you as a cold woman."

"That's good because I'm not cold. The color blue can mean many things."

He leaned forward as she gave him an arched look.

"Enlighten me." He watched her eyes darken.

"Is that possible?" She absently turned the catalog page. Every time Nick looked at her with those dark brown eyes of his, something started fluttering in her stomach.

"Anything's possible, Lauren."

Those words had haunted her after Paul's death. She'd believed happiness was possible. Now, she'd settle for being content. She took a deep breath and closed the notebook. "Blue symbolizes tranquillity, peace, harmony."

He laughed and the deep rich sound filled the half-empty kitchen. "Now I know you've got the wrong color. You, Lauren Hughes, are anything but peaceful."

"What?" Alarm shot through her.

"You've never been peaceful a day in your life. No, you've got purple written all over you."

"Purple?" she echoed. The hand holding her pen loosened and it dropped to the table.

"Unless I was sleeping during that science class, purple is a mixture of red and blue."

Lauren shifted in her chair, suddenly aware that she'd lost control of the conversation. "We could paint the second-floor bedroom purple," she suggested.

"Don't try to change the subject."

"Funny, I was trying to get back to the business at hand." She reached out to gather up the floor plans.

"Aren't you going to ask me more questions?" he goaded.

"No."

"What about mood?"

"What about it?"

"Aren't you interested in what kind of mood I want, Lauren?"

"You already told me. Comfortable, down-to-earth, homey."

"Maybe I've changed my mind," he answered, enjoying the way her eyes sparkled.

"Did you hear that?" she asked, looking toward the back door.

"What?" Nick looked around. He'd heard nothing but the wind against the windows.

She waved her hand. "Guess it was nothing."

He refilled her glass of wine. "You were explaining the characteristics of purple."

Lauren heard it again, a faint high-pitched cry. Not taking the time to explain, she stood up, turned on the outdoor lights, and opened the back door.

"What are you doing?" Nick followed behind her.

"Shivering," she responded, her eyes and ears searching the darkness.

"Lauren—"

"Shh . . ."

She heard the sound coming from the underside of the stairs and would have started down the steps had there not been an arm locked tight around her waist.

Nick didn't hesitate. "Don't move. I'll check it out."

Lauren would have laughed if she weren't so cold. She looked up at Nick. Did he really expect her to go somewhere with his arm around her?

"What is it?" she asked moments later.

She took one look at the pint-sized shivering fur ball in his hands and ushered them into the house.

A half hour later, after giving up his emergency can of tuna, Nick got around to asking Lauren about the homeless cat. "So, you going to take it home?"

"I can't take him home. No pets in the building." That wasn't true exactly. Lauren wanted nothing more in the world than to leave with the precious little bundle, but she couldn't take the cat home only to leave for months.

Its eyes were a deep vivid blue, too fine for an ordinary house cat. Someone was a fool to let the fellow go. She brushed her hand over the cat's slender frame as she studied the little creature. Cream colored with milk-chocolate spots, the short hair was soft to touch and she warmed to the cat's purring.

Nick started getting an uneasy feeling in his stomach as he watched Lauren cuddle with the cat. "Well, I don't know a thing about cats."

"They're independent and quite clean."

"You're absolutely right." Nick rubbed his hands together. "I'm sure he's missing the great outdoors."

"Or missing a home." She shook her head. "He's definitely not an outdoor cat."

"Too bad. My place isn't cat- or people-friendly right now." He had practically no furniture, no plants, and little amenities to offer human guests, much less animals.

She beamed at him. "That's not true at all."

He watched as Lauren excitedly pointed to his recent shipment of French wine. "We can use that shallow wine crate as a temporary litter box."

His mouth dropped open. "But . . ."

Here he was, one of the best sports lawyers in the country, and he was tongue-tied. Lauren looked at him with a Mona Lisa smile and his heart flipped. Then his gaze slid to the cat laid out in her lap and his stomach dropped. Damned if the thing didn't lift its round head and blink at him before rolling over to make himself more comfortable.

"I think we should name him."

"Uh . . ." He shifted his feet and inched away. "That might not be a good idea." He didn't want her to be getting too attached to the animal.

"Why not? I've got the perfect name."

Then she looked up at him with those large brown eyes of hers and his breath caught in his throat.

"We can call him Brooklyn."

He held out his hand and shook his head. "No way. Not happening. This has to be someone else's cat."

"There's no collar."

"Probably slipped off his little head."

"He likes you," she said, standing up and walking toward him.

Nick stared mesmerized as she leaned over and gently placed the cat in his arms.

"Lauren," he warned.

"See how he's purring. His hair is so soft. How can you not fall in love with him?"

Nick opened his mouth to tell her how easy it was not to like the creature. But he made the mistake of looking into her questioning eyes.

This is not happening. Nick shook his head. No way he was going to take care of a cat, no matter what Lauren asked.

He ended up visiting two bodegas, a corner shop, and a grocery store. Nick walked home with one bag filled with cat litter and the other with the smallest, most expensive canned food he'd ever seen. He couldn't wait to crack open a can to see whether it was cat food or caviar.

Shaking his head, he crossed the street. He'd always

wanted a pet but in his mind he pictured getting a big dog, something he could run in the park with. Maybe he'd get one of those Dobermans, huskies, or Labrador retrievers. Yeah, Nick mused, he needed man's best friend, not woman's favorite pet. He'd just have to explain to Lauren that little homeless would have to go to a shelter.

He stepped on the front step of his house and shifted the plastic bags to get the keys out of his pocket. As he stuck the key in the lock, he decided to put the cat up for adoption. Pushing the door open, he inhaled the warm scent of freesia that Lauren had placed in a vase near the doorway. Maybe he'd bribe one of the paralegals at the firm to take it.

Nick nodded and strode confidently toward the living room, only to stop dead in his tracks. Lauren lay curled up on the sofa with her arm around the cat. The enticing scene killed the words in his throat. Stepping out of the room, he went into the kitchen and fought the urge to bang his head against the wall. Mr. Frosty was in hot water and it was going to take everything he had to pull himself out.

Three days and a $150 veterinarian bill later, Nick was still getting over the shock. Brooklyn turned out to be a six-month-old *she* with a habit of sleeping right beside him at night. He was the last person on earth to be taking in stray animals. He'd write a check in a minute, but take in a cat from the streets? He definitely wasn't acting like himself and the reason was Lauren.

However crazy it seemed, she was the most alluring, the most fascinating woman he had ever met. *She is also Alan's girl,* he reminded himself as he applied the shaving gel. He wondered if Lauren felt the attraction. He doubted it; Nick was good at hiding his emotions, but not that good. He couldn't keep his body from reacting to her presence, just as he couldn't keep his lips from curling into a smile just thinking about her.

Maybe he'd talk to Lauren. Find out what was really happening between her and Alan. Maybe he had a chance to win her over. Nick stopped shaving and looked over at the toilet seat. The feline lay curled up looking at him. "Don't get too comfortable," he warned the cat. "I like dogs."

Six

Lauren ran her hand over the smooth flat marble vase she'd had delivered to her office. She could see the flowers and sunlight that would wash over the dining room table centerpiece. The project was becoming more of an obsession. As much as she told herself it was the brownstone, she knew it was Nick's deep voice whispering in her dreams.

"Lauren," the intercom buzzed.

"Yes, Susan?"

"There's a Theresa St. John to see you."

She searched her memory for the name and came up empty.

"Do you know what she wants?" Lauren questioned.

"No, she called about twenty minutes ago and asked to meet with you. Want me to bring her to your office?"

"That's all right. I'll get her." She left her office and made her way to the waiting alcove. She turned the corner and paused before entering the waiting area. A stylishly dressed woman in a burgundy suit with matching clips holding back her long braids sat alone paging through a decorator magazine.

"Ms. St. John." Lauren held out her hand. The woman turned toward her and Lauren watched the stranger's eyes pick her apart piece by piece. "Lauren Hughes. Please follow me to my office." The other woman took her hand and limply shook it.

Lauren closed the door to her office and took a seat behind the desk. "How can I help you, Ms. St. John?"

"Please call me Theresa. Nick has told me so much about you. I feel as though we know each other."

Upon hearing Nick's name on the woman's lips, Lauren allowed a curious expression to creep over her otherwise blank face.

She gripped her pen. "So what can I do for you?"

Theresa crossed her legs. "I've been wanting to speak with you since we bumped into each other at Nick's place."

Lauren shook her head. "I'm sorry, I don't recall meeting you."

"I didn't have the opportunity to introduce myself and you seemed to be in quite a hurry to leave."

Realization hit her square between the eyes: the woman at the door she'd walked past that first day she'd visited Nick's brownstone. "I apologize, I was in a rush to get back to Manhattan that day."

"Well, I just wanted to thank you in person for the lovely job you're going to do on the brownstone."

"Thank you. I take it you've seen the preliminary sketches?" Her hands had balled into fists in her lap. Years of practice kept the smile on her face. She didn't want this woman in that house, much less seeing her designs.

"No, but one of my patients is in interior design. She admires your work."

"You're a doctor, Theresa?"

"I'm a dentist. By the way, I have to say you have nice teeth. Are they caps?"

"No." The word worked its way out from behind her gritted teeth. She looked at the woman hard. Theresa's pretty face, blank of emotion, gave no clue as to why the woman was sitting in her office.

"Nick's father encouraged me to go into medicine,

but it wasn't my thing. Ami, Nick's younger sister, loves it. She's a pediatrician, you know."

"That's nice," Lauren replied impatiently, hoping that Theresa would kill the chitchat and get to the point.

"Nick's father and mine used to practice medicine together. Our families are very close." Theresa blinked her eyes.

Lauren sighed and placed her hands on the desk. "I hate to be rude but I have to get a lot of work done today. What is it that I can help you with?"

Theresa uncrossed her legs and leaned forward. "You can help me by quitting."

"Excuse me?" Lauren could see the gloves coming off.

"Nick is mine, has been since we joined Jack and Jill together. My parents are expecting wedding bells in the spring and I'm not going to disappoint them."

Lauren held up a hand. "Wait, this has nothing to do with me."

"That's where you're wrong. Ever since you started decorating the brownstone, his focus has shifted completely. We hardly spend any time together and I need him to help me look through wedding invitations, not furniture catalogs."

"Theresa—"

"Let me finish. I need time with Nick. We've got a wedding to plan, not to mention the honeymoon."

The other woman's chuckle sent waves of hot anger rushing over Lauren's body. She bit the inside of her lip to keep the rush of words from spilling out of her mouth.

She took a deep breath and replied with a fake calm voice, "Theresa, I'm sorry but I cannot quit this project." And, Lord, did she want to get out of it! But she'd never do it without giving Nick Randolph a big chunk of her mind. "This firm has a reputation to uphold."

Lauren watched as the woman's big smile turned into a frown.

"Is there any way you could finish sooner?"

"That all depends on Nick and the contractors."

Just as Theresa opened her mouth, the phone buzzed. Lauren stabbed the button. "Yes?"

"Lauren, I've got Alan Knight on the line."

She looked up at Theresa. The woman showed no signs of leaving.

"Hey, Alan." Lauren smiled. "Can I call you back in about twenty minutes?"

"Sure. Call me on my cell," he replied.

"Okay. Bye."

"Alan Knight," Theresa murmured. "My, that name sounds familiar. Oh, now I remember, Nick's friend, the very good-looking baseball player."

Lauren's eyes narrowed at the insinuating tone in the woman's voice. "Yes."

"My, my, my." Theresa's delight at the newest tidbit of information was by no means concealed. "I'm sure he's concerned about your spending so much time at Nick's house."

"And that would be none of your business."

"Nick is my business." Theresa gave her a sideways glance.

"I think you should leave now." Lauren stood and stepped from behind her desk.

Theresa picked up her purse and coat. "It'd be a shame really." She sighed dramatically. "To have something happen to their friendship."

Lauren regarded the woman with a hard stare. "What exactly are you implying?"

"Greed is a terrible thing, Lauren. I suggest you stay away from Nick or you might find yourself alone."

Lauren stared at her and blinked. Taking a deep breath, she placed her shaking hands behind her back when all she wanted to do was slap the smile off Theresa's face. If the other woman wanted Nick so badly she'd stoop to such innuendos and threats, then she could have him. If Nick was dense enough to propose to the barracuda, then he could have her. *I hope she makes his life a living hell,* Lauren thought angrily.

She knew her toneless voice didn't match her eyes. Stalking to the door, she threw it open and pointed to the elevators. "Get out."

When the woman disappeared around the corner, Lauren gently closed the door and leaned against it. Letting her head fall back, she closed her eyes and counted to ten as something thick welled up in the back of her throat.

Calmer, she looked at the vacant chair. Theresa St. John was more than welcome to Nick. Picking up the phone, Lauren put in a call to her travel agent.

Making his way through the after-work bar crowd, Nick made up his mind. He'd called at the last minute to arrange the meeting at their regular bar. Spades, with its old-school music, low-ceilinged room, and leopard-print carpet, was always packed, but tonight Nick didn't notice. He was going to let Alan know that he had some serious feelings where Lauren was concerned. Making his way around the small tables, he took a seat on the fat stools across from Alan at the back table.

"How's it going?" Nick asked.

"Good . . . good." Alan nodded. "Therapy's going great and Mom's coming in soon. I got to hand it to you, Nick, you pulled it off."

"Well, let's hope Lauren is still here. She's working like the devil to get everything planned out. She's even managed to get me to spend some long hours looking over the stuff."

"That's my girl."

He's my best friend, Nick had to remind himself. Sometimes he failed to remember that important fact. Every time he touched Lauren accidentally, the sparks would jump up between them, each time more intense than the last. He looked away from Alan as something started clawing at his stomach.

"Your girl is a workaholic. Tonight's my first night off in days," he continued.

Nick wasn't happy about it either. He enjoyed leaving work on time and picking up takeout for the two of them. She brought a texture and depth to his life that he had known was missing. Yet, the time Lauren quit having dinner at the brownstone was about the same time Theresa started coming by with a smile on her face. Nick didn't believe in coincidence, especially where women were concerned, and the thought of going another day without seeing her again didn't sit right.

Sometime after following Lauren through the fifth design store, he'd started liking trailing behind her as she meticulously chose furnishings, appliances, and decorations. He couldn't remember anything sexier than the glow in her eyes when she was seeing something she thought was perfect for the brownstone.

"Hmm, Lauren was supposed to come and drop off an African sculpture," Alan said.

"She didn't?" he questioned before taking a bite of the Buffalo wing.

"Cass came instead. One of Lauren's college friends came into town on business. Apparently he's taking her out to dinner."

Nick choked on his beer. "You're letting her go out to dinner with someone else?"

Alan shrugged. "Nothing wrong with that. Besides, she'll be mad as hell if she knew I was checking up on her."

Nick gave his friend a crazy look. Check up? More like check the man out. Nick's fingers curled up into fists. Alan didn't deserve Lauren—the baseball player could have his pick of women, and here he was letting the phenomenal woman go out on a date with a man he didn't know. Unintentionally, a tiny muscle in his cheek started jumping.

Alan continued, "I trust Lauren. Besides, I got bigger things to worry about. Like this crazy scheme of hers to travel around the world."

"You think her plans to go on vacation are more of a threat than another man?" Nick sat up. "Have you forgotten that Lauren is planning on getting married during this trip of hers?"

"She's just going out with an old college friend. The boy is in town for a computer expo. She won't be thinking about anything but reminiscing on the days he wore his Coca-Cola-bottle glasses and zebra-striped ties."

Alan finished up a piece of chicken. "Besides, I wouldn't mind if my younger sister was dating a guy like Jamal Lewis. Shoot, that'd be an improvement over the lost causes Mama said Rachel keeps bringing home for dinner."

"Little sister?" Nick sat up on the bar stool and looked at Alan.

"Yes, I said little sister." Alan took a swig of beer and stared as his buddy sat up straight. "What's wrong with you? Look like you've seen a ghost."

"You and Lauren aren't . . ." His brow furrowed.

"Aren't what?" Alan frowned.

Nick put his beer on the table. "Seeing each other."

"Man, what have you been drinking? Lauren is like a kid sister to me." Alan stared at his friend in astonishment.

In the couple of years he'd known Nick, he'd never seen him lose his cool about anything. Now just the mention of Lauren's name made the man tense. Alan shook his head and started laughing.

"I thought," Nick said, stumbling, "you were saying that you were interested in . . ."

"Cassandra." Alan bit into a salsa-covered tortilla chip.

Nick's bottom lip fell to the floor. He shook his head and blew out a long breath. "Smart-talking, won't-let-you-get-a-word-in Cassandra?"

Alan's face softened as he pictured the blush that rose to the woman's cheeks every time they were alone at his house. He'd caught himself staring at her for no other reason than that it pleased him. He'd made it his mission to find out her likes and dislikes so he could see her beautiful eyes light up with a warm smile.

"The woman's gotten under my skin. When we first met, the only time she would talk to me was when Lauren was around. Now that she's had to take over finishing up the house, I've been able to get to the lady. She's a wonder, Nick, and she cooks a jerk chicken dish that can make a man die happy." Alan leaned forward.

Little sister. Nick shook his head in disbelief. All this time he thought Alan was in love with Lauren as a woman, and he loved her like a sibling. And she was out with another man.

"Oh, no," he cursed. Not while there was breath still in his body.

"What?"

"There is no way I'm letting another man move in on Lauren." He looked toward his friend for support.

Alan smirked, then picked up another chip and ate it. "It's not like you've laid claim to anything."

"Not yet, I haven't. I was under the impression that you and Lauren were in a relationship."

Alan let out a loud laugh only to tone it down as it drew attention to their table. "That's twice you've been wrong about Lauren. You must really have it bad for the woman."

Nick took another swig of beer. "She gets to me in the worst way. Smart, beautiful, a breath of fresh air."

"Fresh air," Alan echoed. "Before you break into poetry, I suggest you go tell *her*, not *me*, how you feel."

He stood up and began putting on his scarf and coat. "Sorry, bro, but I'm going to have to leave early."

Alan finished his beer and grinned. "No problem. I'm going over to Cassandra's place for dinner in about a half hour. I think I'll just show up early and see if I can get dessert first."

"Talk to you later." Nick gave Alan a nod.

"Good luck," Alan called out.

Nick stopped and turned toward his friend. "Thanks." Where Lauren was concerned, he knew he'd need it.

Why am I here? Nick mused, looking around at the other coffeehouse patrons, and then turned to continue watching Lauren's apartment building. *I only want to make sure she's okay,* he thought, closing his eyes and leaning back into the plush chair. The jangling of spoons on glass and whispered conversations mixed with the whirr of the espresso machine faded away.

"Your Honor, I was looking after a friend," he said, addressing the court.

Nick looked around the packed courtroom. Professor Hanson, his old law school professor, sat on the bench. The man's snow-white, thin wispy hair barely covered his shiny bald head. He'd never forget the way the man's nasal voice scratched at his ears.

"Really, counselor," Judge Hanson drawled, raising his bushy gray eyebrows, "you drank four cappuccinos, consumed two brownies, and sat at the Java Inn for three hours waiting for a friend?"

Placing his hands on the wooden table, Nick nodded hesitantly as the bailiff stared at him in disbelief. "Yes, Your Honor."

"Not because the lady in question is fine as wine and sweeter than your mama's peach pie?"

Nick's eyes about popped out of his head at the man's lecherous look.

"He's lying, Your Honor."

A wave of surprise ran through the jury, but the presiding judge did not seem the slightest bit concerned.

His mouth agape, Nick turned his head to see Theresa stand up from the gallery. The entire Randolph family lined the first row. He was astonished to see his parents' grave and severe faces while his younger brother took pictures.

"I've seen the way he looks at Lauren Hughes. Nick Randolph is a fake. He's been after that woman for weeks."

"Theresa?" He watched as she marched up to the front of the courtroom and came to a stop next to the opposing counsel's table. The red dress she wore seemed to glow so bright it hurt his eyes. Nick blinked twice as he recognized the opposing lawyer. Dressed in a black tuxedo was none other than Jamal Lewis. He watched as the man sent a challenging sneer in his direction.

"Is she telling the truth, Nick?"

His neck swerved toward the witness stand. Lauren sat motionless wearing a nice black dress with the cat sitting in her lap. Her dark brown eyes looked like pools of warm earth that he wanted to cover himself in.

"I . . ." He leaped to his feet and felt his palms beginning to sweat. His heart was beating so fast, he had begun gasping for breath.

"Go ahead. Tell the court, Mr. Randolph," Judge Hanson encouraged with his most obliging smile.

Nick shook his head over and over. "I . . ."

"Sir, are you okay?" came a soft voice.

He focused on the young woman standing in front of him. "Too much coffee."

Eleven P.M. He looked up from his watch in time to see Lauren step out of a yellow cab with a well-dressed man at her heels.

He fought the urge to curse seeing Jamal Lewis. The Michael Jordan of the computer world had been on the front page of both *GQ* and *People* magazines.

He was going to give her twenty minutes before he went up to her apartment.

Entering into her kitchen, Lauren laughed as the two wineglasses she held clinked together. It sounded exactly like Jamal's electronic pager. Placing them in the sink, she leaned against the countertop and smiled. She never would have thought of him as a corporate executive. The laid-back Barbados-born man seemed destined to be a top chef like his father. Now an emergency message had sent him running back to his hotel to use the computer.

Tall, lean, and built, with hazel eyes, Jamal was a handsome man. When he spoke in the lyrical island accent, the contrast of his perfect white teeth and smooth cocoa-butter skin had married women wishing they were single and unmarried women wishing they had his ring on their finger.

If Lauren hadn't known him when his devilish eyes were hidden by thick glasses and teeth locked behind braces, she would have tripped over her own two feet in her haste to fall in love with the man. Then again Nick, with his seductive dark eyes, managed to keep thoughts of other men far from her mind.

For a moment she actually felt a little guilty for spending so much time away from her project. She'd lived and breathed the work plans and furniture placement for so long, it was hard to let go. She'd supervised the carpet installation on the ground floor, hung the heavy damask and muslin sheer window treatments, and walked the house pinpointing ceiling locations for the electrician.

Lauren sighed before pouring out the half-filled wineglasses and stared sightlessly at the running water. She missed Nick.

No. She shook her head and finished washing out the glasses. Brooklyn, she missed the cat. She would follow her from room to room as she made notes or sketched out a more detailed layout of the furniture and decorations. The little feline would jump up onto the windowsill and then leap into her arms, for a good cuddle. *Work, girl, work.* She shook her head. Anything to keep her mind off things she couldn't have.

When Lauren opened the door, Nick wanted to kiss her and shake her at the same time. The curve of her lush breasts drew his eyes like a moth to a flame. That another man might have glimpsed the treasures made him feel as if a whole defensive line had run him down.

"Nick?"

He watched her dark eyes widen.

"What are you doing here?"

"I need to talk to you about the brownstone. May I come in?" he asked, already having stepped inside.

"Of course. Can I get you some coffee?"

"No, thank you." He took off his coat and placed it in her outstretched arms. The thought of drinking another cup of coffee turned his stomach.

"All right. How about some water?" She cocked her head to the side.

"That'd be nice."

"Have a nice night?" He raised his voice, looking around the apartment while she went into the tiny kitchen.

Nick examined the living room, admiring the consciously designed space. Furniture and exotic knickknacks made it warm and inviting. The shelves were crammed with candles, pictures, and delicate figurines. The mix of colors from the indigo curtains to the bouquet of wild-flowers stamped the room with Lauren's own style.

He turned his attention away from the bookcase as she came to a stop next to him.

"Yes, I did. It's always good to catch up with old friends."

"Friends, huh?" Never in a million years would he be-lieve that Jamal Lewis wasn't attracted to Lauren. A man would have had to be dead to look at Lauren in that nice skirt and think of her as a friend.

He reached out and accepted the glass of water.

"What's the matter with you, Nick?" Lauren asked.

"Funny, I was wondering the same about you."

"Me?" she snorted, taking a seat on the sofa.

"Sneaking out before I come home, not returning my phone calls. What's up, Lauren?"

"Nothing." She cut her eyes. The idea of his flirting with her when he was practically engaged to someone else burned her up. She'd avoided him like the plague these past couple of days, going so far as to sneak out the lower entrance when he came in the main door.

"Sounds like something's bothering you."

"Well, get your hearing checked." She moved to stand up.

"Wait."

She looked down at the hand holding her arm.

"I thought you didn't like games," he challenged.

Heat flooded her face and she berated herself for

allowing him to get her worked up. "I don't, but you seem to not only play them but also rewrite the rules."

"What?"

She'd had more than enough. "I thought you were a good man, but this flirting with me while you're engaged . . ." She shook her head.

"Engaged?" he repeated.

Lauren took a step back. "Don't. I expected better of you."

Nick's brows rose. "Wait a minute, I'm not engaged."

"And I'm not in diapers so don't think I was born yesterday," she countered.

"Who told you this?"

"Does it matter?"

"When someone gives you false information it does." Nick took a step closer to her. "Look at me, Lauren."

He gently turned her face toward his. "I did not and will not lie to you. I'm not engaged."

A large part of her wanted to believe him. But she shook her head.

"You know me, Lauren. You may think many things about me, but I'm not a liar."

For some reason she couldn't understand, Lauren believed him. He'd slice the truth and twist it up in knots, but he wouldn't lie.

She met Nick's questioning stare. "You might want to relay that information to Theresa."

"You know Theresa?" he asked, surprised.

"Not before she paid me a visit at the office." Lauren shook her head, not wanting to talk about the conversation with Ms. St. James. That had left a bad taste in her mouth. "I just think that you might want to have a chat with her."

"Trust me. She and I will talk. Right now I'm more concerned about what's missing from my house."

Her heart leaped. "Brooklyn?"

"Is fine." Nick moved another step closer. "In fact, the cat's made a little home for herself on the fourth floor."

"Oh." She turned and strolled over toward the window only to turn and discover Nick had followed her. He took the glass from her hand and placed it on the end table.

"The African chair and stool didn't arrive?" she guessed.

Nick was near enough to see the way her eyelashes quivered. "Came in yesterday and the contractor called to tell me the sofa was delivered this afternoon."

"The painters were finished?"

"Everything's fine, but there's still something missing."

She didn't move as his fingers trailed along the nape of her neck. Her heart beat like a hummingbird's wings in her chest.

Lauren licked her lips. "The dining room furniture should come in a few days." Her voice was a mere whisper.

Nick shook his head. "What's missing is you, Lauren."

Her lips parted in surprise and that was all the invitation he needed.

The hum of desire that always seemed to hang in the space between them rose to a chorus. His lips came down and her arms of their own accord wrapped around his broad shoulders. His mouth locked on hers and his tongue caressed her lips before slipping inside her mouth, drinking in its softness.

He'd been waiting for this moment ever since the day she slammed the door in his face. She tasted of spring when flowers bloomed—lush, vivid, and soft. He held tight as she trembled against him even when her body pulled back.

Who had hurt her so badly she'd run away to look for marriage with a stranger? Nick deepened the kiss and ran his hands down her back to cup her firm bottom. He would write his name all over her body and brand her soul. If passion would keep her bound to him, he'd use it. Nothing was going to stop this, not even Lauren.

"What was that?" Her voice all breathy. The kiss had knocked her for a loop. Her heart beat loud in her ears.

"That was the beginning." After that kiss, Nick could have kicked himself for not doing it sooner.

"Have you lost your mind?"

"Yes, Your Honor, I have." He kissed her again.

Lauren didn't see stars; she felt colors.

Red.

The heat spread from his fingers as they grazed her skin.

Flame.

His kiss burned her lips as his tongue plunged into her mouth. Igniting something deep in her body, sending ripple after ripple of silvery pleasure spiraling through her veins. He was like a drug and the more he gave the more she craved.

Even as her common sense warned of danger, her body sang of love and desire. Lauren was like a blind woman: she read him with her hands. Firm, muscled, and smooth. She was hot, burning, and his body was cool. She wanted to drink of him, fill the empty space his presence brought. It was at his touch, the way she molded into his body and pressed her breasts to his chest. Nick didn't ask, he demanded. Desire ran all up through her and Lauren's ardor matched his. It was that craving that pulled her back to reality.

Lauren broke free from his arms and took two shaky steps back. "I think you'd better go." She turned away and touched her fingers to her swollen lips.

"I promised Brooklyn I'd bring you home."

"Then you'll have to disappoint your roommate, now, won't you?" She moved to walk around him to the door.

"I'll see you tomorrow night. I make a mean steak."

She avoided his gaze. "This can't happen again."

"No?" he questioned with a soft mocking tone.

"I don't mix business with pleasure and I most certainly don't get involved with my clients," she replied firmly.

His lips inched upward. "That's good to hear."

Lauren tossed him a small frown as she opened the door. It was good that he was being calm about this. She could barely look at his handsome face without things going all low and tight.

"Lauren?"

"Yes?" She gripped the doorknob as her heart skipped a beat.

"In the near future I won't be your client."

He bent down and kissed her hard. She tasted like a surprise upset and sweet victory: touchdowns and field goals. He'd never wanted anything more than to make love to Lauren. The touch of her hands and the feel of her lips filled him with the rush of winning. Running his hands over her curves was the best thing in the world. When Lauren's tongue caressed the roof of his mouth, he knew he had it bad. The woman rushed through his defenses straight to his heart.

"Beautiful . . . You and I will be lovers."

Lauren swallowed as her throat went dry. Unable to turn away, she followed him with her eyes as he strode down the stairs. Her heart still hadn't slowed its rapid pace after she closed the door and entered into her small study. Taking a deep breath, she opened the desk drawer and pulled out a world map.

Grabbing something to write with, she started circling and thinking. She tried to fill her mind with travel plans and exotic locations. Her fingers gripped the yellow lead pencil. Nick Randolph with his passionate kisses and knowledgeable hands filled her mind and sent her running for cover. Giving up, she went to bed hoping to escape into the oblivion of sleep.

* * *

"Nick, I've got Theresa on line two." He looked up to see his assistant standing in the doorway.

"Thank you." He gave her a smile. "Could you close the door for me?"

"Sure thing."

Nick waited until the door clicked shut behind her before picking up the telephone.

"Theresa," he started.

"Nick, I was just going to call you. Would you like to meet for—"

He didn't let her finish the sentence. "Why did you go to Lauren's office yesterday?"

There was a strained silence over the line before she answered, "I just wanted to compliment her on the renovations to your brownstone."

"Theresa." His voice was hard and unyielding.

"Nick, I just wanted to talk to her."

"For what purpose? To imply a relationship between the two of us when we haven't so much as held hands in over six months?"

"What the hell else do you expect me to do?" she snapped back. "I've got Mama calling me every other day asking about when she should talk to the pastor and reserve the church for a wedding, Gran just finished knitting baby booties, and Pop's already started a college education fund for his first grandchild."

Nick sighed and bet Theresa was busy biting on the end of a pencil. When it came to business, the woman radiated confidence. Yet, when it came to her personal life . . .

"Theresa, you have to tell them the truth."

"No, no, and no. She'll have a heart attack," she rushed, words tumbling on top of one another. "I can't kill my own mother, Nick. We can just get married for a couple of months. If you want I'll sign a prenup."

"There's no need for a prenup because there won't be any wedding."

After a brief silence, he heard her draw a deep breath. "It'll break her heart."

"It'll bruise her pride," he contradicted. "Your mother has been pushing you and me to get married since I was in second grade. It's way past time that you stood up to her, Theresa."

"Why don't you tell her?" She sounded like a kid again.

He smiled for the first time since he'd picked up the phone. "It'll sound better coming from you."

"Is this payback for my visit to Lauren Hughes?"

"No." He laughed as he heard the sound he'd been listening for. The spunk he thought she'd lost. "This is payback for letting me take the blame for Mr. Campbell's broken window."

There was a slight lull in the conversation. "Tell her I didn't mean any harm."

Nick leaned back in his chair. "I know. Good luck, Theresa."

"Thanks." She paused. "I'll need it."

Two days after finishing the designs for the den, Lauren stood with space measurements and room sketches in hand. She took her time moving from one section to another in the high-end electronics store. The salespeople wouldn't bother her with questions; she knew the owner and half the staff. The interior design firm's clients valued their privacy, their comfort, and above all else their home entertainment systems.

She couldn't help letting out a chuckle as she flashed back to the high-powered corporate executive who had shed tears of joy when his wife surprised him by having Lauren redesign their den. After a minute, Lauren looked down at her watch: 6:45 P.M. Nick was late yet again and she still couldn't keep the silly smile off her face. The kiss they'd shared the other night still lingered on her lips. It was amazing how quickly thoughts of him cluttered her mind. Stopping in front of a set of surround-sound speakers, Lauren chewed on her pencil.

As the hair on the nape of her neck rose, she looked up, aware that she was being watched. Her eyes locked on Nick. He stood a couple of feet away from her. She didn't bother to hide her appreciation of the sight he presented.

Lauren wanted to let out a groan because clothes did not make the man. With his tall muscular physique, Nick made the clothes. He didn't just wear the dark navy suit and burgundy tie; he made them look good.

"You didn't start without me, did you?" Nick teased. He'd run out the door and hailed a cab as soon as the meeting was over. Keeping Lauren waiting was the last thing he wanted to do, but the admiring look he saw in her eyes made him want to leave and come back again just so he could see it one more time.

"Maybe," she teased before leaning down to pick up another brochure.

"I'm sorry. I didn't mean to be late." He took a couple of steps closer.

Lauren gave him her best attempt at a glare as she tapped her pencil against her cheek. "This is becoming quite a bad habit of yours, Mr. Randolph."

"You have to let me make it up to you." He put his arm around her waist.

"Okay, how about you being early next time?" She couldn't keep the twinkle out of her eyes.

Then her eyes widened as a grin split his face. "How about I buy you a drink?"

"I can't," she said, turning to continue down the aisle. "Too much work to do."

"All work and no play . . ." he started but his eyes fell on the big-screen television Lauren had led him to.

"Makes Nick Randolph a happy man." Lauren finished his sentence. "This is what I picked out for the den," she announced.

"Wow." He couldn't find the words as the basketball game started on the screen.

"I do believe I've left you speechless." She laughed.

Nick moved in closer and bent down toward Lauren's ear. "So this is what you do after you've already taken my breath away."

Lauren swallowed hard and took a steadying breath. "You should wait for the encore."

"And that is?"

She moved from the embrace and sauntered toward the back of the store. "Come this way."

Lauren led him to the back and directed him into a demonstration room.

"This." She hit the glowing power button on the wall and stepped back.

Music filled the midsized room as cinema-series rear-projection television blinked to life with the opening credits of the latest Hollywood blockbuster. The entertainment system was a movie and music lover's dream come true. In-wall and in-ceiling speakers delivered excellent surround-sound quality. Lauren turned off the demonstration and leaned against the wall with a silly smile on her face. "Well?"

"You're going to put something like this in my house?" Nick's eyes were still slightly unfocused.

"With your approval of course." Lauren looked up from her notepad.

"I get the game system too?" he asked, remembering the one he'd played at Alan's place.

"Yes, it comes with the 'boys'' package." Lauren tucked her notebook back into her bag.

"Boys' package?" Nick challenged.

"That's what we call the home theater system we're going to install in your den."

"Girls like movies too."

"Not as much as you."

"Oh, I doubt that." His arms came up on both sides of her body.

"Really?" Her voice unintentionally took on a sultry quality.

"Oh, yeah."

She watched as his lips descended upon hers. She thought that this kiss would be like the last but it wasn't. His mouth was sweet and teasing. Lauren wrapped her arms around his shoulders while his finger toyed with her hair. But it was Lauren's own reaction that pushed her completely off guard.

As Nick deepened the kiss and pressed his body against hers, she moaned as her skin tingled with wanting and the fine hairs stood at attention. Everything she had seemed to reach for the man.

When he finally had the strength to pull away, Nick looked down into Lauren's heavy-lidded eyes and thought he'd glimpsed a little piece of heaven.

"Wow," she murmured.

"I think we both need that drink now, wouldn't you say?" he whispered in her ear. He needed something to keep his hands on besides the woman trembling in his arms.

Lauren looked at him for a moment and she fought to regain her composure as a furious blush heated her cheeks. She wasn't some teenager to be caught stealing kisses in public. But when she was around him, her judgment flew out the window.

"I think you could be right," she managed to get out as she watched him button up her coat and straighten her scarf.

"Good, because I know just the place."

* * *

Later, after business was taken care of, Lauren moved past Nick into the lounge area of the bar. The space was beautiful, the lighting low, and as far as she could see, the clientele well heeled and attractive. Lauren stepped into a room with cushiony, velvet-curtained booths, silk scarves hanging from vaulted ceilings and ladies' and men's trinkets peering out from behind Tiffany lamps. The sweet-smelling lounge could have been a more polite version of an old New Orleans French Quarter boudoir.

"I like your taste in bars, Nick," she commented after settling in.

"I felt you might. Something about the place reminds me of you."

"Maybe the music," she said, enjoying the sounds of old-school blues.

"No, I think it would be the lace or the silk. It reminds me of your skin, soft and sleek."

Lauren blinked rapidly and looked away as her throat went dry. Nick was staring at her and the look in his eyes warmed by the candlelight sent a tingle of awareness to all the feminine places in her body.

She took a large sip of the Chianti. The sweet Italian wine flowed down her throat and swept into her stomach. Right away, a warm lassitude seeped into her muscles.

They settled into a comfortable silence after the waiter placed an assortment of appetizers on the table.

Nick ate a small canapé. "So tell me how you got so good at making a man's dreams come true."

"Ahh." A mocking smile graced Lauren's mouth. "But men are such simple creatures. A big-screen television here, video player, stereo receiver, a subwoofer, some nice tweeters, and voilà." She waved her hand. "Instant happiness."

"That's where you're wrong." He sat forward. "I may

have been pleased by the entertainment system, but not for a minute do I think a big-screen television and some speakers will make me happy."

"So what does make you happy?" She glanced at him from over the rim of her wineglass.

He pondered the question for a moment. "Winning. It's one of the reasons I became an attorney."

"The light begins to dawn," she said, leaning back.

"How so?" Nick watched as Lauren bit into a piece of flatbread.

"You have an air about you."

He sat back. "What kind is that?"

"The one that says captain of the football team, star member of the debate club."

"Well, Pop liked to throw the ball from time to time. Mom encouraged me to join the debate team after I achieved a unanimous victory during one of our family arguments."

"You argued a lot at home?" she asked, surprised by the notion.

"Not like that. Mom's being in politics really brought plenty of issues home. So once a week instead of turning on the television, we'd sit and discuss politics, news stories, or community action."

"You liked it?"

"On the contrary, I hated it at first. We'd all take it personally." He chuckled. "My little sister, Ami, didn't speak to me for three weeks after I voiced support for the Republican spending bill."

"And after all that you still wanted to be a lawyer?" She placed her hands on the table.

"No, I wanted what a million other teenage boys wanted: to be a pro football quarterback. I lived, breathed, ate for the game. Knew all the plays, watched all the college games. My coach didn't mind telling me I was good, but I always wanted to be better. My family, my teammates, and the game were extremely important to me. College took it all to a whole new level."

"Went to your head, didn't it?" A teasing smile hovered on her natural brown lips.

Nick finished a jumbo shrimp. "Big time. On the field, we were superstars."

"And I bet that off the field you, Nick Randolph, were quite a ladies' man." If the girls at his university were anything like the way they were at her school, they weren't blind. The man was gorgeous in either jeans and a shirt or shoulder pads and a helmet.

"I won't say I didn't enjoy my four years, but in order to play I had to study hard. Although I went to college on a football scholarship, my parents were strict about the grades. Hitting the books came second to football so that left me with little time for the opposite sex."

Lauren rolled her eyes toward the ceiling. Not for one second did she believe that he hadn't left a string of broken hearts back then.

"What made you leave football after you'd worked so hard to get into the NFL?" she asked.

"It wasn't my choice to make. I ran up against someone faster than I was. The running back for the other team managed to flip me when he made the tackle. What goes up must come down, and I landed at a bad angle and ripped my ligaments to shreds." He took a sip of wine.

"I'm sorry."

"Don't be, because I wasn't. My father was the one who broke the news and he let me feel sorry for myself for about a week. Next thing I knew I was hitting the books again. I learned how to walk again in physical therapy while studying for the law school entrance exams. The rest, shall we say, is history."

Lauren had known from the time they'd met at the hospital that he was a man to be reckoned with. The deep cold fire in his eyes and the forceful presence he projected let the world know he was a man with a mission. The determined way he'd set out to win her forgiveness was another indication of his character. He was a man that would right wrongs and watch out for those in his care.

"Now that I've gone and given you my whole life's story, why don't you tell me yours?" He reached across the table and took her hand into his.

The contact, while unexpected, was not unwelcome. Lauren looked across the table at the man who held her hand as gently as his gaze held her eyes. His touch sent a warmth through her body a thousand times stronger than the red wine.

Something in her wanted to pour out her soul to Nick. Let him drink of her sorrows, joys, and pain. But she had no intention of letting down her guard and allowing herself to be that vulnerable.

Lauren shrugged. "There's nothing to tell really."

"I find that hard to believe," Nick murmured as he caressed the inside of her wrist.

Lauren didn't reply but sharply pulled her hand from his grasp and reached into her purse to grab her wallet.

"Don't even think about it," he ordered.

She froze instantly, obeying the hard tone his voice had taken. She pushed her hair off of her face. "What?"

"My father raised me well, Lauren. Please don't open your wallet."

"All right." She kept her eyes turned down as Nick paid the check. "Thank you for the drink."

"Why don't we make it dinner next time?"

"Nick, I told you before. I keep my business and personal lives separate."

She sighed at the blank look he gave her. "I can't get involved with you."

He grinned. "But we are involved. We only have to be near one another to know that, beautiful."

She opened her mouth and closed it. There was no arguing with the truth as he saw it. So she did the only thing she could except admit defeat: she beat a polite and hasty exit.

Seven

If he weren't so handsome and charming, she'd accuse him of stalking her. After three days of trying, Lauren hadn't managed to shake Nick loose. He'd sent her flowers without notes and a box of chocolates shaped like little kittens. He'd been such a distraction, she'd barely been able to schedule in time to plan her vacation.

Even when he wasn't with her she was reminded of him. Honey walnut with a streak of cinnamon. Everywhere she went now the shade jumped out at her. Somehow he'd insinuated himself in her room. The place in her mind she'd shut everyone out of after Paul's death. The snow-white space filled with possibilities was the only thing that kept her from wanting to join him in the grave.

She looked down at the picture of the light honey-colored chaise she wanted to put in Nick's master bedroom and sighed before closing the book. *Concentrate on the important things, Lauren,* she ordered herself. With her departure date coinciding with Alan's mother's visit, she had too many distractions. *Doctor,* she decided, *I need to make an appointment to get those shots.*

As she moved to pick up the phone, the intercom buzzed.

"Lauren."

"Yes, Ann?"

"There's a woman who says she's your sister on the line."

Lauren slumped in her chair and fought against hiding under her desk or telling Ann to hang up on Sabrina. It was too early for Christmas or New Year's party reminders. If something had been wrong with her mother or stepfather, Nathan would have called.

What was it about her, she mused, that had the last people on earth she wanted to talk with jumping out of the woodwork? Taking the bull by the horns, she rolled her eyes upward and prayed. Had she been Catholic like her grandmother she'd have crossed herself before hitting the button to activate the speakerphone.

"Hello."

"Lauren, dear, how are you?"

Sabrina was only sixteen months older than Lauren, yet the woman continued to treat her as if she were still wearing a training bra and braces.

"I'm fine, and you?"

"Oh, Karl and I are doing beautifully. He's busy with the company and you know me, I have so many activities with the charity groups. This holiday season looks to be our busiest yet. We're helping the children this year; the little ones are so precious, you know. My Karl is almost completely taken by a few of them. I fear we may be looking for nursery furniture soon."

Lauren pinched the bridge of her nose. Same high-pitched falsetto voice that ran like a lawn mower over her nerves. The sugarcoated sweetness lulled you in so she could stab you in the heart. Pushing past the niceties, she asked about her mother's and stepfather's health. "That's nice, Sabrina. Are Mama and Ralph all right?"

"Of course, of course. I was calling because I sent you something in the mail."

Lauren sat up straight and stared hard at the phone. "Oh, what is it?"

"Tickets to the American Entrepreneurship Awards."

"I'm busy," she said, rattling off the ready excuse.

She'd been busy for the last three years. It was the only excuse that got her out of going to Sabrina's parties but didn't break her mother's heart. Nathan knew why Lauren only flew in to Chicago the day before Christmas and flew out the next. Memories of Paul coupled with her stepsister's constant digs and her mother's matchmaking attempts made holidays with the family a thorn in her side.

"No, you're not. I had that nice secretary of yours put the event on your calendar."

Her fingers curled into fists on the desk. "Look, Sabrina—"

The woman cut her off. "Lauren." She sighed dramatically on the phone. "If it's because you can't find a date, don't worry. I'm sure there'll be plenty of single people at the event."

If she could have gone through the phone, Lauren would have dragged Sabrina back four years, just so the woman could see herself without the Mrs. Jackson title and diamond solitaire on her finger. Her stepsister made being single sound as fatal as the Ebola virus. If it weren't for foolish men who thought with their eyes instead of their brains, Sabrina would never have gotten Karl to marry her.

"I really don't feel like arguing with you." Lauren didn't look up from the speakerphone as the door to her office opened.

"Then don't. We won't take no for an answer. Karl told me the other day that he would love to see you. You know how he feels about family. We've got a table near the stage. By the way, he's up for the Small Business Award."

"Sabrina—" she started.

"Oh, I know." Her stepsister's voice brightened. "You could ask Alan. I'm sure he wouldn't mind bringing you."

"I'm sure Alan wouldn't mind, but I would," came Nick's deep voice.

Lauren raised her head slowly like a rabbit sensing escape. Shock rocked through her body, making her forget her next words.

"Who is that, Lauren?"

"Nick Randolph, and you are?" He lazily took a seat on the edge of her desk.

Sabrina's voice always went from high to low at the sound of a man's voice. "Sabrina Jackson, I'm Lauren's sister."

"Stepsister," Lauren mouthed to a grinning Nick.

"Well, Sabrina, I can't wait to meet you at the awards. I hate to cut the conversation short, but your sister and I are late for our dinner reservation."

"Really? Well, you must go."

Lauren shook her head. "Good night, Sabrina." She clicked off the phone and sat back.

"And I thought you didn't lie, counselor." Her frown was about two seconds from flipping to a smile.

"I don't," he replied, moving away from her desk.

"We don't have dinner reservations," she pointed out while purposely ignoring his presumptuous announcement of being her date to the awards ceremony.

"Yes, we do and if we aren't in a cab soon, we'll miss them."

She watched as he took her scarf and coat off the coatrack.

Lauren sighed before looking down at the purchase orders she'd been trying to complete.

"I've got work to do, Nick." She tried to wave him away but he grabbed her hands and pulled her toward him.

"Just turn around so I can put on your coat."

"I've got to finish this," she protested as she put her arms in the sleeves and he placed her scarf around her neck.

"Later. Right now you've got salmon fillet, garlic mashed potatoes, and asparagus waiting for you."

Her stomach betrayed her with an answering growl. He made the prospect of eating Chinese takeout as appealing as dirt. Lauren turned around to give it one more try but as soon as she looked up into his eyes the scarf around her neck tightened and he drew her into his arms. One kiss and work was history, denial philosophy, and the sensation of his tongue caressing hers poetry.

Tomorrow, she mused as he opened the door to the taxi and ushered her into the backseat, she'd avoid him. Cuddled in his arms, she giggled when his fingers caressed her cheek.

Normally it was a piece of cake to look a person in the eyes. People never usually said what they meant, never did what they wanted. The difference always showed in the eyes. Nick had spent the better part of his career learning how to read people. Sitting across from Lauren, he didn't want to read her, he wanted to touch her, then try and understand her.

The candlelight played upon her lovely features, lending warmth to her shadowed eyes. The mere act of looking at her eased the stress caused by back-to-back meetings and deals.

"Is Brooklyn doing okay?" Lauren asked.

"She's discovering the joys of copyright case law."

"Really?"

"She likes to nap on top of them in the afternoon."

"Must be the sunlight," she said, nodding. "That room's in the best location."

"So why did you choose to become an interior designer?" he asked.

Instead of answering, Lauren waved her hand toward the center of the room. They were seated on the top floor of the three-floor restaurant. From the open balcony, they had a clear view of the open kitchen and main dining area.

"This blending of architecture and design. One can always build a perfect space, but you have to fill it to make it beautiful."

She had a long slender neck made for pearls, but she wore a simple silver pendant. Nick returned his attention back to her comments. "So you like to fill up rooms?"

Lauren gave him an annoyed smile as he poured her a glass of merlot. She'd forgotten to be angry with him the moment they'd stepped into the restaurant.

"No, I like to change space, to make it comfortable, relaxing, hot, cold, whatever the person wanted."

"And what did you want?" He buttered a bit of bread and offered it to her.

She took a sip of the dry wine, enjoying the way it warmed her throat. "I wanted to have my own place. I used to envy Thelma on *Good Times*. Although she had to live with those irritating brothers of hers, she could leave the room and slam her bedroom door shut in their faces."

Even as the confession flew out her mouth, it surprised her. It must have been the quiet wood of the ceiling, the smell of hickory smoke in the air, the smooth sound of piano keys, and the tinkling of silverware. Somehow he'd managed to slip in through the cracks, seep into the places she kept locked up tight.

"Like you slammed the door on me?" Nick grinned, recalling the first time he'd tried to apologize to Lauren.

"Exactly. I dreamed of having my own place. I imagined the color of the walls, the curtains, my big bed with just my Raggedy Ann and me." She shrugged. "I became good with finding ways to make people comfortable in their homes."

"Tell me about your home, your family."

"I have an older brother, Nathan. We were both born in Kentucky, raised in Chicago. My father died when I was twelve."

"And Sabrina?"

Just like that, she changed. From a soft pearl to a hard diamond. Even as her buttery-sweet lips begged to be kissed, Lauren's flashing eyes warned him away.

"My mother married my stepfather a year later. Sabrina is Ralph's only child."

Nick sat back as the waiter brought the main course and rearranged the silverware. A maze, he thought as he cut into his steak. Every time he started going one way, he only got so far before hitting a wall and being forced to retreat or change direction. So many twists, curves, and unexpected surprises. One minute he saw a strong ice princess and the next a vulnerable, passionate woman. He shifted in his seat, remembering how she fit perfectly in his arms.

"You do a good job. I'm amazed at what you've done in a couple of weeks."

"Thank you," Lauren said after a bite of salmon. "What about you?"

"Me?" He took a bite of the baked potato.

"What was your home like?"

"Loud." He grinned. "Three boys and a girl. Mom spent so much time in D.C. that Pop stepped in a lot. His being a doctor helped cut down on medical bills."

"I can imagine you didn't lack for trouble."

"No, trouble followed us. Pop saved all of us from making a lot of trips to the hospital."

"Your father sounds like a wonderful doctor."

"In more ways than one."

"Tell me more."

He took a sip of wine to wet his dry throat. The way Lauren looked at him made him feel like the most important man on the earth.

"I've seen boys that couldn't get over their injuries. They saw all their hopes and dreams of turning professional go down the drain. In most cases, my pop would help them find their will to keep going, but some boys just gave up."

Lauren put down her fork. "Is that why you're worried about Alan's knee?"

"Yeah, maybe." Most of the time everything was business, but sometimes things got personal. Alan was one of those. The man just wanted to play ball, not read legal agreements and contracts. No matter what happened, Alan was set for life, he'd made sure of it, just as his father had done for him.

"He'll be fine either way," Lauren commented.

"You sound sure."

"He's family. No matter what happens, he'll get through."

"Especially if your friend Cassandra has anything to do with it."

He watched her fork pause midroute to her lips. Beautiful full lips that quivered with laughter. He wanted to take that fork away and replace it with his mouth. Sexy, he thought. Nick had never imagined that watching her eat could send his restraint straight to hell. He sucked in a breath and focused on gaining control of his clamoring libido.

"So Alan finally figured out that Cassie's in love with him?"

"It must have been the Caribbean jerk chicken." Nick grinned, finishing up the last of the filet mignon.

"Mama always said food was the best way to get to a man's heart." She patted her mouth with the napkin.

"Well, Cassandra must have been paying attention. The man was salivating just thinking about her."

"Hmm." Lauren sighed.

He watched her fanlike eyelashes drift downward before she leaned back in her seat.

"So what's the way to a woman's heart, Lauren?" he asked.

"You tell me," she challenged. "I'm sure you know a lot about women."

Nick raised an eyebrow at the frosty glint in her eyes. He wasn't going to lie; he'd done his fair share of playing around. There'd been beautiful women who had thrown themselves at him solely because of his Super Bowl ring and deep pockets. But Lauren Hughes, she wouldn't take him wrapped in hundred-dollar bills.

"I might know a little something something about women. But I'm only interested in learning about one particular lady." He gave her a searching look.

His father had taught the Randolph boys more than the birds and the bees when they were of age. He and his brothers got schooled on life, love, and women. As Nick leaned against the table, Pop's words seemed to drift over the sound of the piano.

"You know you're in love when the sight of her face and the sound of her voice does something to you. I met your mama as she was speaking into a loudspeaker marching for Dr. King. Nothing mattered but her. You'll know it's love you feel when it doesn't matter if she's screaming, crying, laughing, or giving you the silent treatment. When that happens, you better snatch her up quick 'cause your stuff'll start going bad without her."

After the dinner was consumed and the table was cleared, Lauren glanced away from the hungry look in his eyes. It silenced her when he said things like that. When his eyes seemed to peer into her soul and find it wanting, aching for something that she was coming to believe only he could fill.

She was intently studying the watercolor painting when

the waiter returned with coffee and dessert. "What's this?" Lauren didn't recall having ordered dessert.

"Tart apple pancake with cinnamon ice cream. I took the liberty of ordering it for you while you were in the ladies' room."

"And you ordered?"

"Three-layer chocolate cake." His grin broadened at the way she eyed his plate.

"Oh." She picked up her fork.

"I believe I know the answer to my question," he stated after she had taken two bites of her dessert.

"Oh, what question was that?"

"The way to a woman's heart." He watched her brows sweep upward.

Nick leaned forward and held his fork close to her mouth. His eyes never left hers as she opened her mouth and he fed her.

Her lids fluttered and then she ran her tongue over her lips. "Very good."

"More?" he invited before helping himself to another bite.

"No." She shook her head.

"Afraid?" he provoked, wanting to push her off balance.

"Of what?"

"That I might make my way into your heart," he said quietly.

"No." Her eyes locked on to his, secrets glittered in their depths. "My heart died a long time ago."

"Hearts don't die, they only get a little bruised."

"And how would you know that?" Her chin came up. "I doubt you've suffered from heartbreak." Anger at broken promises and the unfairness of life colored her voice. She'd left Chicago with her parents' and relatives' advice ringing in the back of her head. It's like falling off a horse, they said. Well, this sister didn't have any intention of getting back in the saddle.

He leaned back and placed his fork on the table. "You think you're the only one that has ever gotten burned?"

"I think that you shouldn't be telling me something you know nothing about."

"You could easily correct that by telling me who hurt you so bad." He knew it had to be Paul, the fiancé that died, but he wanted to hear it from her.

"Like that would make a difference." She shook her head. "It's in the past and that's where it'll stay."

"Then why are you so upset?"

She took a deep breath and before she could move her hand, he reached across the table and took hold of her wrist.

"Your pulse is pounding and you're trembling," he said.

Lauren looked around at the other diners, the walls, and the balcony, anywhere but at Nick.

"You can't act as though there's nothing between us, Lauren."

Yes, she could. Part of her wanted to jump up from the chair and hightail it out of there as if the devil himself were at her heels. The other half, the one that was winning, leaned closer and enjoyed the feel of his fingers caressing her wrist.

"Attraction," she murmured, lifting her eyes to his. "Good ole lust, that's what's happening here."

He didn't look away, but held her gaze as tightly as he held her wrist. The scales were falling before her eyes, and she shivered, glimpsing a part of the real Nick, the one that had kissed her the other night. The man she knew his opponents saw across the negotiating table— steely, confident, determined.

"You can walk, you can run, but no matter where you go, Lauren, I'll be there ready and willing to add some wood to this fire we've got burning between us."

"I don't take kindly to threats," she said through gritted

teeth as she snatched her hand away and reached down to get her purse.

His grin widened, flashing her with perfect white teeth. "I don't make threats, just promises."

After paying the check, he moved to her side of the table, taking hold of her arm.

Standing, she gave him an angry glare. "I don't want your promises."

"That's too bad because I'm looking forward to fulfilling each and every one of them," he murmured close to her ear, enjoying the way she shivered. "And I would love to start working on one right now."

They had come to stand at the street corner and Lauren watched car after car drive by. Nick's arm circled her waist and she felt as though she'd found that perfect spot in bed. The one that held the imprint of body heat and it made it all the more difficult to step away.

"Cold?" Nick asked, pulling her back toward him. She turned in his arms and looked up, entranced by the play of light on his face. His fingers lightly held her in check as she felt a gust of cool wind.

"Only my lips," she whispered. The beating of her heart filled her ears, it roared over the sound of honking horns and diesel motors. She swore that all of the Midtown could hear it.

"Then I'll have to warm them up." Slowly, Nick lowered his head and blew a warm breath over her parted lips before taking her mouth with his own. She felt the strength of his fingers at the nape of her neck playing in the short soft fullness of her hair.

No urgency, no demand. It wasn't a dry heat that rose between them, blocking out the world. This kind of warmth curled round and slowly moved up, reaching past her clothing, and clung to Lauren like a second skin. His lips and his scent wrapped around her as he murmured her name and she caught it with her tongue.

It touched everything, leaving her moist and waiting. The shimmering sheen of passion, floating on the waves of desire.

The voodoo that Nick sprinkled didn't punch her in the stomach. It didn't roll over her; instead it lapped against her as his tongue tasted her lips. His mouth was warm and demanding as his fingers gently stroked her neck.

Lauren felt all of her doors unlocking, her wall melting as midnight wishes and morning needs stepped through the doorway. The harsh sounds of cars blowing their horns intruded on the moment. She dragged her lips from Nick as her sense of self-preservation kicked in. Taking a breath, she pulled away and stumbled, only to have his arms catch her.

"It's too late to pull back now, sweetheart." Nick's face was mere inches away from hers.

Lauren gulped in more cold air. The more she breathed, the better she felt.

"I'm not pulling back, Nick," she said, having gained her balance. "I'm walking away. I'm not sure I'm ready for this." She shook her head, not knowing exactly what *this* was. It was more than attraction; he'd awoken something inside her every time she laid eyes on the man. Nick with his handsome-as-sin smile and dark eyes broke the butterflies loose in her tummy and sent tingles to the private spot between her legs.

"I may have a weak knee, but I can sure catch you." Nick chuckled and aimed an arrogant grin her way.

"Go catch a football," Lauren shot back, moving two feet away. She stepped out into the street and held out her arm to hail a taxi.

"Only if you promise to wait for me at the end zone." He stood next to her and before she could move away he reached out and brushed back her wind-tossed hair.

"Your ego knows no bounds. I'm not a football, nor

am I a cheerleader." She glared as a deep chuckle rumbled in his throat.

He loved the way she went from frost to fire. He let out a laugh and pulled her back from the approaching cab.

She gripped her purse and reached out to open the car door. However, Nick was faster. He bent down to whisper in her ear, "If you'd been cheering me on, I'd never have made it to the Super Bowl."

She eyed him curiously as he helped her into the backseat. "You see, Lauren, I have a one-track mind and, beautiful, I'd have rather had you in my hands than a football."

Speechless, she watched as he handed the driver a twenty and gave him her address.

With a grin on his lips and her scent on his fingers, Nick turned up the collar of his coat and started walking down the street. Oh, yes, he reflected on the way Lauren tasted, this was going to be the sweetest victory yet.

Three days later the sound of happy barking signaled the arrival of doggy treats at the large pet store. Lauren looked over at the man standing by her side. Nick had been waiting with the shopping cart when she arrived. For the first time, she saw him in blue jeans and a wool sweater instead of a shirt and tie. Without the silken noose and starched shirt, he was more relaxed and open. And, she thought, if it were possible, even more handsome.

For the second time that Saturday morning, Lauren wondered if she'd made a mistake in agreeing to meet Nick. But instead of dwelling on the thought, she concentrated on shopping as they walked past the pet bedding.

"What about this?" Nick asked, pointing at an over-stuffed pillow cushion for small cats.

Lauren shook her head. "Brooklyn is very fond of the wicker basket I brought over last week."

"Yes, but she can't stretch out in it."

"Cats like to curl up," she pointed out.

"Cats also like to sleep on a man's shirt," he grumbled.

She'd discovered yesterday morning that Brooklyn had somehow managed to drag it into her new bed. Lauren couldn't help smiling at the disgruntled look on Nick's face. "Are you still upset with losing that ugly flannel shirt?"

"My sister gave that to me," he defended.

"As a joke, right?" Lauren raised her eyebrows. The bright yellow garment could blind a person. She knew from the still-hanging price tag that he'd never put it on.

"She said I needed a little more color in my life." Nick couldn't agree more with his little sister. He needed something bright in his life and it wasn't a yellow shirt. That color was Lauren.

"Did you now?"

Nick's eyes crinkled at the smile on Lauren's face. "Ami thought I was getting too staid and uptight in my old age."

"Old age?" she prompted.

"I'll be thirty-five pretty soon."

"Ahh, about the right time for you to have an M.L.C." She followed Nick into the next aisle.

"M.L.C?" He frowned, not recalling the acronym.

"Midlife crisis," she explained. "When sensible men with otherwise high intelligence buy expensive convertibles, new tight-fitting clothes, go to the gym ten times a week, and trade in their significant others for newer models."

"No, no, and no." Nick laughed and took the opportunity to touch her cheek. "I'm not the trade-in type. I plan to find her and keep her."

Lauren blushed and looked away. "What about this?" She reached out and fingered the scratching post.

"What is that?"

"A scratching post."

"Wait." He shook his head. "Brooklyn doesn't have claws. Does she?"

"No, she doesn't, but I read in the book that a lot of declawed cats like to pretend. And we definitely want to give her an outlet away from the upholstery when she has the urge to scratch."

"You've been reading about cats." Nick moved to put the post into the shopping cart.

"Felines in general, Siamese in particular. You didn't think I would just leave you with Brooklyn?"

Yes, he did. Nick knew she planned on leaving *both* him and the cat for her trip around the world. "Well, you know the trend. Women right and left are leaving their men with the pets. Just walking away and abandoning the happy family and leaving us to pick up the pieces."

Lauren played along with the joke. "I'm not one of those women. Brooklyn will always have a place in my life."

"What about Brooklyn's owner?"

She shot him a flirtatious glance. "Him, we'll have to wait and see."

They flirted from picking out a collar to choosing toys. Lauren went for the feminine Queen of Sheba–style colored collars while Nick grabbed the plainest things on the shelf. In the end, they got two of everything. An hour and a half later, Lauren and Nick walked out of the pet store with toys galore. A plastic fishing pole, an electronic mouse that came alive with flashing eyes that could play dead, colorful balls stuffed with catnip, and miniature globes with jangling bells on the inside.

"So now that I have a cat carrier, can I bring Brooklyn over for a visit? Or is that against apartment rules?"

"I think I might be able to work something out," she said, stepping back to allow Nick to open the passenger-side door.

"Or maybe we could go on a little trip. My older brother has a cabin in upstate New York. I think Brooklyn would love to have a taste of the country life."

"And Brooklyn's owner?"

"Would like to spend some quality time getting to know the cat's lovely rescuer."

"Nick," she started and stopped. The tremor in Lauren's voice had nothing to do with the taxicab that had swerved into their lane. "As tempting as that sounds I'll have to take a rain check."

"Afraid?"

"Of what?"

"The big bad wolf."

She smiled. "No, I've spent my fair share of time in the forest. I love nature, but I've got a lot of work to do."

"I've set no deadlines, Lauren. I'm in no rush to finish the renovation."

"I have my own deadlines." And they were coming up faster than she could blink, Lauren added privately.

"Which aren't set in stone," he argued smoothly.

"But they are on paper," she lobbied back.

"Which can mysteriously disappear," Nick added.

Lauren laughed and the sound filled him with a curious warmth. "You're relentless."

"Only when I see something I want." He turned off the expressway and slowed to a stop at the traffic light.

"What do you want, Nick?" Lauren couldn't stop the question from slipping out. From the moment they'd kissed, it had been on the tip of her tongue to ask his intentions.

"Just what I said, beautiful. For now I want to get to know you better, and then . . . we'll let fate decide."

Damn, that sounded smooth. Nick grinned to himself. He'd managed to outdo himself. The part about fate was poetry even if he didn't believe in it. He was a man that believed in cold hard facts, that the future was what you made it. And the future he imagined with Lauren at his side was a nice one indeed.

Lauren fit. In his house, his car, against his body, and in his world. She wouldn't be starstruck in a room with his celebrity clients. She'd be the perfect companion at office parties or dinner with friends. Hers was a face he wanted to see every morning; he wanted his daughter to have her eyes.

For the first time the voice in the back of his head didn't whisper that he was missing something in his life. Its silence seemed to indicate that he'd found it, or rather her sitting by his side.

Two days later, Lauren finished up her last bite of chicken Caesar salad. It had become a habit of Nick's to feed her. Or maybe it wasn't a habit. The only times they could sit down to discuss the renovation plans, one or both of them were hungry. And Nick was forever telling her she was too skinny. It wasn't as though she didn't eat regularly. She'd spend hours cooking for a dinner party with friends, but making dinner for one wasn't worth the effort. Besides, who would keep the takeout places and frozen-food companies in business if she cooked every night?

Taking off her glasses, Lauren put a hand behind her back and stretched. She'd spent the last three hours poring through photos and fabric samples.

"Here, thought you could use some." He stopped next to her side of the temporary kitchen table.

She took the mug from his hand and for a second their hands touched before she drew away. She took a sip and put the cup down. "Perfect."

"What's the rush?" he asked casually as she started gathering her things together.

"I've got to go . . ." She paused.

"Go back home?"

"Vacation." She stood up from the covered kitchen table. "I haven't had one in a long time."

"Where are you headed? The Caribbean's nice this time of year."

"Maybe for you lazy lawyers. Funny, I never figured you for the resort type." She'd had her arms around him. A rock-hard stomach was tucked under that shirt. She'd bet her last dollar it'd been a while since a nice powered doughnut crossed those firm lips.

Nick leaned on the counter. "That's interesting. I picked you for the spiritual retreat type."

"And you'd be half right."

"So you're going to a resort?"

"You're mighty interested in my vacation." She cocked her head to the side.

"I'm just wondering, what's the rush?" He moved in a little closer and reached out to toy with her hair. "You and I have business that won't be finished in weeks, months. To tell the truth, beautiful, what we've got brewing doesn't have a statute of limitations."

"Ever the attorney, huh?" She leaned in closer.

Nick watched her eyes turn cool again. "No, just worried about a friend."

"Well, don't," she bit out. Lauren hurriedly gathered her notes and materials together.

"Sorry." He watched her closely. "Didn't know I was touching a nerve."

"You aren't," she said, not looking at him. The truth was that he'd hit it with a baseball bat. Time was flying, and sooner than she wanted, her birthday was going to be here.

"But I'd like to touch more than that."

His innuendo-laced voice drew Lauren upright, sending documents skittering from the table.

"Hey." She turned and ran into a solid body and stood

there held upright by his arm around her waist as desire flared to life in her stomach.

A thousand watts, Nick thought. No more than that shot through his body when it touched hers. "You okay?"

"I will be once you let me go," she snapped.

"What's this?" Nick bent down and picked up a sheet of paper.

"My travel itinerary." She tried to snatch it from his hand.

Nick took a step back. "Morocco, Turkey, Egypt, Kenya, South Africa, Thailand, Beijing, Vietnam, Australia, Japan. This must be one heck of a tour." He whistled.

"I'm not going with a tour." She took a step back, bumping into the table. "I'm going by myself."

"As in alone?"

"Last time I checked, that wasn't illegal," she defended herself.

"No. It's dangerous."

"Says who?"

"Anyone in his or her right mind, Lauren."

It made her grit her teeth when he said her name that way. As if she were some kid that didn't have enough sense to come in out of the rain. He should have known that his attitude was making her even more determined to go.

Her chin went up another notch. "Just for that, I won't be bringing you back anything."

"And I'm not sharing the Swiss mocha ice cream or the video games I picked on my way home," he countered.

"Selfish." She smiled.

"Stubborn." Nick was so close his scent whispered, tempting her to bury herself in the warmth of his solid body.

"So what video games did you get?"

"Oh, so now she's interested in me?" Nick went to open the freezer and pull out the carton of ice cream.

"Maybe." She reached into the cabinet and brought out the bowls. "It all depends on how well you play."

Nick raised an eyebrow. "Oh, what's this? A challenge?"

"Possibly."

"Football." He turned toward her.

Lauren shook her head. "No, that would give you an unfair advantage. How about basketball?"

"NBA Two-K?" he challenged, scooping the chocolate ice cream into the waiting bowls.

Lauren didn't miss a beat. "You're on."

Three hours later, Lauren moved off the sofa with a smirk on her face. The four-to-three game series had been close but the Phoenix Suns had risen again.

"I think I'll leave you to drown your tears in coffee." She headed up the stairs.

"And where do you think you're going?"

"Home."

"It's late, I'll drive you."

"No, thanks." Lauren smiled sleepily. "I'd rather take the train."

"Is this about my driving?" Nick stood and followed her up the stairs. "Because I'm not Alan." The man drove like a New York taxi driver in the Grand Prix.

"No," she said truthfully. "I like trains." Her father had worked for the railroad. "I've liked riding trains since I was a little girl."

She watched as he reached around her and grabbed his coat. "I'll come with you."

She smiled as he followed her through the door and took her gloved fingers within his own. Ten minutes later as they stepped onto the uptown train, Lauren couldn't help relaxing in Nick's presence. There were no words between them as they rode into Manhattan. He put his arm around her shoulders and she nestled into him as the rhythmic rocking of the train lulled her to sleep.

She didn't protest when he held her tight to his side as they walked from the subway to her door. Giving him a sleepy good night, Lauren couldn't keep lying to herself. She hadn't wanted to leave him at the door. With her head lying on the pillow and her arms wrapped around a stuffed bear, she wished she was warmer; she yearned for the heat only Nick could satisfy.

Eight

She wore violet, not just any old purple. Lauren now knew why she'd spent three hours combing the stores on Fifth Avenue for the perfect gown. The satin silk dress, a bold mixture of red, blue, and cream, clung to her curves like a second skin. She'd been walking past long black evening gowns when it caught her eye. She didn't try it on, just took one look at the size, and carried it over to the anxiously waiting store attendant. She still wasn't thrilled about going to the awards ceremony; was less than enthusiastic about seeing her stepsister, but at least she would look good.

Having spent most of the Saturday afternoon with her best friend getting manicured, pedicured, and a facial, Lauren felt wonderfully refreshed. Spa samples and new shoes in hand, she and Cass returned to Lauren's apartment to get dressed for the night's event. Her skin still held the faint scent of lavender oil and her complexion glowed from the half day of pampering. Taking one last look in the mirror, she turned toward Cass.

"What do you think?" she asked her friend as she took a step away from the mirror.

Cass stood up with a smile on her face. "I think you are going to be beating men off with a stick tonight."

With their deciding to spend Saturday getting ready together, her best friend had brought her change of clothes the day before and spent the night at Lauren's place. Last night they'd thoroughly enjoyed themselves watching videos and munching on sinfully delicious cheesecake.

Lauren eyed the woman's deep red sheath dress. Cass had shown her the garment last night before they'd gone to bed. "And I'm going to have to carry a bat to keep Alan from dragging you back to Harlem."

"You think so?" she asked eagerly.

Think so? Lauren knew so. Cassandra could walk on water as far as Alan was concerned. She'd never seen her best friend so taken with anyone. It was a wonderful feeling to see them happy together.

"Trust me," Lauren said, linking her arm with Cassandra's and pointing them toward the bathroom. "He won't be able to keep his eyes or anything else off you."

"You know, you're too bad." Cass playfully tapped her on the shoulder.

Lauren chuckled at the blush spreading over her face.

"Did I tell you that I've had a crush on Alan since he showed up at your promotion party?" Cass's amber eyes sparkled.

Lauren looked up from her makeup case. Brad had put together the surprise party to celebrate Lauren's second anniversary at the firm. Alan had been in negotiations with the New York team at the time. He'd been the life of the party with men asking about his batting average and all the single women trying to get his dating status.

Cass sighed. "If I hadn't known you, Lauren, I would have gladly pulled every hair out of your head and scratched up that wonderful complexion of yours."

"What?" She paused from applying the opaque eye shadow.

"You heard me." Cass chuckled. "I wasn't the only one. Half the women at the party wanted to wring your neck."

"You could have said something," she defended herself.

Cass nodded. "You're right, but saying something would have meant taking a chance. After all that emotional drama Calvin put me through, my self-esteem was in the basement."

Finished with her makeup, Lauren opened the mirrored cabinet and picked up a bottle of perfume. "I really wasn't too much of a help with the Calvin situation, was I?" she admitted.

She'd disliked the man from the start. Too much flash and cheap charm. She'd seen firsthand the way he treated Cassandra like an expensive watch. Something that he showed off to the outside world. Calvin had liked to be the center of attention and even when he was with Cass, he'd had his eye on other women.

She watched her friend push back her braids. "You were a lifesaver. No matter how much we disagreed, you always told me the truth."

"I'm just glad you came to your senses," Lauren quipped.

"I'm just glad you've finally come to yours."

"Huh?"

"About Nicholas Randolph."

Lauren dabbed the sandalwood fragrance on her pulse points.

"I was only half wrong about Nick," she countered, rubbing her wrists together.

"Which half was the right half?"

"The one that said he was about as tenacious as a school of piranhas."

"What?"

"He's determined to get me to like him."

Cassandra gave her a puzzled glance. "And this is a bad thing? The man is gorgeous, trustworthy, smart, charming, well connected politically and socially."

"Not to mention a client, hardheaded, confusing, and a pain in my rear end," Lauren added.

"He's *your* client, there's nothing in the rules to keep you from dating him."

"You're absolutely correct." Lauren nodded. "But I'm not getting involved with Nicholas Randolph."

Cass shook her head. "Okay, what's really going on here?"

Lauren tried to avoid answering the question by ducking into the closet. She bent down to hunt for her favorite pair of high-heeled shoes.

"I'm waiting," Cass's voice came from behind her.

"Did you want something?" Lauren yelled from inside the closet.

"An answer."

She sighed, rising up with the shoes in her hands. "I've got plans."

"And?" Cass raised a well-tended brow. "You can postpone your little getaway for a while, or better yet, why don't you invite him to go with you?"

She shook her head. "I can't do that. This is something I need to do alone."

"You've done everything alone, Lauren. I know you don't like to talk about your ex-fiancé, but you've held on to the man for too long. He's gone, Lauren. You need to let go."

"I've let go." She flipped back her shoulder-length hair.

"No, you haven't."

Anger rose in the back of Lauren's throat but she pushed it back. Cass hadn't lost anyone as she had, never experienced the waking up morning after morning with the heavy realization that someone you loved wasn't going to be knocking at the door, sharing your pillow.

Lauren pursed her lips. "Look, I'm all about having some fun. But no matter what Nick thinks, this isn't going to get serious."

It had taken a year of counseling to get over Paul's

death. She may have dealt with the grief, but Lauren was sure she would fear getting burned by love for the rest of her life.

"So he's made a move already?" Cass tilted her head to the side.

Her body warmed at the memory of Nick's lips slipping across the nape of her neck. "He kissed me."

"And you liked it." Cass didn't ask a question. She made it a statement. Lauren turned her face away to hide the blush in her cheeks. The word *like* didn't come close to the way she felt about what that man had done. Lauren opened her mouth to deny it when the doorbell rang.

She slipped the shoes on her feet and headed toward the living room. She braced herself for the moment, but opening the door and seeing the man who'd been haunting her midnight dreams made her palms sweat and heart rate spike.

Nick had parked his car a block from Lauren's apartment and walked. He was fifteen minutes early after spending the morning at the barbershop, the afternoon looking over paperwork, and talking with anxious parents. He was more than looking forward to having Lauren in his arms.

Nick liked to have answers. Cold, hard facts. But the things happening between him and Lauren didn't have any answers, just more questions. She took his normal everyday routine and turned it upside down. He thought she'd follow some kind of pattern with redesigning the brownstone.

A strange tenderness spread through him at the image of her caulk-crusted fingers as she had helped tile the bathroom. She'd turned the house and his life upside down even as she asked him about hiring someone to organize his files.

"Hey, Nick!"

Looking up, he waved after spotting Alan walking in his direction.

"What's up?" he asked, thrown off by his presence. Alan hadn't mentioned anything about stopping by Lauren's place while they were at the barbershop.

"Nothing. Cass called me. She wanted me to pick her up at Lauren's place."

"Oh." He relaxed.

"You think this thing is going to be interesting?" Alan asked.

Nick shrugged. "Don't know, but I am looking forward to meeting Lauren's sister."

"Sister?" Alan repeated. "You mean her stepsister, Sabrina?"

"That's the only one I know about."

"Man, that isn't something to look forward to. Sabrina and Lauren have had some bad blood between the two of them."

"Why?"

"Sabrina's always competed with Lauren. I couldn't figure it out. Everything Lauren had, Sabrina wanted. She never gave me the time of day until she thought I had a thing for Lauren."

"Did you?" Nick asked. Although Alan had indicated that he thought of her as a sister, he still found it hard to believe that there had never been anything between the two.

Alan shook his head. "Never. I love her like a sister. So you can quit the jealous husband act."

"I'm not jealous."

"Right. Why don't you quit worrying about me and keep her mind off that trip?"

Nick let loose a big grin. "Don't worry about that. Lauren isn't going anywhere."

Alan patted him on the shoulder. "Just don't hurt her,

man. I trust you with my career and with my money, but if something bad happens . . ."

"It won't." His expression was serious. "This isn't about keeping Lauren from getting into trouble. She's not going on that trip because she's got what she's looking for right here. You're not the only one contemplating settling down."

There, he'd said it. Nick had been thinking about it for the past two weeks. The more of a home the brownstone became, the emptier it seemed. Each room Lauren filled brought the day closer that she might disappear from his life. Quick to size up a situation and quicker at taking advantage of a good thing, he promised himself that he'd keep Lauren with him at all costs.

"You too?"

Nick nodded as they climbed the stairs. "I'm thinking long-term, Alan. Lauren is the kind of woman to take home to Mama. She can keep a man happy for all his days."

"I know what you mean, I feel the say way about Cass. Now, I just have to convince her of that."

"Doesn't listen, does she?" Nick shook his head slowly.

"Not one damn word." Alan put his hand on Nick's shoulder.

Laughing, Nick reached out and rang the doorbell.

When the door opened, the smiles dropped from both of their faces. Nick took one look at Lauren in that dress and felt his left knee go weak as his mouth started watering. The woman was tempting fruit on a plate, a juicy plum waiting for him to pluck.

"Oh, no!" Nick and Alan yelled in unison. A red mist swirled in Nick's eyes at the thought of some man touching her skin, thinking he had a chance. Lauren was his whether she realized it or not.

He watched as Lauren crossed her arms and Cass

dropped her eyes to the floor. "There's no way the two of you are going out like that," Alan started.

"You don't like it?" Cass's small voice checked his temper.

"No, sweetheart." Alan walked past him and took Cass into his arms. "I love it a little too much."

"Really?" Her voice regained some of its earlier confidence.

"Really."

Nick turned his attention back toward a glaring Lauren. He could see from the way her hip jutted to the right that he'd said the wrong thing.

"You have a problem with my dress?" Her hushed tone was hard as steel.

No, Nick thought, clenching his hands. He had a problem with the fact that she was wearing anything. He could see himself stripping her out of that dress and spending the night feasting on her body, making love to her till morning light came through the windows. Then he'd open his eyes and watch her beautiful body in nothing but his sheets and his arms.

He took a step toward her and opened his mouth to order that she change, but Cass jumped in.

"If the dresses bother you so much, you'll have to stick close, because our dry spells are over and these girls are going to have fun tonight," she stated boldly.

Nick watched helplessly as Cass nodded to Lauren and the women walked out the door, leaving him and Alan with open mouths.

Less than a half hour later, Lauren let Nick take her arm as they stepped off the escalator. The elegant reception hall smelled like money, she noted as they entered into the ballroom. Old inherited and newly fought-for wealth. Only a minute passed between the time Nick took her coat and a tuxedo-clad waiter offered her a glass of wine and an hors d'oeuvre. She looked around the large converted ballroom with an appreciative eye. The large crystal chandeliers, brocade curtains, and intricate crown moldings.

She loved the confidence she felt wearing the beautiful purple dress, but what thrilled her more was the way Nick's eyes never left her. The possessive way he held her close in his arms made her feel protected and cared for even though it smacked of male arrogance.

The country's elite, along with their wives who were wearing exquisite designer evening gowns and awe-inspiring jewelry, filled the room. When she'd been new in the design business, the wealth had been intimidating. Now that Lauren had practically lived in their houses, designed everything from their closets to their bathrooms, she was well aware that the rich were only human.

Lauren had just stepped out from inside the ladies' room when she heard her name. The smooth Caribbean cadence was easily recognizable.

"Hello, Lauren."

She turned to see Jamal striding her way. The handsome technology mogul looked fantastic in the black tuxedo.

"Jamal." She smiled. "It's great to see you here."

Lauren watched as his eyes ran up her dress, lingering a little too long on her cleavage.

He reached out and took her hand. "I must apologize again for the abrupt ending of our date. I could definitely understand if you were upset with me."

She waved a hand. "Don't worry about it."

"Then you won't mind if I claim you for a dance after the ceremony?"

She inserted some wit and then replied, "Of course

not. Monsieur Lewis, if I had a dance card, I would let you sign it."

"If you had a dance card, Lauren, I'd take it away so no one else could apply." He gently squeezed her hand. "I'll see you later."

She scanned the room, recognizing one CEO and politician after another, until her eyes landed on Sabrina and Karl. She couldn't miss them. Sabrina was wearing her favorite color: gold. Lauren chuckled at the irony, since her stepsister was often called a gold digger by members of Karl's family.

Moving toward the left side of the room, Lauren rejoined Nick. Cassandra and Alan had long since worked their way up to the head table.

"Ready to take a seat?" he asked.

She glanced at him from the corner of her eye. She noticed a coolness to his voice she had never heard before. Dismissing the thought, she replied in an equally chilly tone, "Whenever you are."

They didn't get ten feet before being stopped.

"Son."

Lauren watched as an elegantly clad older couple approached them.

"Mom, Pop. What are you two doing here?" Nick smiled.

Nick's father, Lauren thought to herself. She moved away and watched the two men hug. She could see the resemblance. Nick was a chip off the old block. The men shared the dark piercing eyes and chiseled jaws.

Lauren had known from the beginning Nick was from a prestigious family. His mother was a much-loved New Jersey state senator and his father a well-known doctor. But it was being in their presence that she could feel the sense of warmth that had nothing to do with the outside world. Nick's parents might be movers and shakers among the African-American elite, but tonight they were family.

Nick moved back to her side. "Mom, Dad, this is Lauren Hughes. The lovely lady I've been telling you about. She's also Alan's childhood friend."

Instead of taking her outstretched hand, Dr. Randolph gave her a tight hug, as did his mother.

"It's so wonderful to finally meet you, dear."

"I feel the same, Senator Randolph. I'm an admirer of your work. You're a true credit to the state of New Jersey, not to mention the senate."

"Please call me Diane. When I hear the name Senator it makes me think of my older white male colleagues who wouldn't know the definition of 'equal representation' if it bit them on the butt."

Lauren was trying hard not to laugh, but kept having visions of state senators jumping up from their seating. Her giggle became a snicker, which grew into a chuckle, and one look at Nick sent her into peals of unrestrained laughter.

Mrs. Randolph patted Nick on the shoulder. "She's absolutely charming, Nick. You must bring her home for dinner this Sunday."

Lauren opened her mouth to protest as the older woman waved a finger at her. "No excuses, young lady. I'll have you know that my husband's pot roast and collard greens are the best in the world, not to mention dessert. I absolutely insist you be there."

Lauren could see where Nick got his forceful personality. It was impossible to say no to his mother.

"Diane—" she started.

"We'll be there at four, Mama. Now you'd better hurry, the host is coming this way."

"Love you." She kissed her husband on the cheek before turning away.

"Lauren, there you are. I've been looking all over for you."

She fought the urge to duck behind a passing waiter at

the sound of Sabrina's voice. Instead she pinned a fake smile on her face and turned toward the approaching couple.

"Lauren, how are you?" The sugar-sweet voice was even more irritating in person.

Trying not to choke from the smell of your perfume, Lauren wanted to reply.

"I'm fine. How are you, Karl?" she addressed her step-sister's husband.

"Doing well." Lauren smiled for real this time. Although the man had married her stepsister, she still liked him. Karl didn't have a mean bone in his body. Too bad Sabrina more than made up for that.

She shook hands and made introductions. "Nick, Dr. Randolph, I'd like you to meet my stepsister, Sabrina, and her husband, Karl Jackson."

"Nick Randolph," she introduced.

Karl vigorously shook Nick's hand. "I followed you when you were playing for Notre Dame. I was real sorry about your knee injury."

Nick nodded, warming to the man. "Yeah, me too."

"Randolph, Senator Randolph is your mother?" Sabrina questioned.

"Yes, and my wife," Nick's father answered proudly.

Lauren turned her attention back to her stepsister. She could see Sabrina's eyes darting between the two of them. Lauren swore she could see the gears turning in her head.

The opening bars of music indicated that it was time for them to take their seats.

"Are you sitting with me, son?"

Lauren felt a sinking feeling when he shook his head. Ten minutes was more than enough time to spend with Sabrina.

"Of course," her stepsister replied with a big smile.

"You just go right ahead, Lauren. I'm sure we'll have plenty of time to catch up after the awards."

After biting back a sigh of relief, Lauren felt as if she were walking on air as their little party moved toward the front. Being escorted by two very distinguished and handsome gentlemen did wonders for a girl's ego.

The only damper on her mood was the sound of the orchestra playing. The haunting music brought back memories she couldn't close her mind against. The low hum of the cello reminded her of the fireman's ball. The cool summer night after food and dancing were over, Paul had taken her down by the water and laid his heart at her feet.

"You okay?" Nick's voice whispered in her ear. He'd watched heads turn as they went down the carpeted aisle. He couldn't blame them—she didn't just walk, she moved with such a graceful confidence that he was sure half the women in the room would give their last dime for it.

Lauren barely managed to keep from jumping out of her skin. "I'm fine," she lied. The gleam in his eyes. Desire mixed with appreciation sent awareness thrumming through her blood.

"Good." He leaned closer and placed a hand on her thigh. "I'm looking forward to getting onto the dance floor."

"I'm sure you'll have fun."

His grin broadened. "We'll have a very good time, beautiful."

It took every ounce of self-possession and then some to keep her in that chair. "I'm not dancing with you." Still smarting from Nick's less than complimentary attitude earlier that evening, she gave him a dispassionate glace. "I've promised all of my dances to Jamal."

Unseen, his fingers tightened on the back of her chair. He'd seen the way the businessman had stared at Lauren when she'd come out of the ladies' room. Nick imagined

it was what he'd see in the mirror every time he looked
at the woman seated next to him. He liked to have control, but tonight Lauren seemed determined to make
him lose it. First the dress, and now it was her attempt to
hold another man up as a shield.

As the audience stood to welcome his mother to the
podium, Nick sat back in his chair and looked stone-
faced at the stage. Even as part of his mind listened to his
mother's speech on the American entrepreneurial spirit,
community building, and corporate responsibility, his
mind was on other things. Jamal Lewis had just thrown
a wrench in this playbook.

He'd made up his mind that his seduction of Lauren
was going to be his best work yet. Aiming a pointed look
over at Alan, he pointed toward his would-be rival and
Nick mouthed, "Defensive positions."

His frown curved into a smile as Alan gave him the
thumbs-up and turned to whisper in Cass's ear. Nick
caught the look of annoyance his father threw his way and
leaned back, spreading his arm over Lauren's shoulder. A
calculating glitter lit his eyes as he turned his attention
back to the stage. Nick Randolph, All-Pro quarterback,
was back in action. Lauren didn't stand a chance.

As soon as the tables were cleared and the orchestra
began playing, Nick grabbed Lauren by the hand and
pulled her out onto the dance floor.

"What are you doing?"

"Dancing with the most stunning woman in the
room." He turned so she couldn't see Alan blocking
Jamal's move toward them. He recognized the classic
football "double cover" play with the receiver using two
defensive players.

Nick couldn't help smiling as Cass got into the act.
Out of nowhere she'd managed to pitch an attractive
woman into his rival's waving arms. Cassandra would
have been a defensive tackle. The way she stopped the

man's run and distracted the opponent would have made his coach proud. His grin widened as he felt Lauren settle into his slow, rocking rhythm.

Two hours later, Lauren stood in Nick's den holding a glass of brandy. She didn't need it—the way he'd touched her on the ride across the Brooklyn Bridge had been more than enough to keep her warm. She'd made the decision as the sounds of the orchestra tickled her ear and his hips moved against hers that she was going to explore the attraction between the two of them.

I'm a grown woman with a woman's needs, she decided. There was nothing wrong with enjoying herself before she went on vacation. Sex didn't automatically equate with love, Lauren reasoned. She was also comfortable enough with her sexuality to enter into a physical relationship with no emotional strings attached. That thinking had brought her to Nick's brownstone at one o'clock in the morning.

"Enjoying the drink?" he asked, coming to stand right beside her.

Leaning against the bar, she took another sip, hoping to moisten her dry throat. "Yes. I like it a lot."

His eyes met hers and her tongue darted out over her lips. Nick's magnetic eyes pulled her in and warmed her up. She watched his eyes darken and gave him her best come-hither smile.

Lauren put her drink down and took a deliberate step closer to him. Like spring come to winter, she moved into him and he into her. Her hands framed his face and she touched her lips to his. Her tongue slipped through and began to explore the recesses of his mouth, announcing her intentions. She wanted him in the worst way. She wanted him to make love to her.

She was tired of thinking and fed up with scraps.

Tonight, she'd fill her plate to overflowing and feast on the passion that flared between them, so that when the time came for her to leave, memories would keep away the wanting, beat back the sorrow of wishing for something she couldn't have.

"Lauren."

She shivered at the way he said her name while anticipation was making her jump out of her skin.

"Yes?" she whispered against his mouth, quickly trying to concentrate on remembering to breathe.

"You're not going home tonight."

"So where am I going, counselor?" She shuddered as his lips nibbled on her neck. Flames roared across her skin as the pad of his thumb snaked back and forth over the silken fabric covering her breasts.

Nick didn't answer; instead he tilted her face up and kissed her. She tasted of brandy and ambrosia. Her sweet mouth, hot and demanding, made him forget about any last-minute acts of honor. "To my bed."

"Can you make it upstairs?" she murmured softly. "My knees are weak."

"Oh, yes, beautiful." He kissed her again, his voice low and husky. "Right now I could carry you across the Brooklyn Bridge if I had to." With that he swept her off her feet and headed toward the bedroom.

"Um-hmm." She sighed, molding herself against him as he climbed the stairs. "This is just attraction, Nick." His strong arms held her as though she were as light as a feather.

"Whatever you say, baby." He began to inch her toward the door to the master bedroom.

"I've got a schedule to keep," she whispered against his chest.

"We'll be right on time," he agreed, every nerve in his body trying to get close to her.

They made it into his room in record time. Lauren

stood looking at him as moonlight slanted through the open blinds.

It was the first time she'd been in the bedroom since the furniture had been delivered. Even in the darkness the slate-gray walls left the room cool and relaxing. She noted that he'd placed the folded quilt at the foot of the bed on the antique leather trunk she'd purchased at a small eclectic store in Manhattan's East Village. Lauren had agonized over the look and feel of the bedroom before settling on comfort. She'd wanted softness, warmth, and privacy. Thick Burmese rugs for cold morning floors, copper-tan muslin panels to frame the long windows.

Of all her shopping finds, Lauren had fallen in love with the bed on sight. It was a rare thing for her to not want to part with a treasure, but the queen-size sleigh bed belonged in Nick's house, in his master bedroom. When she'd first run her hands over the natural knots and beads of the wood, she'd closed her eyes and imagined him lying asleep in the platform bed. A woven bark cloth hung between two bronze lamps over the headboard. The dark mahogany headboard looked black. The cotton velvet gave off a warm shimmer. She ran her hand over the duvet cover before moving away.

She suppressed a nervous giggle as Nick turned and left, headed toward the bathroom. When he rejoined her by the bed, tossing the foil packet on the nightstand, she touched his face with her fingers and he kissed them as her other hand worked on the buttons of his shirt. As busy as his lips were, so were Nick's hands. She felt the brush of cool air at the sound of the back zipper of her dress.

As she pushed his shirt back, Lauren let out a groan. She'd seen his chest a million times in her dreams and fantasies—this was so much better. She ran her fingernails lazily down from his shoulder, skimming over his tight abs, stopping to toy with his belt buckle. Her lips curved into a smile at the sound of his roughly indrawn breath.

"Lauren," he groaned. She was pushing him to the edge of his limits. He looked into her wide-eyed gaze and every thought of taking his time went out the window. He blinked and pulled back to watch her dress float to the floor.

The woman put beauty to shame. Nick would have let out an appreciative whistle if his throat hadn't gone dry at the sight of her standing there. Her skin was brown, flawless, firm. While the dress lay at her feet, the slip clung to her curves, highlighting the beckoning mounds of her full breasts. The outline of her raised nipples, evidence of her arousal, curled his lips with male satisfaction. Her long legs covered in black stockings sent heat spiraling to all the parts of his body.

"Lauren, you humble a man." His voice was hoarse with desire as he reached out and began to inch the first strap off her shoulder.

"Really?" she whispered huskily before moving closer. Throwing caution to the wind, she reached down and placed her hand over his hardness. Her blood heated with the thrill of holding him in her hands, welcoming him into her body.

"Yes, beautiful, you do." Nick's hand came up and cradled her neck as he bent to take possession of her mouth. Her lips were warm and inviting. His tongue delved into the curves and corners as his fingers worked to remove the last of her clothing. He laid her on the bed and stripped off his pants and boxers. Naked, he slid into the sheets and took her into his arms.

He kissed Lauren hard and moved with her. Responding to the signals her supple body was sending through his hands, he fastened his mouth onto her nipples. As they fell into one another, he poured passion over her body that would be so sweet and hot she'd never want to be cold.

His hands moved over her skin, running from her

aching breasts to the sensitive inside of her thighs, and she followed him, mimicking the movement of his fingers. Lauren touched him everywhere and the slowly building tension grew, tightening every muscle in his body, increasing his arousal. Every moan and whimper made him want more. More of the taste of her skin, the sensation of her fingers on his back, the hunger that kept building. He could live for the way her heavy-lidded eyes followed him, the way she arched into his mouth, needing him, wanting him.

Lauren didn't want to breathe. She closed her eyes to everything but the pleasure of his loving her. She moaned and moved against him, seeking release. Nick had seduced her with his eyes, the intoxicating way he smiled. But the bliss of his tongue and hands painted a rainbow of color across her body. Nick was achingly slow, tickling her neck, stroking her thighs, moving closer to her center.

He blew fire in the valley of her breast and added fuel to the volcano between her thighs. Lauren could do nothing but twist helplessly in his arms. And when he left her for a moment, she felt as if she had lost the world. She could barely hear the sound of plastic tearing over the beating of her heart.

"Moan for me, Lauren," he said, moving to cover her body. He heard the passion in her responses, felt her need in the heat of her skin.

She opened her eyes and looked at him. His hands had moved south from cupping her breasts. Every muscle in her body was attuned to the strong fingertips tracing down her stomach to the curls between her legs.

His body tightened with anticipation as his fingers found her wet and waiting for his arrival. Her brown eyes were dark and steady as her lashes fluttered open. He'd wanted to take everything slow, build the fire to a roaring inferno, but his need was too great and the flames from their desire threatened to consume him.

Wanting him more than she ever thought possible, Lauren didn't moan, she opened her thighs to his probing. Nick wanted to take it slow, to watch her face as he pushed her over the edge, but he couldn't. Instead he moved to sink himself in her heat. Arching, she met his downward thrust, bringing him inside.

She cried his name as she felt pleasure laced with an ache so bad it was a hairbreadth away from pain. Nick took that moment to pull out and surge into her. He filled her up and ran her over. Hot and hard. She arched her hips and locked her arms around him, wanting to bring him closer, imprint him on her skin. Lauren clung to him as the thrust of his hips delved deeper and faster into her body.

She could feel his fingers in her hair, his breath against her cheek, but Lauren couldn't see. A rainbow lay across her eyes and it grew brighter with each and every rhythmic stroke. When her release came, the rainbow shattered and Lauren buried her face into Nick's shoulder to stifle her cries as pleasure exploded, rushing over her body, transforming dark to light.

Lauren was fire and she burned him even as he rocked in and out of her. His hands grasped her hips tightly as he pressed deeper inside her. The tight, gripping feel of her around him overcame him as he buried himself in her, pushed through her. He felt her release and as she wrapped her legs around his hips and pulled him toward her, he could do anything else but let go.

Burying his face in the crook of her shoulder, Nick gave out a harsh growl as he experienced his own release.

"Lauren?" he managed to get out moments later. "Are you all right, sweetheart?"

It was everything he thought it'd be and more.

"Nick." She laughed huskily. "If I felt any better I'd be on my way to the hospital."

"I'll take that as a compliment."

Lauren felt the smile in his voice. "You do that," she murmured, trying to fight the lassitude spreading through her muscles. She shifted as he took her into his arms. Her head lay against his chest and her hearing was filled with the beating of his heart as the intoxicating scent of him blanketed her senses. They were still joined together. The intimacy of their embrace filled her with a sense of happiness she hadn't felt since . . .

"Lauren, this changes everything." Nick stroked her hair and gripped her tightly as he felt her body stiffen. She'd given him a taste of heaven and there was no way he could go back to seeing her and not touching her, not wanting to lay her down and make love.

He moved closer and nibbled on her ear, inhaling the sultry smell of her perfume laced with the heavy scent of sex.

Her heart squeezed at his words even as her body wanted to move against him, as a lazy wave of arousal washed over her. Lauren didn't want to hear what he had to say. The promises or declarations caused by too much passion and emotion. Yet, her body betrayed her as her sensitized skin still cried out for more.

"Don't say it." Quickly, Lauren lifted her face and pressed her lips to his, cutting off his next sentence. "Just leave it be."

She needed the quiet of the night to free her mind of a million what-ifs. Lauren wanted to focus on that moment, that feeling, and the intoxication. When his hands and tongue caressed her own, allowing her to press forward as her hands worked to bring him back alive, Lauren allowed herself access to the passion she'd buried alongside her late fiancé.

Curiosity may have killed the cat, but satisfaction brought it back. Lauren sighed contentedly. The exquisite ecstasy Nick Randolph dished out had her coming back for more.

* * *

"What do you think this is, Lauren?" he asked after he'd come back to his senses. Nick hadn't forgotten the way she had avoided talking about what had taken place between them.

"Incredibly wonderful sex." She eyed his naked chest.

With a frustrated sigh, Nick sat up and rubbed his head. That was the last answer he'd expected to receive. "It's more than that and you know it."

"Fine," she muttered, scooting off the bed. "This is a case of good old-fashioned desire. There's nothing wrong with it."

"You're pulling away, Lauren."

She didn't deny it. The longer she stayed looking at him sitting in nothing but a satin sheet, the more she wanted to crawl back into bed and run her lips over every inch of his body. Lauren was smart enough to know that the third time was a charm and she couldn't trust herself to make love to Nick again.

Nick thought her weakness was for chocolate and he wasn't too far off the mark. Lauren liked the sweet stuff as much as any other woman, but what really got her going was cheesecake. Thick, rich, and creamy. Her favorite rested on a chocolate crust topped with a layer of caramel and sprinkled with pecans. Her mouth watered the same way her body did when Nick was near. It was something warm and perfect. A feeling she realized that she wanted to have all the time.

Deciding that she'd rather go home and shower, Lauren picked up her clothes and slowly got dressed. It was only after she pulled up the zipper of her dress that she could face Nick.

"I'm going home."

"You already are," he countered. "There's no need for you to leave."

"Thank you but I'd like to go home," she replied firmly.

"I'm taking you back to your apartment." He got out of the bed and began to dress.

Her stomach turned and she wanted to stamp her feet. She needed space and time to sort through all the feelings that were balling up inside her. Until she could separate and examine the tangled and frayed threads of her emotions, she didn't want to be in the same car with him. Hell, she didn't even want to talk to Nick.

"All right." She slipped on her shoes.

He registered her cool expression and detached tone in the short answer.

"You're awfully silent over there." He grinned, pulling on his pants.

"I don't have much to say." She shrugged, preferring not to say anything at all.

Nick hid his disappointment and aimed one last puzzled glance her way before following her downstairs. The silence between them stretched from Brooklyn to the West Village, and only the sounds of Miles Davis filled the car as he drove toward Manhattan in the late hours.

Just when he thought he was getting somewhere, Lauren stopped talking to him. From the moment she stepped foot out of the bed, he'd gotten the silent treatment. The ride into Manhattan had never seemed longer even though the traffic on the bridge was nonexistent. Nick looked over at her profile as she curled up in the seat. Maybe he should have tied her down in the bed and loved her senseless.

All he'd gotten from Lauren after he'd pulled to a stop in front of her building and walked her to her door were thanks for a lovely evening and a quick peck on the lips. He watched her disappear into her apartment. The heat and passion that they'd brought to the bedroom had cooled to subzero the minute he mentioned his growing feelings. How could she pull away after something like that? The first woman he'd wanted to cook breakfast and dinner for was giving him the silent treatment and he had no idea why.

Shaking his head, he hopped right back into his car and headed for home.

Nine

After the fourth ring, Lauren rolled over and answered the phone.

"Hello." Her voice was slurred with sleep.

"I'll be by to pick you up at two-thirty." Nick's deep voice came through over the line.

"What?" She sat up and switched the phone to her left ear.

"It's about an hour and a half drive to my parents' place in Princeton."

"Can I take a rain check?" She could move amongst movie stars, diplomats, and the world's elite, but the prospect of meeting Nick's family in a more intimate setting bothered her.

"And have my mother showing up at your doorstep wondering what's keeping you from the best meal you'll ever have in your life?"

"If you put it that way." She smiled, remembering the determined glint in the senator's eyes.

"I already got the seven-o'clock-in-the-morning phone call, beautiful. We're expected to be at Sunday dinner."

She sighed and got out of bed. "Then I'd better get a move on."

"I could come over early and help out."

"No, thank you," she replied, shivering at the sexual undertone in his voice. "I'll be just fine. Good-bye, Nick."

She clicked off the phone and put it on the bedside

table. When she'd heard his voice on the other end of the line, her heart had gone from skipping on cloud nine to jumping off. She still wasn't sure she wanted to see him so soon after the night they spent together. Nick had turned her inside out and upside down with his smooth moves and wonderful fingers. Lauren had gone to his bed thinking to indulge in a casual affair only to discover after making love that she was two steps away from losing her head and her heart.

Getting out of bed, she took a quick shower and tugged on a pair of blue jeans and a sweater. No way could she meet Nick's parents without a gift. Now all she had to do was find something she knew his mother would want.

Lauren ran back into the apartment at two o'clock. After looking at everything from picture frames to coffee table books, she'd settled on three beautiful handmade beeswax candles she felt Nick's mother would love.

Standing in front of the bathroom mirror, she brushed her hair back into a ponytail and then curled it into a bun. Once finished, she set to putting on the minimal amount of makeup. The quick shopping expedition through the neighborhood had been enough to add plenty of color to her cheeks and sparkle to her eyes. She was buttoning up her jacket when she heard the doorbell ring.

She opened the door and stood back. "Hi."

Lauren may have managed to sound cool, but she felt her blood rush to her cheeks seeing Nick standing in the doorway.

"Hi yourself." He moved in and placed a kiss on her lips. Taking the keys from her hand, he locked the apartment door and ushered Lauren down the stairs.

Nick moved ahead of her and held open the passenger-side door and almost whistled. Sunday afternoon had never looked as beautiful as the sight of Lauren sashaying down the sidewalk.

Her warm breath sent clouds into the crisp winterlike air. "I didn't mention it last night, but this is not a lawyer's car."

After he got into the other side and cranked up the heat, Nick glanced over. "What kind of car should I be driving?"

"Something safe and sedate." She sat back as the automatic seat belt locked into place. "Maybe a Volvo or a four-door sedan."

He drove onto the expressway and glanced at Lauren as she flipped through the CD carrying case. "I bought the car two days after I joined the law firm."

"This is your first car?"

He watched her hand as she slipped a CD into the player. Moments later the sound of Keith Washington's soft voice filled the car.

"Yes, it is." He nodded. Wanting something low and fast but with style, he'd walked into the dealership with black on his mind and walked out with keys to the last Acura Legend on the lot. "She hasn't given me a bit of trouble since I drove her home." He patted the dashboard with his right hand. "I plan to hold on to this baby for a while."

"Planning on giving it to your son?" she ventured.

"No. Mom and Pop taught us that in order to really appreciate something, you have to earn it."

"My mom also feels the same," she added.

"As good as it sounds, it's tough." He slowed down to pass through the tollgate.

"You can't help thinking of how easy it would have been if your parents had just given it to you."

Nick moved back into the right lane and slowed down. "They could have, but they didn't. Both my parents worked hard for what we had and they expected us kids to do the same."

"My mother and stepfather were giving, but not to the

point where my brother and I expected to have everything we wanted." She paused. "Sabrina, on the other hand, never understood the word no."

"I picked up on the tension between the two of you last night."

She sighed and settled back into her seat. "We've never gotten along."

"Why is that?" It wasn't that he couldn't believe Lauren; he just wanted her to keep talking. He planned to use every opening possible to gain insight into the lady.

"Sibling rivalry, I guess." She shrugged. "Sabrina was used to being the center of her father's universe, and next thing she knew she was sharing him with Nathan, me, and my mom."

"You're very understanding, you know that?" he commented.

"And you have very good taste in music." She blushed, returning his compliment.

"And you are a wonderful dancer, Lauren."

He wasn't thinking of the way she floated on the dance floor. The memory of her moving with him last night was playing through his mind. The way she'd moved her hips, matching his rhythm. They hadn't had sex. Nick knew what that felt like, the emptiness after the act was over. No, he and Lauren had made love and he was still full of how wonderful it had been.

"I go to dance classes," she volunteered.

"Given your grace, sweetheart, I'd have to guess ballet?"

The hum of her husky laughter filled the car and heated his blood. "No, I could only take so much stretching before I fell asleep. I'm taking an African dance class at a studio in the city."

"You like it?"

She smiled. "It was really rough in the beginning since I was pretty out of shape, but you could say I have a passion for it now."

"Before last night I thought winning was my only passion."

He briefly took his eyes off the road to see her half turn toward the window. He noticed the way her brow furrowed.

After a moment he asked, "So when do you take the class?"

"Wednesdays at seven o'clock. Thinking about joining?"

"I could be interested in working up a sweat."

"The teacher's pretty tough."

"Then you'll have to give me private lessons." He reached over and trailed his fingertips against her cheek.

He watched her lean over and turned down the stereo volume. "About last night," she started.

He knew where she was headed and before she could go any further, he cut her off. "Before you close me out, give this a chance."

She shook her head. "It's not fair to start something with you, Nick."

"That's not enough of an answer, Lauren." Nick could feel his jaw clench. Maybe a part of him held out the hope that after last night she'd change her mind about leaving.

The blow to his ego aside, he'd worked too hard keeping his hands off her when he believed she was Alan's to let go now. No, he'd always finished what he started and he'd make sure that it ended when he wanted it to end. The first time he'd laid eyes on Lauren he felt the pull of attraction. Something in the way she glared at him, the way her body had brushed by his as the orderlies escorted her from the hospital room.

"Because . . ." she stumbled. "I can't be in an emotional relationship right now."

"Can't or won't? They carry two different meanings."

"Won't," she stated firmly.

"You know I'm not going to let this go."

She toyed with the seat belt. "Maybe this is going a little too fast for me."

Maybe not too fast, just too sweet, she thought to herself. She couldn't keep it limited to good sex. Not with Nick—he'd want more and she didn't want to go down that road for a while.

"Then I'll wait. I'm a patient man," he responded smoothly.

She narrowed her eyes at him. "Liar, you have a passion for winning, Nick. I see it in the way you walk, talk, the way . . ."

"The way?" He looked down at the speedometer and eased up on the accelerator.

If he could have he would have pulled the car over and looked at her. Visions of Lauren had kept him up all night. The way she felt in his hands, the way her scent lingered on the pillows. He cracked the window and took a gulp of stinging air.

"The way you work," she completed. "You're like a dog with a bone."

"Does that scare you?" He gripped the leather-encased steering wheel and started to slow down as he drove deeper into Princeton. Nick couldn't change the part of him that demanded success and right now he wanted Lauren. Randolphs always did and always would fight for what they believed in. The magic they'd shared wasn't something he could let go of just yet.

"Yes," she responded. "It's overwhelming."

"I got it, honest." He grinned, trying to lighten the mood. "Compared to my mother, I'm a harmless puppy." He reached over and took her hand, wanted to touch the softness of her skin, wanted to feel connected to Lauren in some way.

"Speaking of your family." She leaned toward him. "What should I expect?"

Nick patted her hand. "Good food, good conversation, a lot of questions, and a heaping of advice."

"Advice on what?"

"Everything. You can't have a politician and a physician together in the same room without a whole lot of opinions."

Nick turned into his parents' driveway and got out of the car. Lauren met him on the other side. He took her warm hand in his and couldn't resist sneaking a kiss. Using the ends of her scarf, he pulled her closer. The feel of her soft smooth lips under his turned the icy afternoon into a warm summer day.

Lauren was expecting passion and hunger, and what she got was teasing and sweet. His lips were gentle as his tongue played hide-and-seek with hers. The kiss went on until the sound of a passing car broke the spell.

"Don't do that." She pushed at him.

"Why not?"

The sparkle in her eyes only made him want to do it again.

Lauren looked toward the house. "What if your parents saw?"

"Pop would pat me on the back while Mom read me the riot act for keeping you out in the cold."

Putting his right arm over her shoulder, he walked her up to the three-story brick colonial house. He put his key in the door and paused. "Just remember, beautiful. You can always plead the Fifth Amendment."

Nick couldn't keep from grinning as she swept past him into the house.

Pecans, honey, and vanilla extract. Lauren couldn't keep from breathing deep as she walked into the grand foyer. The smell of cooking and the warm color of the yellow cream walls made the house into a beautiful home. The first floor of the English-style traditional home was spacious with parquet flooring, an open ceiling, and a beautiful semispiral staircase.

As Nick took off her coat, Lauren's practiced eye noted the marble fireplace mantel, intricate moldings, and elegant furnishing. The way light poured in from the upper-level windows and sparkles of rainbows showered the walls from the crystal chandelier. Adjacent to the entrance area was a large formal living room and an elegant dining room.

"Nick, we didn't think you'd ever get here."

Lauren's eyes darted between the three brothers as they enveloped each other in a group hug.

"Yeah, bro. We're starving. Can't you see Chris over here is about to waste away?"

From her vantage point it didn't look as if any of them had missed a meal recently. The three brothers were all big. Lauren felt like a little kid looking up at them.

"Traffic." Nick grinned and turned toward her. Before she could blink, she was tight up against his side. He caught the quick glare she aimed his way before she turned to smile at his brothers.

"Hey, is Ami here yet?" Nick asked.

"Nope, Ami called from the car. She'll be late."

Nick turned back toward the lady at his side. "Lauren, these loudmouths are my older brother, Will, and my younger brother, Chris."

"Nice to meet you." She held out her hand but found herself enveloped in a hug from the both of them.

"Great to finally meet you, Lauren. Heard a lot about you from my brother here," Will started.

Lauren noticed the way his eyes focused on Nick's arm, which had again wound its way around her waist. She wanted more than anything to give in to the childish urge to stamp on his foot and push him away.

"Good things, I hope?" She smiled.

"Oh, yeah," Chris replied. "My brother has been singing your praises for the past month."

"I'm curious to hear about what he's been saying." Lauren slipped out from under Nick's arm and moved toward Chris.

Nick shot his younger sibling a warning glance.

Chris chuckled before turning back to Lauren. "Now why don't you follow me up to the study so we can get back to the kitchen?"

"We?" Lauren repeated, looking from Chris and Will to Nick.

"Yeah, this is the men's Sunday to cook."

"All of you are cooking?" Her eyes widened in surprise.

"Yeah, Pop started the roast this morning and we're working on the sides."

"And what are you going to work on?" She arched an eyebrow at Nick.

His answering grin was so hot it singed her fingers. "Dessert."

Lauren blushed at the snickers from the audience.

"Oh, yeah. Mr. Frosty is melting," Chris joked as he clapped Nick on the back.

"Now, boys, don't harass our guest." Nick's mother entered into the hallway. "Y'all get in that kitchen so we can get dinner on the table. And bring Lauren something to drink, Nick. I know I taught you better manners."

Lauren fought to keep the grin off her face as Nick slumped his shoulders and followed his brothers toward the back of the house.

"Lauren, you come on upstairs to the study with me, dear."

She turned and followed Nick's mother to the second floor and down the carpeted hallway.

"Mrs. Randolph," Lauren began before taking a seat on the love seat. Books lined the shelves of the study as pictures and portraits hung along the walls. The sound of Sarah Vaughn's honey-rippled voice spilled out of the speakers.

"Please, call me Diane."

"Thank you for inviting me." Lauren presented her with the nice gift bag. "I hope you'll like them." She sat up straight and crossed her legs.

Diane sat down on the gold-colored chaise and opened the bag. "Oh, they're perfect," she beamed. "I was looking for something like this for the bedroom. Now that it's getting dark so soon, I've got some ideas that'll go nicely with these beautiful candles."

Lauren blushed at the dreamy smile that lit the other woman's face.

"Here's your coffee, ladies." Nick appeared in the doorway.

Lauren caught the curious look he threw her way and she shrugged. Since she had stepped foot into the Randolph home, nothing seemed to make sense.

"You run along back down to the kitchen, Nickie." His mother made a shooing motion with her hands.

Nickie, Lauren mouthed, as she struggled to keep from giggling. It was such a cute little nickname. He scowled at her before closing the door.

"Oh, this is my favorite song."

Lauren's eyes widened as Diane closed her eyes and sat back on the chaise.

"Go ahead and relax." She waved her hand.

"But," Lauren started.

"Just lean back and enjoy. This is the only time out of the month I get to sit and be."

Leaning back on the sofa, Lauren closed her eyes and took a deep breath.

"That's it," Nick's mother encouraged.

Lauren was so relaxed that when the couch shifted, she didn't open her eyes to see who'd sat down. When the music ended, she sighed and stretched.

"You're late, Ami-bee." Diane pointed a manicured finger toward the miniature grandfather clock.

"Sorry about that, Mama. Got stuck at the office."

"It's Sunday, sweetheart."

"You and I both know ear infections have no respect for women's Sunday."

"Uh-huh . . ."

Lauren stood as she watched the mother and daughter hug.

"Ami, this is Lauren."

"Nick's girlfriend?" Ami asked.

Lauren shook her head vigorously. "We're just friends."

"Not if my son has anything to do with it," Diane responded with a soft smile.

"Hmm . . ." She blushed, taking a sip of the lukewarm coffee.

"Even if Nick hadn't been singing your praises for the past month, I would have known how it was between the two of you." Diane peered over her coffee cup.

"What do you mean?" Lauren crossed her legs at the ankles. She wondered if last night showed. Could his mother have guessed that she had spent half the night rolling around in her son's new bed?

"You have to watch everything in my line of work. I learned early in politics that people examine everything you do from the colors you wear to how many times you wipe your nose." She grinned. "I didn't miss the way his hand lingered on the back of your shoulder as you walked away, young lady. Not to mention the way he watched you last night at the awards ceremony."

"We've built a close working relationship," Lauren inserted. She was stretching the truth and they all knew it.

"Right." Laughter bubbled out of Ami's eyes. "The news about Nick adopting a stray cat made my week. But this . . . this is going to make my month."

"She's perfect, don't you think?" Diane nodded.

"Oh, yeah. He's going to have his hands full."

Lauren threw her hands up. "I'm confused."

"It's the curse of the Randolph men." Ami laughed.

"Or the downfall of the women. My son has been chased by every single socialite from New York to California. You, Lauren Hughes, have not only managed to get the keys to his house, but the keys to his heart in a matter of days."

"Oh, no . . ." Lauren denied, remembering one woman in particular who wanted to lay claim to Nick.

"Oh, yes." Ami patted her sympathetically on her arm. "You are in for the ride of your life."

"They get it from their father," Diane added. "Harold taught them boys to go after whatever they wanted and that included the opposite sex."

"Like you didn't too, Mom."

"Now, hush, Ami."

Lauren's eyes grew round as saucers as she watched one of the most powerful women in the United States blush like a schoolgirl.

"Hmm, I'm not interested in getting involved right now. I'm only redecorating the brownstone," she added.

"You know, when I met my husband I wanted a fighter, not a healer." She shook her head and gazed fondly at the wedding photo on the wall. "But Harold sure taught me. Come hell or high water, that man will always be there for me."

Lauren leaned forward. "I can't imagine how hard it must have been for you."

The older woman ran a hand through her short salt-and-pepper hair. Lauren didn't find it hard to believe Diane had broken many a man's heart. The fire in her eyes and the pride in her face lent her an ageless beauty.

"He believed in me when I couldn't believe in myself.

Harold raised these kids, ran a practice, and helped me get elected into office."

"That's why you and Pop need to take a long vacation." Ami wagged her finger.

"I will once the senate goes into summer recess."

"That's what you said last year."

"Well, this year is different; remember, we've got that family reunion to plan and I expect both of you to help."

Lauren watched Diane's eyes narrow. "And you, baby girl, aren't you working a little too hard?"

Ami rolled her eyes upward. "This from the woman who puts in eighty-hour weeks?"

"We're not talking about me."

"I can handle it, Mama."

"I'm not worried about that. I just want you to enjoy yourself a little, maybe come back to Trenton with me and attend some social functions."

"I love my job."

"You're a pediatrician?" Lauren questioned.

"Yes, and I have the best patients in the world."

Lauren's lips curled into a soft smile. "You must be wonderful with kids."

"Oh, no." Ami shook her head. "Kids scare the pants off me."

Lauren looked at her funny.

Diane leaned forward. "What my melodramatic daughter means is that she prefers her patients to the real children."

"Exactly."

"I don't understand." Lauren's brows wrinkled.

"As patients they're absolutely adorable. I give them a toy, diagnose them, and reassure their worried parents. But the thought of actually having the responsibility of being a parent is terrifying."

"Well, I got through it and did a good job, if I say so myself," Diane pointed out.

"Yes, you did." Ami nodded. "I, however, am avoiding motherhood like the plague."

Lauren fought back a chuckle as Nick's mother rolled her eyes upward. "Now you see why I'm looking to the boys to give me some grandkids."

"Did you know Pop is cooking a roast for supper?" Ami asked. Lauren eased back in the love seat, relieved at the change in topic. The way Nick's mother's eyes focused on her with the mention of grandchildren set off warning bells in her head.

"Uh-huh, Will's making the garlic mashed potatoes and salad, Chris started the green beans and biscuits. Now, what's Nick doing for dessert?"

"He wouldn't tell me."

"What's gotten into that boy?"

Ami shrugged. "Pop said something about the way to a woman's heart. Then they kicked me out of the kitchen."

"If I could be a fly on the wall." Diane laughed, turning up the volume on the stereo.

Lauren sat back and closed her eyes; Nick's words were running through her brain as the music wafted into the air. *Before last night I thought that winning was my only passion.*

Nick took off his oven mitt and leaned against the stove. "Oh, yeah." He gave Chris a high five.

"That good?"

"You know it." He grinned, moving to take the last empty seat at the table.

"Where'd you get the cheesecake recipe?"

"Picked it up from a fellow attorney. This'll beat Pop's brownies by a mile," he bragged. "I might have to bake another once the kitchen gets fixed up."

"Speaking of fixing up." Chris threw open the fridge

and grabbed a soda. "When do I get the keys to my new overnight place?"

"As soon as Lauren finishes the bathroom."

"Man, forget about the house. What's happening with the beautiful designer?"

Nick looked up as Will leaned against the sink. Nick eyed his older brother. "Don't even think about it."

Will shrugged. "Can't blame me for trying to look out for my younger brother."

"No need." He leaned back in the chair and laced his fingers behind his head. "She's mine."

"We know that. Does this mean Theresa's out of the picture?"

"You two know Theresa's been out the picture for months now."

Will nodded. "We might know that you don't want to get back with her, but she doesn't. She's not the accepting type."

"Yeah, well, she didn't have a choice. It's not going to happen."

"So you're that serious about the lady, son?"

Nick turned to see his father walk back into the kitchen.

"Yeah, Pop." He nodded. "I've been thinking about settling down and giving you and Mama some grandkids."

Nick laughed as his older and younger brother started toward the door. Will tugged at his turtleneck sweater. "Whew, it's got a little too hot in here. We'll just go in the den and catch the end of the game."

Nick sat back down at the table facing his father. "Think I'm moving too fast, Pop?"

"Son." The elder Randolph toyed with the pepper grinder. "You see a good thing, you take it and hold on. That's the Randolph creed. Just like every man in the family has done through the years. Just like I did with

your mama. You only get one try at life, Nicholas. Get all
the joy and happiness out of it you can."

A wide grin lit Nick's face. Images of beautiful little
girls with their mother's sweet brown eyes and button
lips. "I'll try."

"And if she gives you sass, don't worry." Pop got up
and moved to open the oven door. "Only makes the
chase even more engaging."

Lauren woke as the car came to a full stop. The wonderful dinner had worked its magic, leaving her relaxed
and full of good cheer even though she'd given Nick the
evil eye every time he looked at her. During the main
course, during dessert. Every time he reached past her,
he'd brushed his fingers against her chest or accidentally
squeezed her thigh. All thoughts of dessert fled her
mind and the chocolate cheesecake he'd spent so much
time preparing could have been cardboard for all the attention she'd paid to the taste.

She opened her eyes to see Nick's face inches from
her own. "We're here, Sleeping Beauty."

She moved her hand to cover a yawn. "I had a wonderful time."

"I'm glad." He reached over and brushed his fingers
against her check, gently cupping her delicate chin,
holding her gaze.

Nick had drunk Lauren's smiles and laughter all day
long, and he was still thirsty for more. But he needed to
know if it could last; if he stood a chance at winning her
heart. "I'm not a subtle man, Lauren, but I want to be."

Her gaze widened at his admission. "As you said earlier
I like to win too much, know too much, and sometimes I
push too hard."

Her lids lowered, with her unable to bear his intense
stare. Her breath quickened.

"But I need you to tell me if I got a shot, beautiful. I can't win if you've given the prize to someone else."

Wrapping her arms around herself, Lauren stared blindly out the windshield. "I didn't recognize his body," she started in a flat tone. "The wedding was three months away, but I spent almost every day preparing for it. We'd just gotten our blood tests the day before Paul responded to fire. His partner managed to get the couple's son to safety. But the roof collapsed and brought down the house before Paul could bring the daughter out." She drew a shuddered breath. "They died instantly."

"I'm sorry, baby." He reached over and, uncrossing her arms, took her cold hands within his own.

"Love hurts, Nick." Her voice was small and forlorn like a lost child's. "Like nothing I've ever felt in my life. It's not some injury that eventually heals. It's a forever kind of pain."

She closed her eyes. "First it was my father. He died when I was twelve and it still cuts deep."

Lauren drew a hard breath while fighting back tears. She still felt as though her dad had abandoned her. She looked Nick in the eyes and the emotions she saw gave her enough strength to pull away from the old memories.

"It'll be okay, beautiful." Nick leaned over and pulled her closer.

"No, it won't, Nick," she sniffed. "And crying doesn't help."

"Then let me help."

"Thank you, but I'll be all right."

To be honest, the last thing she wanted was for him to help. She could see him riding in on his white horse and taking her away from all the fear and anger she'd held on tight to for so long. Everything he did made her want to turn toward him like a buttercup tilted toward the sun. No, she couldn't love anyone like that again. The consequences of giving her heart were too devastating to contemplate.

"I swore I'd never feel grief like that again," she stated more to herself than to Nick.

He stroked her back. Now things seemed to start coming into focus and the new picture made him want her more.

"You're one tough cookie." He kissed her brow.

She pulled back and gave him a soft smile. "You just noticed?"

"No, I knew it from the moment you threw the flowers in my face and slammed the door. My family picked up on it the minute you walked into the house."

She found her eyes following the curve of his lips as they turned upward into a grin. "You have a wonderful family."

"They feel the same about you."

"Even after I spilled water all over Will's sweater?" She smiled.

"That was my fault." He grinned.

"Yes, it was." She smiled back at him toying with her pocketbook strap. His touch on the inside of her thigh had been enough for her to send the glass tumbling.

She needed a man in her bed the way she needed a hole in her head. But want was sitting close, desire shooting through her veins. Nick was becoming an obsession. Not the once-an-hour reminder; it was more the *minute-to-minute want him in the room, in her sight, in her arms, and warm in her body* kind of intensity. She swallowed hard.

"So would you like to come up for a nightcap?" she asked in a fake calm voice. Her heart rate had started rising as soon as she looked at him.

"No," Nick bit out.

Lauren's eyes widened as he turned the ignition and started the car. She'd been thinking about being alone with him since she got out of bed this morning. The game he'd started at dinner was still playing on her skin.

"Why not?" She fluttered her eyelashes.

He sighed and put his hands on the steering wheel. "If I come upstairs with you, Lauren, we'll be sharing much more than a nightcap."

"What else did you have in mind?" She tilted her head and unfastened the lap belt. She was openly flirting with him and it felt good. Like opening an old box and rediscovering a much-loved toy. This was what she missed, the give and take, the anticipation of a stolen kiss, the way possibilities and desire swirled in the air. Lauren missed playing, had more or less forgotten the heady power of her own feminine wiles.

"Breakfast," Nick said.

Her mouth went dry at the look in his eyes. The glow from the streetlight enhanced the heated stare as the scent of his aftershave sent memories of their lovemaking across her skin.

Picking up her handbag, she opened the car door and stepped out into the cold, then walked to the driver's side, tapped on the glass, and patiently waited as Nick rolled down the window.

Before he could say a word, she kissed him, slow and teasing, until they both had to come up for air. This was what she yearned for, the fire in her blood, the pounding of her heart, and the need for that substance only Nick could provide.

Giving him a sultry look she leaned in closer and whispered in his ear, "I like to have a bagel with my coffee."

She didn't recall how fast he got them up into the house, up the stairs, and into her bedroom, but they'd broken the speed record. Once they were in the bedroom, Lauren took off her shoes and strolled over to Nick, loving the way he watched her, the way his eyes followed her every step.

"Are you sure about this, Lauren?"

She moved in closer and began to toy with his turtle-neck. He still smelled of the outside cold and of earth. The heavy smell of wood and smoke mixed with the spice of aftershave. She'd loved watching as Nick and his brothers carried wood into his parents' house. The strength of his arms and the proud set of his shoulders.

"What an interesting question," she murmured, reaching underneath his sweater to run her nails down his hard chest. She watched his eyes darken, and the sound of his roughly inhaled breath sent a satisfied shiver down her spine.

She stood on her tiptoes and placed a long, wet kiss on his neck. "You see that nicely made-up bed, Nick?"

"Yes, darling, I do." His voice was low with a husky edge.

Lauren rubbed her body against him, her teeth nipping at his earlobe. She let out a small breath. "It's empty and cold."

Pulling back a fraction, she looked him in the eyes. "You've been in my head all day. Right now, I don't want you running through my mind, Nick."

"Where do you want me?" he teased, cupping her hips.

She licked her lips, marveling at her newly found boldness. "I want you in my bed; I want it full and messy with you and me. I want to wrap you around me and rest my head against your chest with your heartbeat as my pillow."

She could look upon all the colors in the world, vivid rich hues of every shade of the rainbow. But only Nick could give her glimmering white stars and red-hot fire.

"Beautiful, I'm yours." Nick raised his hands in a mock surrender as his eyes locked with hers.

Lauren laughed and it was a free sound that echoed lightly through the room. She helped him pull off his sweater and then tossed it on the floor.

Seeing him shirtless, proud, and visibly erect stole the breath right from her body. It left with a whoosh, leaving her with nothing but a honeyed desire so sweet it made her body ache. Reaching up, she pulled his head down and kissed him. Nick opened for her, and the hand caressing her neck drew her closer and allowed his tongue deeper access into her mouth.

Standing back, Lauren unbuckled his pants and pushed them down. She'd reached for his boxers when he grabbed her hands.

"Now, it wouldn't be fair if I was the only one undressed," Nick whispered hoarsely as his hands moved to hold her still. Lauren was driving him nearly insane with her teasing.

"I'll undress . . . eventually."

"It's lonely being the only one without any clothes on, darling."

"Maybe I could use some help," she teased, but she wanted more than his assistance, she craved his fingers and his tongue, the hardness of his flesh, the fullness only brought by his joining her body with his.

He didn't so much as reply but took command. Nick turned her around and pulled her back tight up against his chest. The warmth of his lips on the back of her neck while his fingers cupped her swollen breasts took away all thought. The rough feel of his four o'clock shadow on her hypersensitive skin sent a violent shudder over her.

What might have been minutes turned into eternity as he undressed her slowly. She made a sound that started as a purr. Then pleasure followed the trail of his fingertips over her skin. Then the hum turned to a moan when his hand covered her sensitive heat and the rapture turned her legs to jelly. She arched forward, pressing against his hands as they caressed her breasts.

Lauren didn't know where she found the strength to

pull away but she took him by the hands and led him to the bed. The outside world had fallen away as soon as they'd stepped into her bedroom. Nothing but the sound of their breathing stirred in the room.

"Lie down," she ordered, her voice trembling. She felt her heartbeat go crazy when Nick raised an eyebrow and languidly stretched out on the bed all the while watching her. Lauren paused, taking time to study his perfect body and memorize the moment. She'd wanted him there, in her bed, the way he ran through her mind from the time she opened her eyes that morning.

She didn't just slide into bed beside him. Lauren lightly ran her fingernails up and down his body before moving to straddle him. She looked down into his face and found herself captured by the tenderness in his eyes. She bent down and placed kisses all over his body. Putting all her need and passion into her mouth, she drew a deep breath. Nick tasted of crisp pine and wood smoke, but under all of it was him and he was sweet, smooth, and hard.

As her lips trailed over his chest, his hands moved over her, calmly stroking, encouraging, leaving her wanting more. Her tongue licked his nipple while her mouth blew out a soft cooling breath. She was rewarded with a harsh moan.

Lauren echoed his groan as pleasure ripped through her, jagged and searing, as his fingers found her wet and wanting. She threw her head back and closed her eyes, feeling the tightness start to grow low in her body as her breath came faster. Ripples of fire ran over her skin, bowed her back, and took her breath away.

"That's right, baby. Let it come."

His heart pumping as if he were running laps, Nick wanted nothing more than to bury himself in Lauren. Her desire-laden eyes looked right back into his dark ones. He stroked her tiny sensitive nub with one hand while the other reached, opened the nightstand drawer, and pulled out a foil packet. She took it from his hands, and slowly covered him.

Nick drew in a rough breath, trying to retain a measure of restraint. He wanted to let her set the pace and intensity of their lovemaking, but the sensation of Lauren's fingernails against his sensitive skin was almost too much.

"Lauren," he said roughly.

The sound torn from his throat was somewhere between a curse and a hymn. The kitten had claws; Nick dragged his hands through her hair. He groaned, feeling the combination of rough scratching and softness of her warm skin moving over his body, coming into intimate contact with his hardness.

The moment of feeling her slide against him snapped his control. Nick pulled her up for a kiss and then with his hands on her hips, guided her as inch by inch she sheathed herself. She cried out his name as he filled her completely.

Her body moved with his kiss, rose, and fell with the thundering of their hearts, matching the rapid rhythm of harsh breaths. Lauren wanted to make the night last forever, to draw out the way he filled her body, putting his name on her room, marking her soul with his presence while he drove into her hard and deep. She clung to him as everything around her fell away and in that space there existed nothing but him, nothing but the feel of need and pleasure, friction and heat.

The warm tension started low and grew until it covered her body. It built into a crescendo as he moved in and out. She squeezed her thighs together, wanting to catch him and hold him. Just when she thought it couldn't get any better, intense pleasure exploded low in her body and surged along her nerves, filling her veins, and pushing her over the edge.

Lauren locked her eyes with his as he sat up and wrapped her legs around him, deepening his possession and positioning her so that his next thrust found that perfect spot and every muscle in her body contracted.

"Nick," she cried out loud as sounds of love spilled from her lips. Her fingers clutched at his shoulders as her nails bit tight into his skin.

She collapsed into his chest and rested her cheek on his shoulder. Her body felt like lead, weak, heavy, and it was wonderful. Still locked together as Nick lay back down, she found the strength to squeeze her legs when she felt him move away, forcing him to be still.

As her eyes drifted closed, Lauren wished for this always, the passion, the fire, but most of all the warmth, the fullness. She wanted him to stay as he was, buried inside, connected to her.

Nick didn't believe lightning could strike the same place twice or a man could get more than one taste of heaven, but his own release was better than the first time. Struggling to draw air into his oxygen-deprived lungs, he groaned her name as Lauren collapsed on top of his body. Nothing made him feel more content than to have her light frame covering his own.

Sated beyond belief, he wrapped his arm around her and rolled them so that she curled against him. Lightly stroking her hair, Nick breathed in her soft scent. He knew beyond a shadow of a doubt, he loved her. Twice, the lady had brought him to his knees even as she'd unknowingly laid claim to his heart.

Her sleepy sigh brought a smile of pure male satisfaction to his face and he tightened his arms around her. She was the one. He knew it deep down in his gut. What he felt would never waver or fade. Randolph men only had one love of a lifetime, and for him that was Lauren.

Nick wasn't a betting man; he liked a sure thing just like everybody else, and what he wanted at the moment was for Lauren to open her eyes and whisper words of love and forever. He'd be there to fight her ghosts and battle her sorrows. The love and commitment he felt would last this side of forever. It was a fact that Lauren could trust him with her heart.

Now all he had to do was convince her of that.

Lauren woke to the sound of chirping. Not the bird outside the window, but a high-pitched repetition only a ringing cell phone could produce.

"Shh . . ." Nick whispered before she felt his hard lips gently cover hers. "Go back to sleep, beautiful."

Obeying his tender command, Lauren snuggled deeper into the pillow. When she next woke to an empty bed, she sat up and surveyed the evidence of their lovemaking. Rumpled pillows, her down comforter hung off the side while the sheets lay bunched at the bottom. She hugged the pillow tight and smiled. Mornings didn't get better than this. Her body still bore witness to Nick's lovemaking.

She got up and walked to the bathroom. She stared at her reflection in the mirror. Swollen lips, flushed cheeks, and dark eyes. She looked thoroughly loved. It was only then she noticed the silver pendant around her neck. "Cass was right," she murmured to herself. She hadn't let go of Paul completely.

Slowly she unclasped the necklace he'd given her for her twenty-fifth birthday. She closed her eyes and felt a weight lift off her heart. It was time to move on. Time to let the past go. After showering and getting dressed for work, she walked into the kitchen and stared. Next to the full coffeepot lay a perfectly round bagel and a note. She felt something melt in the region of her heart. She stared at the scrap of paper. Nick's confident scrawl took up the page.

Good morning, beautiful. Have to go out of town on business. Be back soon. I love you. Nick.

All her newly found bravery vanished as her throat went dry. Lauren sat down hard at the kitchen table, forgetting about breakfast and the fresh smell of coffee that lingered heavy in the air. His three handwritten words almost choked her. *I love you.* A heavy lump settled in her stomach as she stared blankly at the paper.

She shook her head over and over. Not this time. She wasn't going to stay and get her heart ripped out. She stood up, put on her coat, grabbed her purse, and was out the door.

Nick Randolph might have pulled the stars out of the sky and made her dance till daybreak, but she wasn't going to lose her heart the way she lost her mind. She had a job to do and no matter what was happening between them, the day she finished her half of the brownstone renovation, she'd be ready to step on the plane.

Ten

"Ladies and gentlemen, on behalf of our Miami-based flight crew we'd like to welcome you to New York City. The captain has turned off the fasten-seat-belt sign and you are now free to exit the plane. As a reminder, please use caution when opening the overhead bin as objects tend to shift during flight."

Three hours and two minutes. Nick looked at his watch. He'd never wanted to get off a plane faster than he did this evening. He'd pulled out his laptop computer and finished up all the little details during the flight.

As of the time the plane touched down he was a free man, and all he wanted to do was spend time with Lauren. The writing was on the wall: his bachelor days were over. He'd rather have the good stuff and he knew without a shadow of a doubt it was right at home.

The contract negotiations had hit an eleventh-hour snag but he'd pulled off another coup. Next season would see the Miami football team with one of the best starting lineups in years, thanks to some last-minute concessions on both sides. For the next two weeks all he had on his schedule was loving Lauren and reading up on the newest salary cap proposals.

Taking his place behind a young married couple, he walked down the jet-way and exited onto the airport concourse.

"Nick, over here."

With briefcase in hand he turned toward Alan and the smile on his face froze. Alan's mother stood right beside him, and the sight of the woman with her hands on her hips and a frown on her face set alarms to ringing in his head.

"Mrs. Knight, how great to see you."

Dropping his briefcase, he gave the older woman a hug. Even as he said the words his eyes looked at Alan over her shoulder. The expression on his friend's face didn't bode well for a happy meeting.

"Don't Mrs. Knight me," she said. "I'm not happy with either one of you. Alan told me all about your little scheme for Lauren. The both of you should be ashamed of yourselves."

Marva Knight glared up at him from underneath a pair of round glasses. Her light auburn hair was pulled back in a bun and her smooth pecan-colored skin was still unmarked by the wrinkles of worry or time.

Nick rubbed his brow and the pained expression on his face was soon to match the one that Alan wore. All the way through the airport to baggage, Mrs. Knight's scolding took him from professional sports attorney back to an elementary schoolkid caught with his hand in the cookie jar.

From baggage to the car, the lecture continued. And the farther they walked, the more his shoulders slumped. Alan had been dead wrong—if it were up to his mother, Lauren would be on a plane tomorrow. Nick hopped into the front seat of Alan's SUV and buckled his seat belt.

"Nicholas Randolph, I'm going to have a serious talk with your parents. Here I was thinking that you'd rub off on my baby, give him some of that good common sense." Marva pointed her finger before settling back in the leather seat.

She shook her head and tried hard to stifle the laughter that threatened to erupt out of her chest. "I can't believe you'd go along with this nonsense Alan's cooked up."

Marva had suspected that Nick was more than just being a good friend from the minute Rosemarie had talked about the boy at church last Sunday. Lauren's mother had been overjoyed with the prospect of her daughter being happily settled with a new young man.

The expression on Nick's face the moment she mentioned Lauren had confirmed it. The way his eyes softened and he got that dazed look. Like a kid with the promise of ice cream.

Oh, yes. She nodded to herself. The boy had fallen for Lauren. She wasn't surprised, that girl was a chip off the old block and it was a pretty one. She'd watched her blossom from a shy, skinny thing to a beautiful woman and it about broke her heart to see her suffer after her young man's death.

Usually she didn't like to meddle in the affairs of others, but she was tired of sitting back and letting them waste some of the best years of their lives waiting for love to kick them in the pants. No, she was going to be a thorn in these kids' sides until they buckled down and got serious about bringing some love into their lives.

"Mrs. Knight, we were only looking out for Lauren," Nick explained.

She put on her best glare, as he turned halfway around in the seat to look at her. "Oh, no, you weren't." She waved her handkerchief. "I know my son Alan's overprotective. He's been that way toward Lauren since Paul's death. What I can't understand is why you went along with the nonsense."

Nick felt sweat start to bead on his forehead. Lawyers, judges, intermediaries he could handle, but this? He didn't know what to do.

Alan jumped in. "Mama, Nick only did it 'cause I

asked him to and it doesn't matter now because Lauren isn't going anywhere."

"And how do you know that?" She leveled a glare into the rearview mirror. At least her only son had the decency to look guilty.

"Tell her, Nick." Alan nodded.

He cleared his throat. "I'm in love with Lauren, Mrs. Knight. Thinking about asking her to marry me."

"Well, I hope she tells you no," Marva huffed. "The two of you tricked the girl. If it wasn't for your scheming she'd be traveling all over the world."

She was so happy they couldn't see through her right then. She could never play a good game of cards. The twinkle in her eyes would always give her away when she was fibbing.

She'd spent the last three hours on the plane imagining all sorts of horrible things only to find out that her son was playing Cupid. Oh, she was going to have fun with this one, and the stories she'd tell at the women's luncheon had her covering her mouth to hide the smile on her face.

"Mama," Alan protested, "why'd you want Lauren to leave when you thought we were seeing one another?"

"Watch the road," she scolded, putting a stern expression on her face. "I always knew that you and Lauren were putting on. She wouldn't have you. No, that girl needs a strong hand."

"That's right." Nick had to jump in before things got even worse. "She needs a strong hand, not some man she picks out from her travels."

He started feeling more guilty and uncomfortable at every passing minute. He hadn't lied, but he hadn't disclosed the full truth either. There were a lot of things he still didn't know about Lauren, but it hadn't taken him long to figure out that she wasn't going to like what they'd done.

Marva crossed her arms and sat back on the leather seat. "The girl was done grieving. Didn't either of you two college-educated gentlemen pick up on that? She wasn't actually going to pick up some stranger off the street."

"But, Mama, she was serious about getting married before she turned thirty." Alan exited off the expressway.

"Maybe, maybe not, but what you boys are doing is still wrong."

Nick shot Alan a frantic glance. This was not turning out anywhere near what they'd planned. His friend had been so sure that his mother would be on their side and now everything looked as though it was going to blow up in their faces big time.

"Mama—" Alan started again.

"Don't Mama me. Thought you were going to use me to talk her out of going, huh? You wait. I'm going to talk some serious sense into that girl." She nodded.

Nick almost let out a sigh of relief, but the woman's next words snatched his breath back.

Marva continued, "Lauren should have invited me. I would have helped her find a young man and train him right."

Oh, this was getting good, she thought to herself. Marva could see the wheels spinning in Nick's head. If that boy didn't put a ring on that girl's finger by the time she got back on the plane to Chicago, she'd quit playing the lottery.

Alan slowed the car. "Mama, Lauren didn't even invite Cassandra on the trip."

"Speaking of the young woman, I can't wait to meet her." She turned toward her son. "It's way past time for you to start minding your own business and give me some grandkids. I need a little body to rock in my lap at church on Christmas Sunday. Not to mention some playmates to go to Orlando with since you and your sister are always too busy. Your father doesn't like to fly, won't take Amtrak, hates Greyhound, and I won't sit for that long drive."

"Mama," Alan mumbled her name for what had to be the fifth time before pulling to a stop in front of Nick's brownstone.

"Don't Mama me. Here I am after flying halfway across the country to look after you and you're busy trying to run somebody else's life instead of looking after your own. I plan to have a nice long chat with this new young lady of yours."

Nick unbuckled his seat belt and moved to get out of the car. For one minute he felt sorrier for Alan than he did for himself. Nothing like someone else's mother to make you feel slightly better about your own situation.

"It was great seeing you, Mrs. Knight. We'll have to have dinner while you're in town."

"Of course, I can't wait to have you and Lauren over, I got this new catfish recipe I know she'll love."

Marva gave him one of her best smiles. It did her heart good to know that Lauren was going to be taken care of. The child had had more than her fair share of grief, but Marva knew from the set of Nick's shoulders everything was going to be fine. Now, she only wished her youngest child would get her act together.

Pursing her lips, she felt a little worried about leaving her husband and daughter alone. What were they going to do about that girl?

Rachel had had half the eligible bachelors in the Chicago area and beyond calling on their house only for her to turn them away. Her husband loved their baby girl to distraction, but the thought of having that nice big house to themselves . . . Maybe she could send her to live with Alan once he settled down, she mused, closing her eyes for a little nap.

"Alan, can you help me get my bag out the back?" Nick shot the man a pointed look.

"Yeah." Alan unbuckled his seat belt and got out of the car.

Nick hopped out into the cold and walked to the back of the truck. "Look, man, you've got to keep your mom away from Lauren or we'll both be in the doghouse."

"I can try, Nick." He watched as his friend shifted from foot to foot. "But you might want to go ahead and tell her."

The thought of her being mad at him made the contents of the first-class dinner he'd had on the plane shift in his stomach. "You think you might be able to get your mama to change her mind?" he asked.

Alan shook his head from side to side. "Not a chance."

Nick reached in and grabbed the wheeled carry-on. "Wish me luck."

He took the stairs slowly and went into the house. Before reaching into his pocket for the keys, he rehearsed what he was going to say. First, he'd lay out the facts and tell her he and Alan had done it for her own good. *Yeah,* he mused, swinging open the door, *and if she doesn't believe me, then what? Then I'll beg.* He nodded and stepped into the entranceway.

The first thing that registered besides the warm silence was a sign on the mirror Lauren had hung in the foyer.

Follow the yellow brick road.

His lips curled into a smile at the large childlike handwriting and arrow sign. Taking off his coat, he deposited his briefcase and suitcase next to the closet and headed toward the back of the house. The trail of yellow sticky notes started at the banister and led upstairs to the second floor.

The sight that met him as he gently pushed open the double doors leading to the room they planned to make into a study made his knees weak. What had once been an empty room was an office that any man would be proud of. But it wasn't just the room that got to him. It was Lauren curled up by the window that did it. Any thoughts he had of confessing got pushed to the back of his mind.

Nick didn't consider himself to be a selfish man, but the last thing he wanted was to have Lauren angry with him. Nothing was going to ruin the perfect homecoming she'd planned for him. She'd managed a miracle in three days and he couldn't begin to wonder how she did it.

He walked into the middle of the room and stopped as the cat hopped down from the windowsill and pranced over to wrap its tail around his leg. Nick reached down and scratched Brooklyn on her little head while he looked around his new home office.

College and pro football pictures stood next to his undergraduate and law degrees on wall-mounted shelves. A walnut-stained credenza, filing cabinets, and bookshelves lined two of the walls. A flat-screen monitor, printer, and scanner sat looking like an ad out of a catalog on top of the desk of his law school dreams. The big heavy wood desk and hutch with drawers sat next to a big black leather chair.

Nick tiptoed over to Lauren and gazed down at her sleeping on a cushioned bench. Tiny specks of paint dotted her cheeks like errant freckles and her hair lay covered by an oversize bandana. He stood over her for a moment, relaxed by the mere sight of her chest rising and falling, the whisper of her indrawn breaths.

Carefully, he leaned over and gathered her in his arms. She sighed and settled back into sleep with a soft smile. He carried her to the bedroom and laid her down on his bed before taking off her clothes and then his own. Holding Lauren tight, Nick placed a gentle kiss on her lips. *I'll tell her in the morning,* he thought as he closed his eyes.

* * *

Lauren woke the next morning to the warmth of his arms, the feel of his strong chest against her back, and just lay there with her eyes closed. Smiling, she turned and trailed her fingers over the nape of his neck. "Good morning," she whispered.

Her breath caught in her throat as he opened his eyes and looked at her as though she were the alpha and omega: his beginning and end.

"Sleep well?" he asked.

"No," Lauren answered with a straight face.

"Bad dreams?" He moved to pull her closer in his arms and began to play with her hair.

"Someone's snoring woke me up." She looked away to keep him from seeing the way her eyes sparkled with laughter.

"What? Brooklyn slept in here last night?" Nick pretended to look around the room for the Siamese cat.

"No." Lauren giggled as his finger tickled her skin. "It was you, silly."

A boyish smile lit his face. "Probably because I was freezing since someone pulls all the covers."

"I guess Brooklyn got cold," she answered in a prim and proper voice.

"Or maybe it was Lauren that got cold," Nick murmured against her throat.

"I missed waking up with you beside me." She closed her eyes, luxuriating in the warmth he was bringing to all the parts of her body.

"I would have loved to have you with me in Miami, sweetheart, but even if you'd been there, we wouldn't have spent any time together."

Her eyes grew round with concern. "That bad?"

"We were spending some long hours at the office. I don't think I got more than ten hours of sleep during the entire trip."

"All work and no play makes Nicholas Randolph an

awfully tense boy," she said softly, enjoying the way his lips curved upward.

"I wasn't the only one keeping busy. I saw the new office, baby."

"You like it?" She watched as his beautiful lips curved upward into a grin.

"I love it," he said before kissing her.

"I'm glad. I wanted to surprise you."

It was a little more that that. Lauren had wanted to see his face light up as he walked into the room. To see the glow in his eyes as he looked upon the place that had been but four bare walls before he left for his trip.

In most cases, interior designers never got involved in the day-to-day actual implementation of the changes, but this renovation was different, personal. Last-minute changes and two sick employees had forced her to step in. She'd spent every waking moment putting everything together. She was so exhausted that what she'd planned to be a quick nap had turned into a deep sleep.

Nick kissed the tip of her nose. "I'd hoped that I'd be here to help you, but the contracts had to get hammered down; training camp's right around the corner."

"Everybody's gotta relax sometime. Join me tomorrow for my dance class," she invited. She gave him a searching look while her hands caressed his back.

"I'm not much of a dancer, baby," he murmured, drawing her closer. This was exactly what he'd missed while in Miami. Even though the weather never dropped below seventy-five degrees, the heat he felt lying next to her body made the Florida weather seem freezing cold.

"That's because you're so tense."

He sighed. "We were up until three in the morning and then I had to be back at the table at seven o'clock the next morning."

"Poor baby," Lauren cooed. "We'll just have to make you feel better."

"Uh-huh." Nick gave her a wicked grin.

"So why don't you turn over, big boy?"

Nick opened his eyes slightly to look into Lauren's serious face. "Huh?"

"You heard me, sleepyhead. Roll over onto your stomach." Just to emphasize her command, Lauren tickled him on the rib cage.

"All right, woman." Nick scooted over and then settled back down as he felt Lauren straddle his back.

"And what do you think you're doing?" He attempted to turn his head, but the pressure of Lauren's hands kept his neck still.

"I'm giving you what you need."

"I don't think that'll work in this position, sweetheart." He grinned.

"I meant a massage," she retorted. "Now close your eyes and take a deep breath," she softly instructed.

"You don't have to do this, Lauren."

"But I want to do this." Before she finished the sentence her hands had started their work on his shoulders. Fanning her hands out on his upper back, she used the pads of her fingers and thumbs to moved inward, upward, and outward on Nick's hard muscles.

A soft smile played on her lips. She loved the feel of his muscles under her hands, the heat of his skin. That this man could rock her world one minute and purr like a kitten the next.

She moved slowly to relax his muscles, repeating the movements until the tension dissipated from his shoulders. As her fingers worked their magic and she smoothed out the hard tension in his muscles, she grew more and more aware of his body snug underneath her own. Lauren slid down in the bed and started to work on Nick's lower back.

"Feel good?" she asked twenty minutes later, after she'd progressed down the middle of his back using her knuckle to gently rub along his lower back. Careful to skim along the border of his lower back, she used the tips of her fingernails to stimulate his senses.

"Hey, don't go falling asleep on me, counselor," she warned after not getting a response.

"I'm wide awake, beautiful."

Lauren's lips curled upward in a confident smile. Flipping her hair back over her shoulder, she bent down and using the inside of her forearm began to rub slowly across the indentation that marked the border between his lower back and rear.

"Lauren," Nick breathed heavily.

"Yes?" she murmured.

"Come up here."

"Say please." She laughed huskily.

"Witch," he murmured. It was the truth. Nick couldn't think of a time when he'd been so relaxed and aroused.

Taking her cue, Lauren rubbed her palms up his back and stopped at his neck. Applying a light pressure, she stroked in a circular motion behind his ears and then gently stretched his earlobe. She was about to reach her seventh repetition of the movement when Nick had had enough of the sensual torture. Cursing, he flipped over and rolled Lauren underneath him.

The thin line Nick had been holding on to ever since Lauren had settled herself on his back snapped at the erotic sensation of her whisper in his ear and her skin like a warm blanket on his back. Moving quickly he rolled over and placed himself on top of her.

"Woman, where did you learn to do that?" he asked.

"You liked it?" With a provocative look in her eyes and a wicked smile on her face, she could have been Eve holding out a big red apple.

"You'd best believe it," he said, moving to kiss the hollow of her shoulder.

Lauren felt her breath catch in her throat as Nick's

lips trailed downward toward her breast. "My dance instructor suggested I take a massage class."

Nick looked up into her heavy-lidded gaze and smiled. "Remind me to thank the woman."

When he'd opened his eyes that morning all Nick could think of was how he could tell the woman he loved that he'd deliberately kept her from leaving on her trip. Yet, all the things he'd planned to say got lost in her eyes and in the sensation of her fingernails on the inside of his thighs.

Every rational thought faded as his lips kissed her flesh and the need to bury himself in her warmth grew. He'd wanted to confess, but the touch of her hand on him took all thoughts away and he made love to her as the sun rose in the sky and the rain started to fall lightly to the ground.

While Nick was on his business trip, every morning when she'd gotten up and gone over to the brownstone, Lauren had thought of him. Every color, every cloth, and every paper she'd put away, she missed him. Even Brooklyn had seemed a little less frisky.

The only thing that kept her from getting down in the dumps was the thought of his surprise at the home office she'd put together. She could picture him sitting at the desk typing on the computer or poring over some of the books that lined the shelves in the apricot-cream-colored room.

When dreams came at night, she could only see his face, feel the emptiness of his place in the bed. She could have cheerfully hit herself or killed him for leaving her, for loving her, for forcing her to feel his absence. She felt it the way her grandmother sensed the coming of rain. It was in her bones. His face, his smell, no matter where, would stay with her.

Now that he was back, she'd thought the emotions would go away. But as she stood stretching her hands down toward the hardwood floor, the man still stood at the forefront of her thoughts. Her eyes looked on unfocused as the other women in the class gracefully curved their backs and raised their arms.

"Okay, ladies, shall we get started?" came the voice of her African dance instructor.

Lauren shook her head to clear her thoughts and turned her attention back toward the dance instructor, noticing for the first time that class had not started. Following the looks and whispers of the other dancers, she looked over toward the doorway and her heart stopped to see Nick standing there.

She'd seen more than her fair share of good-looking men in her lifetime, but seeing him barefoot with the African grab just about undid her. The way his lips curled up into a smile and his eyes bored into her sent warm waves up and down her body.

Even if she could have lied to herself before, Lauren couldn't now. She hadn't fallen; she'd dropped and hit hard. She loved Nick, way down deep in her soul. As he walked toward her with that grin on his face, she knew love was trying to kill her once again, but this time she'd die a happy woman only to have his arms around her.

Having left the office early and gone shopping in Harlem to pick up the appropriate outfit, Nick stood in the doorway watching Lauren from the doorway as the class started the second song. He'd heard the beat of the drums coming up the stairs. His eyes zeroed in on the woman he loved.

Her bare foot tapped to the sound of drumming, pounding in tune with the player's hands. She was a bright light of summer in November. Her white peasant blouse topped off a long pale red skirt. A scarf covered her hair, and a small silver cross dangled in the air above her chest.

He'd spent the better part of the day thinking about her and then Alan's phone call had disrupted what could have worked out to be a great day. His mother was going to invite them over for dinner tomorrow night. The weight on his shoulders seemed to have gotten heavier. He'd spent the entire time with Lauren in denial and now his and Alan's best intentions were going to bite them in the butt.

Nick watched as Lauren gestured for him to come inside. Since two women had taken up residence beside her, he walked to the back of the room and stood in a place directly behind Lauren. He joined in the stretching and soft warm-up session and made an attempt to concentrate on the teacher's instructions.

He began to feel his muscles loosen and slightly protest from the heavy use. His breath came faster with the turns and kicks, steps and jumps. The heavy beat of the drums and the sounds of bare feet moving across the floorboards, hands clapping, and the teacher's shouted encouragement filled the room.

Nick spent most of the class enjoying the sight of Lauren shaking her hips to the rhythm of the drums. Then as the beat got into his blood he joined in with the easier patterns. Nick shook his head and concentrated on the instructor as sweat started to bead on his brow.

He watched as Lauren and her fellow classmates not only moved easily through each routine but also did it with such a professional finesse. As the drummers increased the tempo and the instructor kicked it up another notch, Nick struggled to keep up. *I definitely need to get back into jogging,* he thought.

* * *

After two days of relaxation and long wonderful nights of passion, it was time to get back to work. Standing on her tiptoes, Lauren hung the last metal pot on the hooks over the stove. The brownstone kitchen was nearly completed and she couldn't help being proud of the job she'd done. She stepped back and looked over at her lover as he leaned against the wall with his arms crossed

"Looks good, doesn't it?" She smiled.

"Oh, yeah." Nick grinned broadly. She felt her body flush from the heated look he sent her way.

She shot him a mock serious look. "Don't you be getting any ideas over there. We can't be late to dinner; Mrs. Knight's cooking up some of her signature catfish."

Lauren took a step back from the kitchen island and surveyed the newly redone kitchen with pride. "All this and I still have two weeks left on my assignment. Cass will be able to finish up in less than a month."

She leaned back against the countertop and tilted her head. "When all this is finished, you'll have a beautiful home."

"No, Lauren." He shook his head and moved to stand in front of her. "I'll have a beautiful *house,*" he corrected. "I need you here to make this place into a home."

He reached out and tucked a stray lock of hair behind her ear. "I think it's time we talked about our future."

She tensed and took a couple of steps to the left. "I don't."

"Why is that?" Nick looked her in the eyes.

She dropped her gaze and surveyed the floor. "Because there's really nothing to talk about."

Nick reached out and cupped her chin, bringing her eyes level with his own. "You think our relationship amounts to nothing?" he asked incredulously.

Lauren shook her head. "That's not what I meant."

"But it's exactly what you said," he argued quietly.

"Look, Nick, I don't want to discuss this right now."

His voice dripped with sarcasm. "Well, I don't want you leaving me to go and find some foreign Casanova."

Shock brought her body uptight. "What?"

Nick was never one to shy from confrontation and it was way past time they cleared the air. Lauren's future was with him, not on some plane heading to God knows where. Life was short and now that he'd found the woman he didn't want to live without, he was physically, mentally, and emotionally ready to commit to a long-term relationship.

"You heard me . . ." He scowled. Unable to take back his rash declaration, he pushed forward. "I don't want you going on a vacation and picking some stranger off the street."

"How long have you known?" Lauren held herself rigid with betrayal.

"From the beginning. Alan asked for my help the night we bumped into one another at his house."

"It wasn't his place," she said hoarsely. She wasn't as much angry as she was hurt that Alan would betray their friendship.

"Don't get mad at Alan, he was just looking out for you."

"I can look out for myself." She clenched her fingers.

"No, Lauren, you can do bad all by yourself. But you're not alone, baby."

"The house, the renovation . . ." Her voice trailed off.

"I was going to get the stuff done anyway."

"He made you do it," she accused.

"No," he denied. "Alan only pointed out that you were the best person for the job."

"When were you planning to tell me?" She took a step away from him.

He cursed under his breath as her eyes turned colder than the icicles hanging from the eves outside the brownstone. "Never. The last thing I ever wanted was to hurt you."

"Why?"

"Because I love you and I want you here with me," he said simply.

She ignored the last part of his explanation. "No, I want to know why the sudden confession."

"Because Mrs. Knight—"

"Alan's mother," she managed to get through gritted teeth. The anger that had started as a simmer in her stomach kicked into a rolling boil.

"She was not too pleased that Alan and I were keeping you from leaving."

"You were expecting something else?"

"Yeah, Alan thought she'd talk you out of the idea."

She drew in a deep breath as another more insidious idea crept into her mind. The love she felt for him had become less of a miracle and more like a double-edged sword.

"Don't even think it," Nick warned, seeing the look of suspicion in Lauren's eyes. "What's between us has nothing to do with your plans. I wanted you from the moment I saw you by Alan's bedside and I know you love me but you're so afraid of getting hurt you won't give us a chance."

She held out her hand, stopping him from coming too close. "Oh, so that's supposed to justify lying to me?" She turned and started stuffing papers into her briefcase. They'd moved her around like a puppet on a string and it was the easiness of the manipulation that fueled her growing anger.

"I didn't lie, just withheld the truth," he defended.

"You manipulated me. The both of you." She hadn't forgotten about Alan's role in this. She planned to give her friend a piece of her mind.

"We wanted to do what's best for you."

"I decide what's best for me." She opened the hallway closet and roughly pulled her coat off the hanger. "And

I don't appreciate deceit from friends, much less my lover."

"No, you need a good dose of reality. Paul isn't coming back and you aren't going to the grave," he said brutally. "You hold his death in front of you like some kind of shield. And I'm here to tell you it might have worked with other men, but I don't give up, Lauren."

Her head reared back as though she'd been slapped. "How could you?"

"How could I what?" Nick countered, taking a step closer. "Love you? Easy. Want to keep you with me until we're old and surrounded by grandkids? Simple."

"I forgave you once because it was a mistake, but this . . ." It took her breath away to know that their whole relationship was one big fabrication. "This . . ." Her hands were shaking. "This was deliberate and self-ish. You trivialized my goals, ran over my intentions. You tricked me and now you have the nerve to throw Paul's death in my face."

There was little he could say in the face of her hurt. "I'm sorry, Lauren." He tried to take her in his arms.

"No," she said harshly. "Don't touch me."

Lauren gave the man she loved one last evil glare before turning on her heels and heading for the front door. She didn't even take the time to button her coat. Just walked out into the street and hailed the next passing cab.

However glad he was to have gotten everything out in the open, Nick couldn't help cursing as he watched her storm out of the house, leaving both him and Brooklyn to stare at the slamming door. He frowned with anger at the idea that she would think he'd ever hurt her. Bending down, he picked up the cat and headed back to the kitchen.

He'd reached the point that he didn't know what to

do. The sex was great, they were compatible, he loved her, and even though she'd never said the words, he knew Lauren loved him. Nick was used to getting everything and anything he wanted easily, especially where the opposite sex was concerned, but Lauren . . .

He ground his teeth as a headache starting right behind his eyes. The woman messed with him so badly he couldn't tell if he was coming or going. Walking past Tiffany's the other day, he'd seen the perfect engagement ring in the window. All he needed was to pick it up.

He stared unseeingly at the breakfast nook, as doubt filled him. Maybe he was wrong to push her, maybe it was a bad move on his part to mention her ex-fiancé's name, but what was he supposed to do? He'd anticipated she would react badly to finding out about his role in the scheme to keep her from leaving on her husband-hunting trip around the globe. But the way she'd looked at him when he mentioned her ex-fiancé's name . . . He'd made a colossal tactical error and he hoped she'd forgive him for his foolishness.

Not one to dwell on a problem, but concentrate on the solution, Nick quelled his negative thoughts. A grin appeared on his face. Damn, Lauren was beautiful when she was mad. His body tightened at the fire in her dark eyes.

Nodding, he put Brooklyn down on the floor and reached over to grab a can of cat food. Taking a glance at the half-finished kitchen, he smiled. It might take a while, but he'd win her back, he mused. Yep, he'd have to do some fancy footwork and show Ms. Hughes about passion and how a Harlem-bred brother loves.

Eleven

"Thank you again, Mr. Randolph. I cannot believe you did it."

Nick walked around his desk and extended his arm upward and shook the young man's hand. At seven feet two inches, the Norwegian college senior towered over most of his classmates. Jacob Yousav was on his way to becoming one of the best point guards the NBA had ever seen.

"Remember, you can always change your mind," Nick added. "The NCAA draft rules give you thirty days to back out of any deals without losing your amateur eligibility."

"I will telephone my family tonight, but I have dreamed of nothing but basketball since I was eight years old. I have the chance to play as Michael Jordan did at the 1984 Olympics in Los Angeles. My father took us to see the games. I will never forget seeing the American ninety-six-to-sixty-five victory over Spain in the gold medal game. At only twenty-one years of age, Jordan scored twenty points and led the team to victory. Mr. Randolph, I will play like that." His eyes took on a feverish glow.

Nick grinned, remembering the time his eyes held that same fire. "We'll test the waters, Jacob, but I'm pretty sure that after watching your performance last season, I have no doubts that you'll be a top pick in the drafts."

"Is there anything else I can do, Mr. Randolph?"

"Just keep the grades up." He watched as the young man put on his jacket. "There's a car downstairs ready to take you back to the hotel. Any plans for the weekend?"

"My older brother is attending a conference at the United Nations. We will go to the Statue of Liberty today."

"Well, enjoy." Nick led the young man to the elevator and then went back into his office and shut the door. Another satisfied client and future blue-chip player. Sitting down in his leather chair, he turned on the desk lamp, determined to read.

It was only after the light in the office started to dim that Nick looked down at the latest edition of his favorite sports law journal and realized that he'd been reading the same article for the past half hour.

Lauren, her name seemed to whisper in his ear.

He'd thought that he'd give her a day or two to cool off and then she'd be willing to talk. Not happening. He shook his head. She wouldn't answer his calls, return his e-mails, or come by the brownstone. He could have dealt with the silent treatment if she were coming by the brownstone. At least that way he would have been able to see her.

Nick's first thought was to talk to Alan and see if his friend could get Cassandra to put in a good word for him. But it seemed as though his lady wouldn't talk to him either.

All he thought about was her face, her voice, her smile, her scent. He hadn't had a good night's sleep since she slammed out of the house. He wasn't one to wallow in self-pity, but he didn't know what to do.

"What do women want?" he said out loud, throwing the periodical down on his desk. He'd found himself pondering the age-old question. Better yet, what did Lauren want? Unable to sit still any longer, Nick stood and started pacing. He did his best work wearing a path in front of his office desk. What a tangled mess he had on his hands.

What could Lauren need that he couldn't give her? he mused. Looking down at his fingers, Nick ticked off the potential answers one by one: love, sex, money, marriage, kids, and family. He could give it all to her, but he still felt he was missing something. He wished she would talk to him, tell him what to do, what to fix. He didn't have any idea about what to do in these situations. How do you negotiate when the other person won't pick up the phone, answer the door, or hit the reply button?

Now they'd had their first fight and he didn't have a clue as to how to make it up to her. Nick strode across the hall and into the firm's library. Most of the firm's attorneys had long since cleared out for their homes in Connecticut or New Jersey. There he stood surrounded by thousands of law books, but none held the answers he needed.

For a second he thought about giving Will a call and then decided against it. Ever since he'd made the mistake of letting his ambition get the better of his common sense, his older brother had been silent on the subject of women. Nick was close to both of his brothers, but Will was one Nick went to when he needed advice. And boy, did he need it now!

Sitting down in the high-backed leather chair, he closed his eyes and sighed in frustration. It wasn't as though he'd killed the cat or something. Little Brooklyn had taken over the house; all Nick did was live there.

The only thing he'd wanted to do was keep Lauren close, to keep her from leaving, and she acted as though he'd committed a crime. All those thoughts swirled through his head but the more he tried to understand her, the more his head started to ache.

"The woman's going to give me migraines," he muttered.

Three hours later in the comfort of his newly renovated den, Nick knew he'd hit rock bottom when he lost the National Championship and the Super Bowl. Looking over at his older brother, he finished off his beer and sat back on the sofa.

"So how's business?" he asked casually, dropping the game controller to the floor.

"Slow," Will replied. "Market volume always slows down the closer it gets to the winter holidays."

"That's good," Nick replied. "Less stress, right?"

"Of course, so why don't you stop beating around the bush and tell me what's going on?"

"What makes you think something's up?" Nick asked, picking up a bread stick.

Will sighed. He hated it when Nick switched into his "something's wrong and I want to talk about it but I don't want to come out and say it" mood. "The New York Giants are playing the Atlanta Falcons up at the stadium, little brother."

"So?" Nick shifted on the leather sofa. Here was something else he'd forgotten about, the football game.

"Your favorite football team is playing a home game and instead of sitting in the owner's box snacking on caviar and lobster, you're losing video games and eating chicken wings, nachos, and bread sticks. This is food only a man with lady troubles would eat."

For the first time since Lauren had stormed out the

door a genuine smile appeared on his face. "Nothing wrong with spending time with my older brother."

"Yeah, right," Will sarcastically replied. "Are you ready to tell me what happened?"

Nick watched as Will turned off the video game system. His shoulders slumped. It took him two more beers and a plate of nachos to spill the entire story.

"So you lied to her," Will stated bluntly.

"Technically," Nick started.

"Stop." Will raised his beer. "This involves a woman, right?"

Nick nodded slowly.

"Okay, then there's no 'technically' about it. You lied plus she found out equals she's angry and you're miserable."

"If you want to put it that way." Nick reached over and grabbed a Buffalo wing and dipped it into the blue cheese dressing.

"Bro, there's no other way. I thought you were smarter than that."

"Look, I got a law degree, not a Ph.D. on women. I thought I was doing the right thing."

"Well, now that we know you were dead wrong, what are you going to do about it?"

He shrugged and bit into another nacho. "Wait until she cools off, I guess."

"Didn't you tell me she was planning to leave the country?"

"For three months," Nick answered.

Will's brow creased. "You sure you want to wait until she gets back? Women have long memories and if you don't work this out before she leaves, she might come back but not to your waiting arms."

"What we've got is a bit stronger than . . ." His voice trailed off.

"Nick," Will interrupted. "All the money, success, and

pride don't mean much when you're coming home to an empty condo filled with things she left behind. Things you can't stand to throw away because you're hoping she'll surprise you by walking back through the door."

"Man, I'm sorry." Nick put his hand on his brother's shoulder. The last thing he wanted to do was bring up bad memories.

"Yeah, well, so am I. Mainly because it was my mistake and I'm having a hell of a time living with it."

"Have you talked to her?"

"No." Will shook his head. "Toni's moved on with her life as she should have."

"How can you be so sure?" Nick could see that his older brother was still in pain.

Will took a pull of beer. "Look, little brother, I can't go back and correct my mistakes. She was the best thing that walked into and out of my life. Don't make my same mistakes."

Nick sat back on the sofa and nodded. "I've learned from my life in law that mistakes aren't bad things. What really gets you is if you don't learn from them."

"And what have you learned this time?" Will asked.

Nick lifted his hand as though he were placing it on top of a Bible. "To tell the truth, the whole truth, and nothing but the truth."

An hour later after his older brother had returned to New Jersey, Nick stood outside the work-in-progress that used to be one of the brownstone's bathrooms. Every pro had the games when he played like a rookie. He'd run the football in some tight situations, but every time when the pressure increased he'd held the line. He stared fixedly at the unfinished floor. If he couldn't get through Lauren's defenses, he'd just have to do an end run around them.

* * *

She'd woken up hurt and angry three days straight. That Nick could keep something like this from her hurt, but his accusation that she still grieved over Paul cut her to the core. He'd been wrong of course. She was afraid of losing him, terrified that she'd wake up one morning with the knowledge that she'd never see him again.

Yet, she still struggled with leftover fury. Every time she thought of what they'd done, Lauren felt like the world's biggest fool. Only Alan's mother with her chocolate-laced coffee and homemade banana nut bread had kept her from killing him the moment he opened the front door.

She sat across from Alan and his mother at the kitchen table.

"Look, Lauren—" Alan started.

"Alan," Marva warned, sending him a glance. "Don't say a word. What you've done to poor Lauren is unforgivable."

"But . . ." he floundered at his mother's unexpected scolding.

"But nothing." Marva put down her coffee cup. "She could be at some fancy resort, sitting on the beach with a nice tall, dark, and handsome man right now."

Alan's woebegone face moved Lauren to pity. "It really wasn't that kind of vacation."

"That doesn't matter." Marva waved, cutting the young woman another slice of pound cake.

She didn't miss the way Lauren softened toward Alan. She'd called them the "terrible two" when they were kids. Lauren would come to his defense. The littlest child on the block would always be there to help her oldest son even if his younger sister wouldn't waste a second before running home to tell on her brother.

"What they both did was wrong, but I can only take up for this knucklehead." Marva gestured toward her oversize son, who at that moment was slumped down in his chair like a prisoner on death row.

On the outside, she was as stone-faced as a Catholic schoolteacher. But on the inside, Marva was cackling with glee. "Now when are you leaving and is there anything you need?"

She shook her head. "I'm expecting the tickets to come any day now."

"Wait, Lauren," Alan burst out. "All this is my fault. You can't blame Nick."

She schooled her features so as not to reveal the hurt she felt when Alan mentioned Nick's name. She'd never felt more lonely and cold than she had the past couple of nights. She'd tried everything from her favorite foods, to hot chocolate, and warm, relaxing baths, but nothing seemed to warm her up. "And why not? He went along with you, didn't he?"

"Yeah, but it's deeper than that. The man loves you."

She folded her arms and sat back staring at Alan. "Really? If that were true, then he couldn't have lied to me."

"He wanted to spend time with you." Alan tilted his head and gave her a pleading look, which Lauren ignored.

"Then he should have asked," she fired back, steeling her heart.

"That's right." Marva looked at Lauren. The wicked gleam in her eyes could have set the whole brownstone on fire. She was going to play devil's advocate even if it killed her. Lauren needed to get some of that anger out so she could move on back to the love Marva had seen in the girl's eyes.

"Mama," Alan eyed her over his mug before turning back to an unsympathetic Lauren. "I asked you to stay and you told me no. What kind of chance did Nick have?"

"A pretty damn good one before the other night." Lauren took a big bite of cake.

"Sorry," she muttered from behind her hand after catching Marva's sharp glance. Each passing day she'd spent with Nick had sent thoughts of her vacation further and further back into the recesses of her mind.

Alan reached across the table and grabbed her hands. "Lauren, you're like a little sister to me. Life has hurt you in some of the worst ways possible, but I've seen you and Nick apart and I've seen you together. It doesn't take glasses to see that you two got something special. Nick feels the same way about you that I feel for my Cassie. The thought of her being mad because of something I'd done makes me feel like the day big Tyrone kicked me in the stomach."

Lauren couldn't help smiling at the childhood memory. "Alan, I can't handle loving Nick as much as I do. I don't think I'm that strong."

"You took on the biggest bully on our block and you're saying you aren't strong enough?" His eyes twinkled.

"Not like that. Emotionally."

"Well, emotionally Nick is a wreck and you aren't too far behind. The boy is miserable without you."

"Well, let him be miserable. You men have been making my baby miserable for the past month," Marva cheered.

"No," Lauren countered. "I wasn't unhappy at all. I love Nick, I don't want to hurt him."

"Then forgive him and take a chance on love, Lauren," Alan urged, seizing the opportunity. "For the first time in my life I'm in love and I have you to thank for that. None of us want you to be unhappy."

Lauren stared into the milky depths of her coffee. "I'll have to think about it."

"Could you think fast? Cass won't talk to me until she gets your approval."

"What? You have got to be kidding."

Alan shook his head and reached out to pour another cup of coffee. "Mama, am I kidding?"

"No, he isn't," Marva confirmed. "That friend of yours is something else. Had this boy practically begging for her to scream at him and she still didn't say a word."

"She did that?" Lauren laughed. Knowing how hard it was for Cassandra to bite her tongue, she thought it must have been close to impossible for her not to speak with Alan.

"Yes, she sure did. Taught you a lesson, didn't she, Alan?"

"Mama." Alan stopped stirring his coffee. "This is serious. The woman I love won't speak to me, my attorney isn't returning my calls, and my best friend looks like she wants to kick me to the North Pole. Can I get a little motherly support here?"

"I'll talk to Cass tonight." Lauren got up and walked over to the other side of the table and bent down to give Alan a hug. She wished she could talk to her older brother, Nathan, as easily as she spoke with Alan. Their conversations had become more and more infrequent since her move to New York.

"I owe you, Lauren."

Looking over his head and catching Marva's wink, Lauren smiled. "Yes, you do."

All week Alan's words ran through her mind. *Take a chance on love.* After showering and getting dressed, Lauren entered the kitchen and poured herself a cup of coffee.

As she was looking over at the overnight package on the kitchen table, a frown formed on her lips. She should have been happy or at least excited—she'd bought her luggage, gotten her visas, and treated herself to an impulsive shopping spree. But even the sight of her airline tickets and travel itinerary didn't lift her spirits.

One week and she would be stepping onto a Morocco-bound plane, beginning a round-the-world three-month adventure. Nice hotels, exotic restaurants, museums, castles, and secluded beaches. Lauren finished the coffee and picked up her briefcase, ready to go to work.

An hour later she sat at her desk and looked through a set of photographs for a third time.

"Lauren." Ann peeked her head in the door.

"Yes?" She looked up from the color samples.

"I've got Henri on line two."

"What's up?"

"He mentioned something about the master bathtub not fitting."

Lauren put her pen down and smiled before picking up the phone. She had confidence that the French contractor would be able to finish the necessary changes to Nick's brownstone without her supervision.

"Tell me, Henri."

"Lauren, how can you expect me to fit this beautiful tub into this small corner? It is sacrilege, I cannot do it."

She rubbed her brow. "I measured the space three times. The tub will fit fine in the right-hand corner nearest to the window."

"Oh, that is not the only problem. How am I to install tiles when I do not have all the materials I need? I am missing tiles. This is quite unlike you, Lauren."

She sighed and sat back. "Give me an hour. I'm on my way over."

"I shall be waiting."

She put the phone down and gave in to the temptation of laying her head on the desk. The day just kept getting better, she thought sarcastically.

* * *

Lauren exited the train in Brooklyn thirty minutes later. *I don't love him,* she lied to herself, getting out of the subway car. *It's just the sex and confusion.* She climbed the stairs, shivering with the strong blasts of cold air. *Old-fashioned case of passion,* she continued to lie to herself.

But as she trudged down the leaf-lined Park Slope sidewalk remembering the way he had held her on the uptown train, she could no longer fool herself. For the past few weeks, she'd seen Nick and his brownstone more than she'd seen her own apartment, and the last couple of days she'd been miserable and the nights she'd tossed and turned herself into a restless sleep.

She had loved her father with all her girlish heart only to visit his early grave to lay down flowers. Paul was a dream come true, her dream of happily ever after, and she hadn't hesitated at the opportunity to be his wife. Her future had been full of possibilities until the night all her hopes burned to the ground and dreams turned to ashes.

She knew Nick Randolph would give it all back but only if she had the courage to take a chance.

Lauren noticed the quiet the moment she entered into the brownstone and closed the door. *Oh my word,* she thought upon finding the foyer of the brownstone transformed by candlelight. She walked into the living room to see a warm blaze in the fireplace, the glow of flickering light on crackling flames bathing the area in a seductive glow.

"I love you, Lauren." Nick's sudden pronouncement filled the otherwise silent air.

She turned around slowly to see Nick standing in the doorway. Her eyes ate him up as her skin tingled with a dormant hunger of a passion denied. The sight of his strong body and the confident set of his shoulders. She could still feel the touch of his broad fingers in her hair stroking the curve of her neck, the searing heat of his lips.

It was as if he'd never left her side. A cloud passed over her face as she remembered the reason for their being apart.

Nick drew in a breath. Something way down deep inside him responded to the sight of Lauren standing before the fireplace. He continued, "The last thing I ever wanted to do is hurt you, beautiful."

It was the closest thing he could come to an apology. He'd spent the past three days second-guessing himself only to discover that if he'd had the chance to do it all over again, he would take whatever risks necessary to have Lauren in his home, in his heart, and in his bed.

He looked at her as she stood in the middle of his half-empty living room staring at him, still wearing her black leather coat and red scarf. Aiming the remote control, he pressed play, activating the portable stereo on top of the mantel. A riff of saxophone rose to the ceiling and bounced off the walls.

Lauren gave him a serious look. "So where is Henri?"

"Probably back at his apartment opening my best bottle of red wine and whispering sweet French nothings to his newest girlfriend."

"Oh." She dropped her gaze and turned back to the fireplace. Holding her hands out toward the flickering flames, she realized her hands were shaking.

Moving to stand beside her, Nick reached out and took her wrist and brought it to his face and rubbed it against his cheek. Lauren watched as he tasted the inside of her wrist, his tongue lapping at her furiously beating pulse. A quiver ripped through her body as her lips parted slightly to emit a sigh.

"I miss you, beautiful."

The icy walls that had slowly crept around her heart during the cold nights alone in her bed melted in the wake of his words. As her shaking subsided, so went her reservations as her whole body seemed to relax with a peace she'd never known.

Nick cupped her chin and moved it until he could look down into her beautiful visage. As her eyelashes swept upward, he saw the unguarded emotion simmering in the depths of her eyes. It might have seemed like a small gesture, but the feel of her plum-colored nails sliding over his jaw let him believe again.

Lauren gazed at Nick's handsome face, wanting to imprint the image on her soul. She traced the shape of his jaw, enjoying the prickle of stubble underneath the pads of her fingers. This was the face she'd seen behind her eyelids at night. His lips, his piercing brown eyes and angled cheekbones. She wrapped her arms around his neck and pulled his mouth within centimeters of her own. As he held her gaze, the vulnerability she saw held her still.

"I love you," she whispered into the heated air between their wanting mouths, and before he could give voice to the response she saw in his eyes, Lauren kissed him. She pressed her lips to his and put all her doubts and fears, passion and feeling into the kiss. What she could not say with words she would show. She would bury herself deep within his soul and warm herself in his arms always.

They took their time that night. Lauren writhed and moaned as Nick painted her red with passion. The way he said her name was framed with magic. He moaned her name like a smoke-shadowed jazz club. The way the blues poured out of a singer's mouth and washed over the microphone, filling the room, taking the oxygen out of the air. Melancholy long notes turned into razor-sharp, short staccato beats as he came into her body.

The rhythmic music of his thrusts cut her to the bone and stabbed her through the heart. Over and over, her body danced to his beat, arched to his tune, only to shatter the moment he nipped her throat, and pleasure broke over her body, making her hair stand on end.

Words, promises, "I love yous" crowded in her throat, spilled off her tongue, and clapped in her ears as wetness pooled behind tightly closed eyelids.

As they lay nude covered only by the flickering candlelight, Nick looked down at Lauren's dreamy face. The love he made to her that night shouted, "This is the real thing, the good stuff, and no matter how far you run, you'll always want to come back to his arms, back to his heart."

Lauren snuggled into his chest as he rolled away, wanting to keep him close, keep him warm inside her. As sleep slid silently into the bed and Nick kissed her cheek before cuddling into the nape of her neck, Lauren felt like giving up. Surely love would succeed in killing her this time.

"I'm not him, Lauren."

She shifted in his arms, suddenly glad that the fire had long since died out, leaving the room in darkness.

"Who?"

"Paul. I won't leave you ever."

"I know you're not him, Nick," she whispered, her voice soft with sleep.

"You sure?"

"No," she admitted more to herself than to him. Knowledge sat like a stone in her heart. Lauren knew he'd leave her bleeding, just like her daddy, just like Paul.

Nick woke slowly the next morning and looked over his shoulder to see if Lauren was still asleep. Seeing the empty space beside him, he quickly threw off the covers, put on a pair of pants, and hurried downstairs.

The smell of coffee met him on the bottom stair. Following his nose toward the kitchen, Nick stopped dead in his tracks at the sight that greeted his eyes. He loved seeing Lauren in nothing but his sheets, but the woman could wear the hell out of a man's shirt.

He couldn't decide what he wanted more. To take her back to bed or the coffee cup in her hand. Maybe he'd do both. When he came upon Lauren reaching into the kitchen cabinets with nothing on those long legs of hers, he had some serious doubts.

"You know, you made this too easy," he said, coming up behind her and pulling her back toward him. The feel of her round bottom sent his body temperature up forty degrees.

"What are you talking about?" She giggled.

"You've made it easier for us in the future—there'll be no need to redecorate after you move in."

His sheer confidence took her breath away even as it aroused her. "Oh, yeah?" She turned and raised an eyebrow. "What if I wanted to live at my place?"

"Then we'll have two places to make love in." He grinned. "I like the idea of spending my lunchtime at your apartment."

"Really?"

"Uh-huh." He placed kisses on her long, slender neck. "Maybe get a bite or two before heading back to the office."

"There's nothing in my fridge."

"That's fine because all I want is what I'm holding right now." To prove his words, he pulled her tight against him.

"You're insatiable," she murmured.

"No, just hungry, beautiful. Now how about we go back upstairs?"

"How about we fix some breakfast?" She slipped from his arms. "This woman can't live on love alone."

"Well, this man can feast on you, darling." He nibbled Lauren's neck and held tight as she laughed.

* * *

"Marry me," Nick whispered in Lauren's ear some time after their second round of lovemaking.

The moment the words left his mouth he felt as if he'd kicked a winning field goal with five minutes left in overtime. Lauren had made a home of his empty brownstone and his waiting heart. Life hadn't been the same since she walked through the doors, and he didn't want to let go of the wonder she brought to his days and the fire she brought to his nights. Nick never minced words or wasted time. It took red and blue to make purple; now he had to have Lauren to have happiness.

Her body stiffened as Nick's proposal echoed in her mind. Her breath caught in a strangled sob as a part of her wanted to turn in his arms and happily consent to be his wife. However, the thought of dedicating herself to him sent a ball of fear from her stomach to her throat.

"What's wrong?" His voice was a soft caress over her skin.

She opened her eyes and stared at the window curtains. "I can't marry you, Nick."

He pulled back from her as though he'd been burned. "I thought you'd forgiven me."

"I have."

"Then why won't you marry me?"

She looked at him and Nick could see the glimmer of unshed tears in her eyes.

"What is it, Lauren?"

She rolled out of the bed and walked out of the bedroom and into the bathroom. Her breath coming rapidly, Lauren leaned against the closed door and let her head fall as tears streamed down her face. Her moment of courage had all but ended with his proposal of marriage.

Half of her wanted to run out the door and head straight for the safety of her apartment. But her love for Nick kept her still even as the fear beat at the back of her mind. Lauren sniffed and wiped away her tears as one truth emerged from her thoughts. Two was company and three was a crowd. Fear had no place in the relationship between them.

"I'm leaving," Lauren announced in the quiet kitchen. She'd made the decision in the shower. Nick deserved better than a scared little girl. She knew in her heart of hearts that he'd never leave her. That was why she would be the one to go.

Her announcement caught him with a coffee mug halfway to his mouth. He put it down with a bang.

"I'm not your father or Paul, Lauren. I love you just like they did, but I'm not going to disappear."

She stood next to the table, close enough to see the tick in his cheek but far enough away so that she would have to reach out to smooth the worry lines from his brow.

"My head understands, but in my heart I'm not sure I can give the kind of commitment you and I both deserve." She smiled sadly.

"You survived, beautiful. You're alive and we're in love. Draw that into your heart and when you have doubts, lean on me, don't run out on me." Nick got up and went to her.

She curled her arms around him. "I love you. I love you and Brooklyn so much I can't see straight and it scares me to death."

"I'm not leaving you and I'll never let you go."

"I need some time alone." Lauren was amazed at the sound of her own calm voice.

He rubbed his head. "Is this because I asked you to marry me?"

"Yes." She laid her cheek against his chest. "I caught myself looking for a way to kick you out of my heart even though I know that you've made that impossible." She'd wanted to grab hold of something to keep herself from being happy with him.

"Damn straight," he growled. "I'm in your blood, like you're in mine."

"I know, but I need you to let me out of the contract early, Nick. I need to go away for a while and get some things sorted out."

"No," he said roughly. First, she said she wouldn't marry him. Now, she wanted to leave. "I'd do anything for you, Lauren. Adopt a stray cat, paint the walls, and let you sleep on my side of the bed. But this is pushing it."

Her eyes filled with unshed tears at hearing the pain in his voice. "This is pulling me apart. I love you, but I'm not going to lie and say I don't have doubts and fears. You deserve better. *We* deserve better. I've fallen so deep that I don't know which way is up. All I know is that a part of me, the part that's terrified of you, wants out and I need to come to peace with that."

"Then let me in, Lauren. I want to go down with you. I want to pull you into my heart because you have mine, beautiful. You can't say you love a man and then tell him you're leaving."

"But I can't say I love a man and still have reservations. I'm not leaving you, Nick. This is something that I have to do for me."

"And it's selfish."

"Yes, you're right." She nodded. "But it's something I need. I don't expect you to like it or even understand, but I couldn't leave you even if I wanted to, Nick. I'm planning on leaving behind that part of me that's afraid so when I come back there'll be no doubts."

"How long?" He pulled away from her and put some space between them. He felt like a yo-yo. This morning he woke up and everything was as it should be. Now,

Lauren threatened to pull up the foundation of his new-found happiness.

"Two weeks, maybe three." She faltered.

The poker face that served him well as an attorney slipped smoothly into place. He'd put everything on the table and none of it mattered. Lauren still planned to leave. Not saying another word, Nick turned around and walked out of the room.

Twelve

As the plane took off down the runway, Nick closed his eyes and relived the conversation he'd had with Alan the day before. Instead of letting Lauren's absence and the onset of the holiday season get him down, he'd met his friend at an exclusive health club.

"You know, I saw something on a sweatshirt when Cass and I were walking through Union Square the other day," Alan had said through clenched teeth as he exercised his injured knee.

"What did it say?" Nick had asked.

"If you love something, set it free. If it doesn't come back to you, hunt it down and kill it."

His arm stopped in midcurl. "Are you suggesting that I kill Lauren?"

"No, all I'm saying is if the mountain won't come to Mohammed, then Nicholas Randolph should go to the mountain."

Nick put down the hand weight. He knew from the copy of Lauren's travel itinerary that she would be in Marrakech, Morocco, for the week. "In this case the mountain happens to be ten hours and an ocean away."

"So?" Alan finished a repetition.

"I've got your endorsement renewal contracts on the table, the preliminary draft notifications are coming out . . ."

His best friend picked up his towel and wiped his head. "When was the last time you had a vacation?"

Alan's question had lingered in his mind all the way back to Brooklyn. It had been far too long since he'd had a real vacation, a relaxing trip that didn't include his cellular phone, laptop, and a briefcase full of documents.

Nick was brought out of his reverie by the captain announcing that they would be turning off the fasten-seat-belts sign as soon as they reached their cruising altitude of 36,000 feet. The very next morning after that conversation with Alan, Nick had picked up the phone and called his travel agent. By the Friday evening, he'd been packed and ready to go.

Turning toward the window, he watched New York's shimmering skyline disappear as the plane headed up into the clouds. Nick looked down at the black velvet ring box he gripped in his left hand. He was ready to prove that love was stronger than pride. He only hoped that love could conquer Lauren's fears as well.

Two days after telling Nick she was leaving, Lauren stepped off the plane into a new world. Morocco, a country of twenty-four million, 65 percent Arab, 35 percent Berber, and 100 percent beautiful. This was to be the start of a journey she'd spent so many weeks planning. The size of California, bordered by the Atlantic Ocean to the west and the Mediterranean Sea to the north. Algeria stood vigil to the east while the desert spread out to the south.

She'd come to the oldest city on the northern part of Africa to wander and buy. Lauren planned to spend her evenings in Marrakech drifting through the city square watching it come alive with acrobats, dancers, snake charmers, and musicians. At daybreak she would head out to explore the busy marketplace and the narrow streets of the city.

Djemma El Fna, the Times Square of Marrakech, was a place where treasures lined endless tables and rugs. Amulets, rugs, embroidery, handwoven baskets, leather, pottery, and tile. The souk, as her guide called it, was a market, a vast complex of covered streets and alleys that rambled north through the city.

The day after tomorrow, she was to go into rug shops to be served endless glasses of mint tea as merchants brought brightly covered mats woven by nimble fingers of young native women. Eager to purchase something upon her arrival in the city, she couldn't resist buying a handmade caftan from a small stall close to the hotel.

The guidebook spoke of paradise-like weather in Morocco. But it didn't come close to describing the country's warm days and cool evenings, the scent of night-flowering jasmine, courtyards with splashing fountains and shimmering lanterns. A hidden oasis thick with wildflowers, orchids, and swimming pools like lakes. Yet in all the beauty, something was missing and she knew what it was even though she didn't want to admit it.

Lauren woke the first morning to the Muslim call to worship. The muezzin's call resounded from the tall temple tower. She'd groaned out loud when she'd gotten up. For all the comfort of the beautiful bed, she hadn't slept well at all.

Here it was the second day of her round-the-world adventure, and she was heavy-eyed from a night of little to no sleep. Blaming it on jet lag, she put her guidebook back into her day-pack and continued to trudge up the steep path to sun-bleached battlements in the early morning sunshine.

The attendants at the palace gate had been half asleep as she'd walked through the ornate entranceway. She glided through the outer precincts of the grand estate where Muslim kings and queens and nobles of the royal courts once treaded. The air of mystery and romance still clung to the walls. She lingered in the courtyards and halls until she walked into the heart of the palace, the harem. Each different-sized room she visited accentuated the Moroccan architectural motifs she'd studied in school.

Lauren had wanted to throw herself into the moment and the place. Soon, she knew the building would be crowded with tourists from all different parts of the world, but for the moment the halls stood empty but for the sound of intermittent footsteps and the gurgling of water. Yet even as she stood entranced as water splashed delicately from sculpted fountains, she was unable to muster any sense of required admiration.

Pillars rose from cool marble floors and met sculpted arches. Lauren looked up at the thousands of intricately carved honeycomb-shaped cells of the dome overhead, then to her right. While arched windows allowed a picturesque vision of the snowy heights of the Atlas Mountains and the scent of rose gardens and orange blossoms lay heavy in the room, she wanted to see Nick's face, hear his voice, and feel the warmth of his smile.

That evening Lauren bypassed the temptation to order room service and decided to go out instead. Hoping to lift her spirits, she put on a long burgundy dress and wore it with her favorite pair of silver earrings and an emerald pendant. She went down to the lobby of the hotel and was speaking with the concierge about recommended restaurants when someone tapped her on the shoulder.

"You wouldn't happen to be looking for a dinner partner, by chance, would you?"

Raising a delicate eyebrow, Lauren turned to look at the stranger. At first she'd thought he was British, but upon closer examination of his rugged face she recognized that the man's reddish brown color was a more permanent tan versus a vacation one. Australian, she surmised.

"Yes, I am." Her response was rather cool.

"Well, then, Connor Burrows at your service." He tipped an imaginary hat at her.

Lauren couldn't help the giggle that escaped her throat. She shook his outstretched hand. "Lauren Hughes."

"American?"

"You guessed it."

"I'm from Sydney, myself."

"That must have been a long flight," she commented.

"Not that long. I came on holiday from a company in London and I've been here with nothing but a bunch of French and German tourists for the past week."

"Sounds awful," she teased.

He wagged his eyebrows. "It's a bloody nightmare. I thought I'd have to spend another dinner bored stiff talking to myself when I heard your voice."

"Madame," the concierge interrupted. "The car is out front."

"I have reservations at the best restaurant in Marrakech," Connor tempted.

Lauren looked from the concierge's stone face back to the Australian's grinning one. "Best in Marrakech?"

"Absolutely." He grinned.

Deciding to throw caution to the wind, she let the big Australian escort her outside to the waiting transport and the promise of a wonderful dinner.

"There is no love sincerer than the love of food," Connor assured her after they were seated in the exclusive eating establishment.

"Did you come up with that yourself?" Lauren smiled for the first time in three days.

"No way. Some other brilliant bloke came up with that."

"Why does it have to be a man? Maybe it was a woman." Lauren started on one of the eight appetizers laid out before them.

"No, dear girl. Only a man could love food so much. You'd think we invented the stuff."

She quickly discovered that the man led with his stomach even though he was as skinny as a bean. Connor was an avid food lover and amateur chef. He didn't give a flying bat about the history or the buildings. After spending half a year under Britain's cloudy skies and constant rain, he'd come to Morocco for the weather and the food.

The meal, in the Moroccan way, was substantial, relentless, and delicious. A volley of salads came, then a tagine or chicken, stewed in lemon and olives, and then a mound of couscous. It was more than her stomach could bear.

Connor continued to extol the virtues of the dinner. "This place offers dishes from all over Morocco, particularly those from here in Marrakech and Fes. They've got a right strong tradition of cuisine."

Lauren covered her mouth to hide a yawn. "There certainly was a royal quality to those large servings."

Connor's eyes studied her svelte frame. "Why, you barely ate enough to feed a starving chookie."

Lauren have a blank look.

"Chookie is Australian for chicken," he clarified.

"Connor." She let out an extravagated sigh. "If memory serves me right we finished the chicken on the second course."

She laughed as he patted his nonexistent stomach and leaned back on the opposite divan. "You know, you could be right."

After most of the dishes had been cleared from the

table, the waiters in fezzes and djellabas produced dessert dishes like magicians from round platters, to a background timp of drums and a thrum of guitar. Faced with multiple sweets and puddings, Lauren simply reclined and used the best of the divan.

"You don't seem to be enjoying this virtual feast we have here, friend." Connor pointed at her empty dessert plate.

Lauren watched as her dining companion proceeded to pop a fresh-baked pastry into his mouth.

"I'm taking a rest," she lied. Truthfully she wasn't hungry for what lay on the table. She wanted something that didn't come on the menu and that was Nick Randolph.

"Look, Lauren, I may just have met you but I'm not blind."

"What do you mean?" She put down her water glass.

"The only reason a lady as pretty as you is alone and not eating has to be because of some bloke."

"That obvious?" She sighed.

"Only to those of us versed in the signs. I've been there a time or two myself. So what happened? Did he leave you for an Italian lasagna?"

Lauren had to think for a moment. All the reasons she'd had for taking her trip seemed trivial at the moment. "He asked me to marry him."

"That's bloody fantastic," Connor exclaimed.

"And I couldn't give him an answer," she finished.

"Oh." Connor's smile disappeared. "In love with someone else, are you?"

"No, that's not possible." She smiled. "He's the one for me. I thought that a little time away would help me settle some things."

"And you're settled now?"

The corners of her mouth curled upward. "Yes, I am. I just hope he'll have me back."

Connor lifted his hand and signaled for the server to

bring over a fresh pot of tea. "I believe this calls for a toast."

Lauren watched as the tea was poured into the serving pot twice and then returned. The server then raised the pot five feet above the small tray of glasses and poured. Lauren could have clapped at the performance. The man was so good, not a drop spilled outside his target.

Mint tea was to Moroccans what wine was to the French. It was served when people met, when they were together, and when they said good-bye. She had quickly discovered that the green tea, mint leaves, and sugar drink was an easy addiction.

Connor raised his petite gold-trimmed glass.

Lauren sat up and raised hers as well. "To good food and happy lives."

Connor added, "To the future bride."

After returning to the hotel, they exchanged e-mail addresses and phone numbers along with promises of drinks when one of them was in the other's city. Lauren returned to her hotel room, kicked off her shoes, and started packing.

She reminded herself that she would have to send a special thank-you gift to Mitzi. The travel agent had booked her into a beautiful room. The comforts of the modern age blended skillfully with the traditional Moroccan style of cedar and antiques.

Her suite was elegant but the bedroom decorated with paintings, tapestries, and local objects was worth the trip. The iron bed lay at the center of the room. Weaved with colorful percale, a cloth twice as silky as cotton, it made sleeping into a decadent luxury and she loved waking to the smell of the world-famous white roses of Marrakech.

Brown doorways and white designed arches. Tea service at noon. The Moorish-style bathrooms with silver basins, marble floors, and large bathtubs, access to the upstairs terrace.

The next evening greeted Lauren as she looked over the white-washed terrace listening to the haunting melodies of the musicians and singers. Lord, she hoped Nick would hear her out, she thought. She was scheduled to leave on the first nonstop flight back to New York the next morning. The look on his face as he had kissed her good-bye sat like a stone in her stomach.

The hotel was located in the old part of the city. She could look over and see the labyrinth alleyways and rampart walls that had guarded Marrakech for centuries.

The setting North African sun cast a reddish gold film over the city of stone buildings while bathing her in its gentle warmth. Her heart wasn't in it. No matter how hard she pushed herself, she always came back to the same feeling, misery.

It was a magical place and she'd miss it when she left, but denial wasn't a state she could stay in long. Her original around-the-world departure date along with her love for Nick had crept up on her unexpected and unwelcome just like a Monday morning. She'd known she'd made a mistake the moment the plane had lifted off the ground from JFK Airport.

Regret had sat beside her on the jumbo jet, had given her the silent treatment on her way to the hotel and the evil eye when an Australian businessman asked her out to dinner. Wherever she went Nick was there. She saw his walk in men dressed in djellabas or long robes, his dark eyes in the faces of shopkeepers and guides.

"Madame," came a male voice.

She'd come up to the rooftop terrace wanting to spend time alone. The gregarious Parisian travel group kept trying to adopt her as their own. She schooled her features before turning her somber gaze in the direction of the voice. A hotel attendant had come to stand five feet away from her.

"Oui?" she called out automatically.

He replied with a melodic French-Arabic accent, "A special dinner will be served upstairs tonight."

"Thank you." She smiled. "But I'm leaving earlier than I expected. In fact, I leave tomorrow. If I could have the meal in my room, please."

He shook his head, sending the red tassel on his hat whipping through the air. "I'm afraid that cannot be, madame."

"What?"

"Tonight's dinner is a traditional Moroccan event," he added quickly. "Our other English guest requested the chef's world-famous dishes served on the top floor."

Lauren hesitated. She didn't want to socialize, but she hated to turn down the opportunity to listen to Connor's stories about the Australian outback. The tales of bare untouched country and landmark signs that warned travelers of camels, wombats, and kangaroos.

The hotel attendant held out his hand. "Before you make a decision, please come look at what has been provided for you to wear."

Curiosity got the best of her as she followed him back into the building. There hanging by itself on an iron rack was the most exotic caftan she'd ever imagined. She ran her fingers over silken threads of mauve, blue, gray, brown, and black. The robe was a reflection of the traditional Moroccan palette. She reached to take the gown.

"I'll take it to your room and send someone to help you dress." He nodded.

An hour later, Lauren exited her suite wearing a cotton shift, the caftan, and a half veil, which covered everything but her kohl-laden eyes. She looked down at her hands and feet in amazement.

Fetma, the hotel attendant's sister, had generously used henna to paint the palms of her hands with a beautiful web design. She'd also been gifted with hand-embroidered babouches, or heelless slippers. Feeling as though she'd fallen through the looking glass into the pages of *The Arabian Nights*, Lauren followed the servant through the long, narrow arcaded reception rooms to a set of gilded doors.

They entered into the ryad, or enclosed open-air courtyard. Four beautiful orange trees and a fountain stood vigil among small round tables and chairs. White terra-cotta walls and covered arches progressed up wide stairs to the upper-level floors of the hotel.

"In here?" she questioned, noticing for the first time that they were alone. "Where are the other guests?"

"Inside, madame." He waved her inside. Lauren stepped into the room and jumped at the sound of the door closing.

Her eyes grew large as she scanned the room. It was the most romantic scene she'd ever laid eyes on. The low table and chairs were strewn with rose petals. The walls were striped with turquoise and tangerine, offset with Marrakech red. She glanced upward to view the elaborate stucco and carved wood ceilings.

"Hello," she called out. "Connor?"

"Come out onto the terrace," came a masculine voice.

Lauren turned and walked toward the open doorway. Her babouche-clad feet silently moved across the carpeted floor. She stopped dead in her tracks at the sight. Standing by the railing of the candlelit roof-terrace stood an elegantly clad Nick.

"Hello, beautiful."

Those words were all she needed. Lauren launched herself into his arms and pressed herself against him.

"I was going to come home," she said moments later after the initial excitement of seeing him had settled.

"I know," he replied.

"Then what are you doing here?" She snuggled deeper into his arms.

"Just thought I'd indulge in a little prehoneymoon vacation." He grinned, holding her close. "Next time you decide to take a trip, love, I'm coming with you."

"Promise?" She smiled.

He kissed her and then pulled back slightly. "You have to promise me something, Lauren."

"Anything," she said recklessly.

She watched as he went down on bended knee. "Marry me."

From within the deep pockets of his robe a ring appeared. She placed her lowered hands on the sides of his face and drew him upward. She felt the tears of happiness slip down her face and simply answered, "Yes."

Much later, after the dinner had been consumed, lovemaking savored, and sleep taken, she slipped from the bedchamber and went to stand on the terrace. Lauren gazed out at the starry night and the Koutoubia Minaret. The oldest of the three Almohad towers rose over the low city buildings to dominate the skyline. Everything seemed more exotic and wonderful now that Nick was there.

When hands fell to her shoulders, she didn't jump. Lauren leaned back into Nick's warm body, smiling as his arms encircled her. He pressed his cheek against hers, sleep warm against night cool.

"So what shall we do tomorrow, beautiful?" Nick murmured. He was in awe of the old city, but the feeling of having Lauren back in his arms eclipsed everything he'd ever seen.

"We're going to the marketplace," she said excitedly.

"And what are you planning on buying?" He brushed his fingers against her cheek.

A soft smile played on her mouth as she looked down at the engagement ring Nick had placed on her finger hours before.

"A wedding chair," she said, tilting her head upward to look into his eyes. "In traditional Berber villages they craft a special chair to carry the bride, veiled and hidden, to her new husband."

She turned and took his hands within her own. "I want one in our home so that I can tell our daughter about this night. The happiest of my life."

"Lauren," Nick started, not knowing what to say. This was what he'd wanted from the moment she walked through the doorway to the brownstone.

"I love you." She smiled into his eyes. She had been more than ready to return to Park Slope, Brooklyn, back to the brownstone that they'd designed together. But as Nick pulled her into his embrace she knew now and forever that she was already home.

Dear Reader,

After all is said and done, Lauren and Nick have a home, a cat, beautiful memories of sunsets in Marrakech, and the love of a lifetime.

As their story closes, another opens, and this time, Lauren's older brother is soon to discover that the price of ambition could prove too high a cost when love is on the line. A tangled web of secrets and loyalty converge when Hon. Nathan Hughes joins Alyssa Knight's quest to discover the truth about a friend's accidental death.

Warm regards and best wishes,
Angela Weaver
E-mail: angela@angelaweaver.com
Web site: www.angelaweaver.com

COMING IN NOVEMBER 2003 FROM
ARABESQUE ROMANCES

__FOOL FOR LOVE
by Kayla Perrin   1-58314-354-8 $6.99US/$9.99CAN
Kelly Robbins can't believe it when Ashton Hunter calls her out of the blue. She's never forgotten the one passionate night they shared—or that he left town the next day without contacting her. This time she's determined to stay practical. But when desire proves irresistible, Kelly and Ashton must face their insecurities and past fears.

__NOT THE ONE
by Deirdre Savoy   1-58314-386-6 $6.99US/$9.99CAN
When her boyfriend marries somebody else, Nina Ward wonders if pediatrician Matthew Peterson might be who she's looking for. He's handsome, stable . . . and he stands to inherit a fortune if he weds before he turns forty. But Matthew has a secret—and even as he and Nina are falling for each other, his secret threatens to destroy their love.

__TANGO
by Kimberley White   1-58314-410-2 $5.99US/$7.99CAN
Kendall Masterson has finally recovered from a serious car accident. But Kendall soon discovers her scars aren't just physical when the prospect of getting into a car again—with a handsome new admirer, no less—fills her with panic. She wonders if she's even ready for a relationship yet—but despite her fears, she's going to find out. . . .

__TABLE FOR TWO
by Dara Giraard   1-58314-452-8 $5.99US/$7.99CAN
Cassie Graham has always been drawn to sexy men with beautiful eyes and a wicked smile, but when she meets reclusive restaurant owner Drake Henson, she does her best to deny her attraction. The last thing she needs is an arrogant man who'll offer the promise of marriage with no love, and she's determined to resist Drake's charms at all costs . . .